SECOND LAW

PAUL H RAYMER

Salty Air Publishing
www.PaulHRaymer.com

Second Law/Paul H. Raymer — 1st ed.

ISBN (Print edition) 978-0-9906781-7-5

ISBN (Ebook edition) 978-0-9906781-8-2

❀ Created with Vellum

For Kate

"You want to talk about this letter. Then talk, and I will know from your talk whether I can offer an honest opinion or whether it is better to reassure you in your own."

— LEE - EAST OF EDEN - JOHN STEINBECK

"Heat cannot of itself pass from a colder to a hotter body."

— RUDOLF CLAUSIUS - SECOND LAW OF
THERMODYNAMICS

ALSO BY PAUL H RAYMER

Death at the Edge of the Diamond

Recalculating Truth

Residential Ventilation Handbook

PROLOGUE

TILLEY, CAPE COD—AUGUST 1984

*I*t was a killer August evening, one of those evenings that seduces tourists and compels them to want to keep coming back to Cape Cod to spend their hard-earned vacation dollars and stay forever. The katydids chirruped merrily in the trees. Bats swooped and swerved soundlessly, chasing insects. It was late enough that there was only the occasional rumble of a distant truck on the highway. The air was perfumed with manure and mown grass with just a dash of chlorine and sea salt.

Two figures shuffled down the drive, away from the festival's reception at the institute. They appeared to be chatting, although one seemed noticeably intoxicated and stumbling. By the time they reached the dimly lit parking lot, their voices had grown discordant. They stopped by a white box truck. The lettering on its side read, "Grady's Foamrite–Keeping the Heat in. Keeping the Cold out." One figure jumped onto the truck's back bumper, flung up its roll-top door that screeched in protest. The drunk struggled to follow, clambering into the truck. Their voices grew louder and more threatening—until the thunderous sound of machinery abruptly drowned them out.

The drunk then lurched off the truck, stumbled a few steps, and dropped to the curb. The other figure followed, dragging a hose out of the truck, and stood there, confronting the drunk. Although they both seemed to shout, their voices could not be heard over the sound of the machine. A substance began to shoot out of the hose and the machine started a rhythmic *click, clack; click, clack*. When the foam hit the asphalt, it expanded like toxic shaving cream. The figure with the hose kept moving it closer and closer to the drunk, in a sweeping back-and-forth pattern, click, clack; click, clack.

The drunk scrambled to stand up. Rapidly expanding foam had already trapped its feet and legs, and the foam continued to expand rapidly, engulfing one body part after another, growing like an alien creature. The victim fell to the asphalt screaming and tried to cover its head, but the foam continued to grow, mindlessly and mercilessly, determined to swallow the victim whole. And the figure finally could no longer scream with a mouth and nose filled with foam. With a flick of the wand, the killer blew the victim's cap into the bushes with the pressure of the spray.

The killer holding the hose continued to layer the foam thicker and thicker until the grotesque mound stopped moving. Then the killer stood for a moment regarding the massive pile, coiled the hose, climbed back in the truck and shut off the machinery, pulled the door down, and walked back up the drive toward the institute.

In the parking lot, the quality of the silence felt different as the katydids attempted to regain their rhythm. The foam crackled and whispered as it hardened, and the smell of burning flesh supplanted the perfume of the Cape Cod summer night.

CHAPTER 1

SANDWICH - AUGUST 4, 1984

*T*wo days earlier, Jon Megquire was driving Maybelline, his MG Midget, toward the Sagamore Bridge thinking, I hope nobody dies this time. Five years earlier, the last time he had been on the Cape, a guy was murdering people with carbon monoxide or CO. And a few years before that, his parents came for a wedding and his mother died of CO poisoning in their motel. Death could put you off all the great Cape Cod happy times—happy times like playing minor league baseball, and working construction with Ace Wentzel. And there was Lisa.

For the thousandth time, he asked himself why he'd felt the need to drive all the way from Fort Lauderdale. But Maybelline was running well on this delightful, early August day. Besides, this little sports car connected him to his best Cape experiences, and she wasn't quite ready to finish that story.

He was also thinking about what his father had said about his future. At twenty-seven, he wasn't a kid anymore. It was time to make some choices—one of those obvious statements that parents make. Of course, he knew that. This time... this time he was going to find his true path in life and nothing was going to get in his way. He was going to attend this festival... this conference to learn about buildings, energy efficiency, and solar heating. For some reason, this felt right.

And that included Lisa—the girl he'd left behind. Since he'd last seen her, she'd graduated from UMass Boston's Crime and Justice program and joined the Massachusetts State Police. She was following in the footsteps of her father, Mark Prence, who had been the only police officer in the town of Tilley when Jon was last on the Cape.

From Jon's point of view, theirs had been a long-distance romance of convenience. It was easier to nudge it along rather than let it go. They had talked to each other on the phone. They had written letters. He congratulated her on her successes at UMass and her job with the State Police, but they had lived different lives for the past five years. No doubt she had dated other people. He certainly had. He wasn't a monk, and five years in the Florida sun and hanging out with athletes and athletes' women does not encourage celibacy. Jon wondered if he was making the wrong choice, rekindling what had been a short summer relationship. When he called to tell her he was coming up for the festival, she had sounded... distant? Neutral?

For a moment, he wondered if he should just keep going. He was on the Sagamore Bridge now. He could keep driving down the Mid-Cape Highway to Tilley. But the exit for Sandwich Road came up immediately. No time for choosing. His hands pushed Maybelline to the exit instead of toward the highway. He had to do it. He had to see if there was anything to their relationship.

MAYBELLINE SLID EASILY around the ramp, one hundred eighty degrees, and stopped at the lights pointing north, facing the Canal, back toward the mainland. Jon followed the directions Lisa had sent him, driving under the bridge and along the Canal. This was a strange section of Route 6A—no glitzy tourist places, only a few houses, a forgotten spot, bypassed by the highway.

Jon pulled into the apartment's parking lot and checked his watch. Working with Ace had trained Jon's eye to evaluate buildings. These were a dozen simple two-story units glued together, all the same with balding patches of grass. Sheathed with unpainted cedar shingles and white trim, the apartments fit into the neighborhood. Bright yellow and red plastic children's toys were scattered about. Among the cars and pickup trucks, a two-tone Massachusetts state police car stood out, proclaiming Lisa's presence. These were the homes of the teachers, firefighters, police, and the "help" that earned just enough to cling to the Cape side of the Canal and weren't forced to cross one bridge every day to go to work.

On this warm Saturday evening, part of the parking lot was taken up with an enclave of folding lawn chairs and a charcoal barbecue grill. The occupants looked up as he pulled Maybelline into an empty slot.

Jon got out, smiled and waved, and scanned the doors to locate unit numbers. He didn't expect her to come running out to greet him, but because he didn't know what she would do, he felt queasy.

He hiked up his pants and ran his hand back through his hair. Jon had the stature of an athlete—broad shoulders, thick neck, and square jaw. A face you might find on a baseball card. He had scrubbing-pad curly hair and his hazel eyes flashed when he smiled. He was grinning now in anticipation.

He walked up the steps to Lisa's unit and rang the bell. What was making him nervous? Jon was not vain, and he didn't know if his appearance had changed. There was no one in his life to reflect on how he looked back at him. Maybe a little extra weight. He rubbed the stubble on his chin. Had Lisa changed?

Then she opened the door. There she was, dressed in a red V-neck floral dress, her silky auburn hair loose to her shoulders, and that heady perfume she still wore. She had put on some weight. Jon didn't know if you could call it bulk, but her police physical training had changed her body shape. He thought she looked gorgeous. His mouth opened, and he was momentarily speechless, except for one word: "Hi."

Then there was that smile.

"Hi. You made it."

"I did," he said. "Yes. Traffic was horrible."

"It always is at this time of year."

"You look great."

"Thanks." She looked up at him while she held the door. "So do you."

He tried to read what was going on in her eyes. Then she pushed the door all the way open and said, "Come in. Good to see you."

"Good to see you too," he mumbled, stepping into the apartment.

God, this is awkward, he thought. Maybe he should have grabbed her in his arms, glued his lips to hers, and dipped her toward the floor right there in the front hall.

"So you're a cop now," he said.

"Yes. I am. Does that bother you?"

Challenging right from the start. He looked back at her, paused, and laughed nervously. "Of course not. No, really, it doesn't bother me."

This was one of those moments when the right words should just flow… but rarely did.

"Still driving Maybelline?" she asked, following him into the living room.

"Yeah. She's burning a bit of oil."

"I guess that was a stupid question," she said. "I mean you're here. She's here. You drove her all the way up from Florida?"

He grinned. "Yah. Risky, huh? I had to stop partway. Not exactly a luxurious ride! But she made it. We're a team. The two of us."

He looked around the room. The building was tucked into the trees, which made it dark, but kept it cool. There was nothing glamorous about the stacked boxes of these apartments. They were utilitarian shelters.

"Nice apartment," he said.

"No, it's not. It's dark. There are water leaks. The dishwasher doesn't work. But I'm not here much. Basically, it's a place to sleep."

They hadn't touched. Jon didn't know what to do with his hands. He thrust them deep into his pockets as if to put them away.

She moved toward the kitchenette. It was all part of one room—

kitchenette, dining area, eating area, living room with the television. Bedroom must be upstairs, Jon thought.

"You need a bathroom?" She pointed back toward the front door. "Just don't get confused with the closet." She snorted. He smiled.

He stepped back to the bathroom door, entered, and stood for a moment, thinking. He used the toilet and then washed his hands and stared at himself in the mirror. The bathroom had pale yellow wallpaper with dainty little flowers sprinkled all over it. Analyzing rooms, spaces, buildings was an annoying disease that Ace had infected him with. The face that looked back at him appeared confused. Who are you? He asked himself. You have been working with millionaires, famous sports figures, and fantasy women who pushed out their boobs in their tight dresses, blinked their painted eyelashes, and licked their fat red lips. Yet Lisa makes you feel like a schoolboy!

When he stepped out of the bathroom, she asked, "How about a beer?"

"Great."

She handed him a cold bottle, and their hands touched. He swallowed, even though the beer had yet to touch his lips.

They sat side by side on the sofa and she curled her legs around under herself. They started talking about what they'd been doing. She told him about her years at UMass Boston. About the Crime and Justice program.

"Well, that was a natural," he said. "Growing up. Your father was the only cop in town, right? It's bred into you."

She acknowledged his comment with a laugh.

He talked about working in Florida, trying to get the major league baseball franchise up and running. Lot of money involved, he said. Lot of legal barriers to get through.

"Did you like doing it?"

"Some of it," he said. "It was fun to meet the stars."

"You could have been one of those. You could have become a professional baseball player. Do you miss it?"

"No," he looked down at his beer. "I made that choice. And seriously, I don't know if the Angels really would have let me play. And there's always the chance of injury—career-ending injury. And then where am I? No, I made that choice to not go pro. I made the choice to work in Florida. I made the choice to leave Cape Cod; to leave you."

"Aw," she replied, putting her hand on his forearm. "That's sweet. I appreciate the sentiment, but don't get gooey on me now. That's not in your character. No, really, you came back for a building conference? Is that right?"

"No, I mean, yes. But they call it a festival. The First International Helios Festival, and it's in Tilley, at that institute they built there - ITI."

"They like getting international in the title, don't they? I've always wondered what they did there."

"I honestly don't know much about the place, but they have some great speakers coming, so I thought I could learn new construction stuff. And I couldn't resist coming back to Tilley."

"But construction? Why? Seems like a major leap from professional sports. Getting bored with sports stars and beautiful women?"

He laughed. "It was Ace's fault, really. He made me see buildings differently. And energy's a big deal. I mean, there is all this solar science going on. And they're talking about another energy crisis, like we're going to run out of oil for real this time. And the earth is warming up and the climate changing, and I got kind of bitten by it, you know?"

Jon surveyed the living room, wondering if Lisa enjoyed the no-frills quality of the space. No family pictures graced the walls or the shelves, just a couple of framed posters, one of a Woody with surfboards on top on a beach and one of a Cape Cod Baseball League game.

"I guess we should eat. Do you have plans? I've got some fish." She went to the refrigerator and pulled out a package of fish. She looked at it, then held it up to her nose. "Pew! On second thought, maybe I've had this too long."

John came over and sniffed the package. The smell of the fish mingled with the aroma of her perfume, and he couldn't sort it out. "Don't know," he said. "I'm no expert."

"Neither am I. So let's go out. But you haven't given me an answer. Do you want dinner or do you want to keep heading down to Tilley?"

Jon didn't have any plans. For anything. Maybe that was why he had hesitated at the exit. His life was filled with hesitations and stops and starts. He just waited until pieces fell into place in front of him, and he had to stumble over them. Baseball, construction, Lisa, even murder.

"No," he said. "I don't want to keep driving." He smiled. "I want to spend the evening with you."

She smiled back and there was an extraordinary natural warmth in that smile, a path into her heart, and he suddenly realized how much he had missed that smile. Maybe there was a plan in that smile.

"Let me buy you dinner," he said.

As they left her apartment, Lisa waved to the people in the parking lot.

"They know everything," she said. "It's a little village. You can't have a private life. But sometimes it's good."

The apartment building in Fort Lauderdale Jon had been living in was a high rise, full of hundreds of people. He occasionally recognized some faces, the hair, the perfumes of other tenants when he rode the elevator, but they remained strangers.

They walked in silence along the gravel surface to where Lisa's street intersected Route 6A and the parking lot for the Canal Side Inn, a big old building that looked like it had been there since the days when stage coaches traveled the road on their way to Barnstable and further down the Cape.

In the parking lot, Jon spotted a large white box truck with "Grady's Foamrite" painted on the side.

"What?" Lisa asked.

"Nothing," he said. "But I think this guy is supposed to be speaking at the festival. This is one of the new techniques people are talking about. Using spray foam for insulation."

"Uh-huh."

"No, seriously. This is state-of-the art. I wonder what he's doing here?"

"Having dinner?"

They entered the inn, and the hostess greeted Lisa. "I come here a lot," she told Jon.

It was an inviting space, with a white tin ceiling, a long counter with stools, and doorways into other rooms. A couple of large ceiling fans rotated lazily. Pictures of local sports teams hung on the walls. There was a sign that read 'No Dancing' and another with the mandate: 'No shoes. No shirt. No service.' Servers wearing shorts and black aprons rushed between the tables, pushing through the swinging doors into the kitchen. The air was saturated with the smell of fried food with a hint of cigarette smoke.

It was a Saturday night in early August on Cape Cod, so the place was bustling. "Want to sit at the counter, hon?" the hostess asked. "It's going to be maybe fifteen, twenty minutes for a table or booth."

"We'll wait in the bar," Lisa said. Jon followed her between the tables, dodging the servers, and trying not to bump into diners' chairs.

The bar was darker, with a mirror behind the bottles, and a long, ancient wooden counter with a shiny chrome footrail and swivel stools. Some patrons were hunched over eating. Others toasted themselves in the mirror as they drank. Jon and Lisa slid onto two stools near the cash register.

They ordered a couple of Narragansett draft beers. "I haven't drunk this stuff in a while," Jon said as he clinked glasses with Lisa. "Oh, I've got to tell you about this thing that happened down there in Florida. It was actually one reason I came up here. I had to wine and dine this guy from Toledo, Ohio. You're not going to believe it, but his name was Marty Robbins."

"No?" Lisa said with a grin.

"Yeah, really. Marty Robbins. Like the country singer. He was a building product accessories millionaire, who seemed to have endless stories about manufacturing joist pocket brackets, brick ties, fire wall hangers, light capacity U-shaped hangers, and what he called a *slopeable* and *skewable* rafter hanger that you had to see to believe." Jon attempted to imitate Marty's voice.

"That's what he told me, anyway. He had an overweight hand and a flabby handshake. He thought the appropriate attire for a July evening in Fort Lauderdale was a blending of Walter Cronkite and John Travolta—white suit, white shoes, white nose brush mustache, and a big, Midwestern grin."

"Could he sing?" Lisa asked.

Jon laughed. "I didn't ask. Anyway, we went to this fancy place called Caesar's Famous Steakhouse and Lobster Palace. They had all these white-faced busts of Caesar, Claudius, and Nero, and their faces glowed purple from the mood lighting. They had Dean Martin on a loop singing 'Volare' and Perry Como trying to 'Catch a Falling Star'. It was really crowded, so they put us at a table right beside the lobster tank. I mean, all those lobsters in there climbing over each other, waving their claws and antennae."

"Yeah. I hate that," Lisa said. "Seems cruel. In some places, they make you point to the one you want to eat!"

"The menus in this place are like encyclopedias and the wine list is a vast computer print-out. You're supposed to pick your steak by its age and thickness and you never, ever order it well-done. I saw a guy try that once. The waiters are like storm troopers! They took him into a backroom, and he never reappeared."

Lisa laughed and sipped her beer. "Not really?"

"Well, I didn't see him come back. Maybe I got distracted. Anyway, I was supposed to sell Marty on backing the baseball franchise. He was a big fan of the Toledo Mud Hens. The thought of owning a piece of a major league franchise made him drool. A major league franchise in the Miami market almost made him wet his pants, and I almost had him when BAM—the lobster tank just exploded!"

"What?"

"BANG! Yeah. The whole tank just seemed to fall into pieces all around us, and all the water poured out onto our table. Dozens of escaping lobsters were wriggling and squirming their way across the tablecloth, waving their antennae and swinging their rubber-banded claws, heading for the floor, dropping off the edges of the surface like drunken caterpillars."

"What? What's a 'drunken caterpillar' look like?" Lisa asked. She was full-out laughing now.

"Damned if I know," Jon said. "I just made that up!"

"So what the heck happened?"

Jon was afraid she was going to spill her beer. "I jumped up and knocked over my chair, but Marty just sat there and watched them drop into his lap. And he said, 'Oh, my!'

"People at the surrounding tables dropped their forks and put down their wineglasses, and when I looked around the room and through the wreckage of the tank, I saw a guy with a gun."

"Shit!" Lisa exclaimed.

At that moment, the server appeared and said, "There's a table for you guys now." Jon and Lisa looked at her as though she were an apparition. "Unless you want to eat here?"

Lisa finally said, "Oh, right. Great," and they picked up their beers and followed the server to the booth.

"You've got to finish the story," Lisa said as they settled onto the vinyl padded benches and opened the food-stained menus.

"Yeah. So… someone started yelling 'Gun! Gun! He's got a gun!' and as you can imagine, that didn't calm things down at all. I ducked and so did Marty."

"Who was the guy shooting at?"

"I don't know. Don't think I'll ever know, and I wasn't about to hang around to find out then. Marty had reached up and put his hands on the broken glass at the edge of the tank to peer over. So now his hands were bleeding. All around us, diners were rushing the doors. I grabbed some napkins and wrapped them around Marty's hands, yanked him by the sleeve of his John Travolta jacket, and headed for an exit. There was a lot of noise—screaming, glasses and plates crashing to the floor. But when we got outside, people were hanging around, as though someone was going to come out and explain every-thing—like they do on television—a celestial voiceover. But that wasn't going to happen."

Jon swallowed a gulp of his beer. Lisa was leaning over the table on her elbows.

"I started more or less pulling Marty down the street toward his hotel. It was a muggy night, and he was puffing and sweating like a pig, and he stopped, bent over and put his hands on his knees. He was gasping. There was blood on his suit. And the bloody napkins around his hands were flapping like a mummy coming unraveled.

"It occurred to me it was probably not the best idea to stand there, Marty and his gold Rolex, white suit, bloody napkins waving. And me in my seersucker suit and wet pants. We were ideal tourist class targets for a dark city street. Then Marty started laughing. He let out this huge guffaw I thought would wake the entire neighborhood. And he wouldn't stop! He thought I had staged the whole thing for his benefit."

"What?"

"Really! He thought it was a staged adventure. Like something from a Disney theme park! He said he'd never been in the middle of a crime before. 'It was so real,' he said. 'I thought I was going to wet my pants.' But, of course, they *were* wet!"

"Jesus!" Lisa said.

"It was the lobster water, of course," Jon said. "Lobsters escaping the palace! I wondered if Marty might have had one in his pocket!"

"What did you do?"

"I got him back to his hotel. He had to go upstairs to change, and I waited in the lobby. I had lobster water on my pants too, and that was embarrassing. I covered it up as best I could with my jacket, but you know it's there, right?."

"Sounds like quite the night."

When they had finished eating and were waiting for the check, Jon remembered one more thing he wanted to tell Lisa about the crazy night with the exploding lobster tank "Marty told me I should come to this festival."

"Really. Why?"

"He said his wife wanted a retirement place on Cape Cod. When I mentioned that I'd worked up here for the summer. I think he thought

I could build it for him. He said his wife had seen the pictures of the Cape and heard the stories. She'd read all those fancy home and garden and architectural magazines, and her head was full of ideas about a house on the water."

Jon said he'd told Marty about playing in the Cape Cod Baseball League and working for Ace Wentzell, and about Ace's passion for excellence.

"Well, did he wind up buying into the baseball franchise?" Lisa asked. "Were you successful?"

Jon looked down at his hands and then sighed. "I guess my heart wasn't in it. And Marty may have been a kind of dork, but he was pretty perceptive. I think he knew better than I did that sports promotion was not my gig."

"I can see that," she said. "So you told him about this festival?"

"I did. And he said I should go."

"Why? Why did he tell you that?"

Jon looked at her, studying her face, thinking about her question. "I guess he could tell that I wanted to go."

THE DAY WAS FADING as they walked back to her apartment. He took her hand and felt the strength of her fingers and the smoothness of her skin. He asked her about living here in Sandwich. What her neighbors were like. Did she have to go off-Cape for shopping? They talked about the upcoming presidential election. Did she think Reagan would win again?

And while they talked and walked, Jon found he felt relaxed and comfortable with her. He liked the way she thought. He liked the way she talked. He liked the smooth sound of her voice and it surprised him how quickly they reached her apartment.

People were still sitting in the parking lot, drinking, smoking, chatting. One guy had a guitar and sang calypso songs. Jon recognized something that sounded like a Harry Belafonte tune. Someone waved at them to come over.

Lisa looked at Jon and said, "It's polite."

Jon didn't object.

Lisa let go of his hand to walk over to the group.

"Well, well," said the guy with the guitar. "So the lady cop has a boyfriend at long last?"

"Don't make any trouble," Lisa said. "I've got all your names in my little book."

"Cop to the core," one man said with a smile. "Got to get the facts right. 'Just the facts, ma'am. Just the facts.' Want to join us, or do you have other things on your minds?"

Lisa said, "We have a lot of catching up to do. But thanks for the invite. Rain check?"

"Can you sing?" the guy with the guitar asked.

"What?" Lisa replied.

"Can you sing? Soprano? Alto? Bass? Anything We could use some harmony."

"We could use something musical," one woman laughed. "Sometimes it sounds like fighting foxes out here."

Lisa laughed. "I don't think I'm the one to improve what you're hearing. Maybe another evening."

"What about you…?" the man asked, looking at Jon.

"Oh, I'm sorry," Lisa said. "I didn't introduce you. This is Jon. Jon Megquire. He used to play baseball. He had a shot with the Angels."

Jon smiled and executed one of those stupid chill waves. "Long time ago," he smiled.

"But can you sing? How about 'Stay the Night'," and he started the disco drum beat on the body of his guitar. Boom, da boom. Boom, da boom! "Stay the night. Stay the night. Da, da, da, da."

"Uh, no," Jon said. "I don't think so."

Lisa laughed. "But, hey, he's a friend of Marty Robbins!" she explained.

"Really?" the guy with the guitar asked. "Really? What's he like? Now he can sing."

Jon choked. "No. No. Not THE Marty Robbins. I was just telling

Lisa about a guy I met who is called Marty Robbins. Completely different person." Jon laughed.

There was a general, knowing "Oh" from the group in the lawn chairs.

"And he's been doing a lot of driving today," Lisa further explained.

Another understanding "Oh." Punctuated by an "Uh, huh!"

"Got to put the boy to bed, do you?" someone asked.

Lisa grabbed Jon's hand and guided him back to her door.

Jon called back over his shoulder, "Nice to meet you!"

"Say hi to Marty for us when you see him again," someone shouted.

Back in the living room, Lisa kicked off her shoes. "Beer?"

"Nice people," Jon said.

"Nosey," Lisa replied. "I told you. You can't get away with anything."

While she pulled two beers out of the refrigerator, Jon poked around the living room.

He found her cassette player. "Wow," he said. "No turntable?"

"Too much trouble," she replied.

She came over, pushed the button on the console, and the cover flipped open. "I don't have a lot. Pick out something."

Jon squatted down to look through the spines of the Norelco cases and found one called "Saturday Night Jazz."

She sat on the sofa. He sat beside her and they listened to the music. The conversation they had begun while they had walked from the inn continued to flow.

"Is your father still the only cop in Tilley?" he asked.

She told him there wasn't much crime in Tilley and thus no need for more police. She told him that four years ago when they built the institute, ITI, it had brought outsiders into the town—outsiders like interns, researchers, and the press. The residents were used to tourists, but these people were different. The locals thought of ITI as a commune or a cult, and that made them nervous. The visitors and the staff were not noisy, and they didn't cause trouble, but they connected Tilley to the outside—off-Cape, the rest of the world. There had been a bit of vandalism on the property that was blamed on ancient Wampanoag land rights.

He told her about working in Florida, with celebrities and athletes, trying to get them to invest in the baseball team, trying to get authorities in Major League Baseball to approve Fort Lauderdale for a franchise. About Joe Robbie, the owner of the Miami Dolphins, wanting to move his team out of the Orange Bowl and building a stadium. It was hard to compete with someone with those connections and reputation.

"Then along came Marty Robbins and the Lobster Palace episode!" he said, and they laughed. She asked him if they'd caught the shooter and what it was all about. And he said they'd never know—at least he would never know. "It isn't like on TV where it's all wrapped up in an hour."

"Do you still want to play baseball?" she asked.

He told her that his short stint with the Fort Lauderdale Suns was enough for him. "Hurting my knee was the last straw. It was kind of part-time gig between the other work I was doing."

"You weren't really serious about playing anyway," she said. "Did that guy from the Angels ever contact you again?"

Jon felt himself bristle at the non-serious accusation. "I *was* serious," he said. "And it was fun." He took a swig of beer.

Lisa laid her hand on his arm and her touch sent tingles up to the back of his neck.

"How's Ace?" Jon asked, changing the subject.

"I guess he's busy. I don't hang around the town much these days. But from what I hear, he's built some less traditional houses recently. You should talk to him. But you're not a great communicator, are you?"

Another sting to his character. Maybe he deserved that one. "I plan to talk to him. He's one reason I came back. I gave Marty Robbins his name."

They nursed their beers and looked at the floor and time seem to take a deep breath. Finally Lisa said, "Where did you think this would go?"

"What?" The change in conversational direction was so abrupt that Jon mentally staggered back.

"Tonight. Whatever it is between us? I mean, were you planning on driving the rest of the way to Tilley tonight?"

"I… guess," Jon said.

"There must have been girls you dated in Florida."

"Um. I guess."

"What do you mean 'I guess'? You're a stud muffin. Girls must fall all over you."

"Nah."

"Jesus, Jon. Sometimes you can be so blind. You probably didn't notice."

"Sometimes it's hard not to notice." Jon grinned. "I mean, man, they don't wear many clothes down there in the southern sun."

"So?"

He tried to read her face and deflected the conversation. "What about you? College boys? Handsome cops? I hear there's a lot of hanky-panky that goes on in those police barracks. And you're beautiful."

Color flushed her face. "Friends," she said. "Nothing serious."

"There was this one girl for a while," he said. "She came from Atlanta. But it went nowhere." He said that the girl was nice and she was pretty, but he could never figure out what she wanted because, he realized, she didn't know. She spent a ton of time fixing her face, trying on different outfits, asking him what he thought of them, and whether certain things made her look fat! "You just can't answer questions like that," he said, rolling his eyes. Then he asked again, "What about you?"

She got up and moved back toward the kitchen. For a moment, he thought she was ignoring his question. "Friends," she repeated and then turned to look at him, "Except one."

He grinned at her from across the room. "Yeah?"

"Yeah. I guess. After you left and went to Florida. College is a big change… and Boston is a big change from Tilley. I was lost there at the beginning. First semesters away from home can be brutal. It was a long time ago."

"Not that long," Jon said.

"Well, it seems that way."

"So, what about this guy?"

"He was a junior and seemed to have it all together. Knew what he wanted to do. Wealthy parents. Great hair. Nice ass."

"What did he want to do?" Jon asked.

Lisa laughed. "I don't remember! Some kind of a business thing like a technical start-up. But he was really confident... And I wasn't."

"So what happened?"

"I thought he was the one," she said. "You know? God, it seemed so right. Like the missing puzzle piece that has all the right colors and shapes and you think, 'This has to be it', but then it just doesn't quite fit."

"Oh," Jon said.

"I eventually came to my senses and realized he was an egotistical ass! There was no way he wanted to be connected long term to a small town cop. He needed a Barbie on his arm to show off to his friends."

"So, what happened to him?"

"He graduated. He's probably a politician now."

"Oh," Jon said again.

"Look," she said, "I can't let you drive tonight. It would be ethically wrong for me as an officer of the law to let you drive, since you've been drinking. And besides, it's getting late. You'll sleep here."

Jon looked at what he was sitting on. "Oh. Okay. Thanks."

"So, how about another beer?"

"Sure. Why not? I'll get my bag from Maybelline."

"Your long-term girlfriend! She must be getting old by now."

"Don't talk about her that way! You'll hurt her feelings and she'll start acting up."

"Just go get your bag."

Back outside, the twinkles of twilight kissed the sky. It always surprised Jon how late it stayed light this time of year. He looked up at the stars, the crescent moon, and Venus glowing brightly. A dot streaked across the sky and he wondered if it was a comet or something man-made.

He pulled his bag out of Maybelline's trunk and slammed the lid back down.

~

LISA RAN upstairs to brush her hair back from her face, considered if she should add make-up, ran back downstairs, and tried to think how she should stand when he returned. Then she berated herself for generating a sweat, running up and down the stairs.

Five years earlier, when she'd first met Jon, she had been a kid—naïve, star-struck by his status as an athlete (although she never would have admitted it then), as well as the hunkiness of his body. She had tried to be very cool and aloof, although she hadn't always succeeded. Even then, he was indecisive. He didn't seem to know where he was going or where he wanted to go, and she was compelled to help him.

It surprised her he hadn't pursued a professional baseball career and instead had gone to Fort Lauderdale to work as a sports promoter working for his father's company. And although she knew it was just a childish romantic fantasy like princes and pink ponies, deep inside she was disappointed that he hadn't wanted to stay with her in Tilley. Jon had to follow his own path. And she had to follow hers, which had led her to her life of fighting crime and working for justice.

She had shoved those college romance thoughts onto a dark shelf in the back of her memory closet and knew now that it had just been a rebound reaction to Jon, piled on top of all the other pressures of early days of college life.

But he was here again.

~

WHEN JON CAME BACK INSIDE, Lisa asked, "Do you know how to dance?"

He put his bag down. "Sure," he said. "I mean, it's basically just shuffling around."

She laughed. "Let's try it. If I was using a turntable with one of those automatic drop spindles, we have to put a stack of records on and let them drop and we might not like all the tracks on the record but we would have to manually lift the tone arm up to the next track. My parents had a machine that actually tried to flip the record over like those gadgets in juke boxes but it would fling the record across the room instead. I don't like everything on this Cyndi Lauper album —and we still call them albums. Isn't that amazing? They haven't been albums since our parents bought 78 rpm records where you could barely get one track on a side!"

Jon thought that was one of the longest explanations he had ever heard Lisa deliver. "Me too," he said.

"What?"

"Oh, I don't know. Albums. I have a cassette player in my car."

"I know," she said. "You played it for me when we drove out to First Encounter Beach five years ago." She paused. "And walked along the beach. And you didn't want to get sand in Maybelline."

"I know," he said. "I remember."

They looked at each other, uncertain. Then she fast forwarded the tape, skipping "Girls Just Want to Have Fun" to get to Lauper's "Time after Time" track , and stood close to him, looking up at his face. He put his arms around her. She reciprocated, and they started moving in time to the music.

It had been a very long time since he'd danced with anyone at a wedding reception, and that had been pounding rock and roll, bouncing around, not this slow, rhythmic, swaying. This was a body to body embrace, and it felt wonderful. He'd never liked Cyndi Lauper's music before. He used to think she was whining.

He refocused on Lisa's living room.

"You still think too much," she said, nestling her head into his shoulder.

They fit together well, he thought. He could feel the straps of her bra through her shirt. She was rubbing her hand on the back of his neck, making his hair tingle. He wanted Cyndi to just keep singing—

time after time after time. By the time the song ended, their lips had joined. With the abrupt beginning of the next pounding song, they pushed apart and started bouncing to the rhythm. They laughed and spun around and jiggied and joggled all over the room.

Jon came close to knocking over the coffee table, stumbled back, and she caught him, still laughing. When the next slow and melodic tune began, they hesitated to come together, but the mood wasn't the same. Lisa stopped the cassette, and they stood there, breathless, looking at each other.

"You don't have to sleep on the sofa," she said finally.

"Great. The floor?" He smiled.

"The bed's upstairs."

"Oh. Your bed? I've never slept with a cop before."

"Neither have I," she replied.

"I'm not a cop."

"I know."

That confused him, but he grabbed his bag and she turned out the lights in the living room and awkwardly led him up the narrow stairs to her room.

As LISA LED Jon up the stairs, her head spun—just a little, the fringes of an alcohol buzz. She had never brought a man to this bedroom before. It was her sacred space where she could be as soft and gentle as she liked and not the hardened police officer she had to portray every day. Day after day. She liked her job. She loved puzzling out the crimes she had to solve, but she could never, ever, not for a moment, show a sign of weakness or softness to her fellow officers. It was tough enough being a woman in this man's world and even tougher to be a female state trooper. Most of the men resented her. She made them uncomfortable. She had to watch every word she said and how she said it.

But here, here in her bedroom, she could take on that other role as the female of the species... and she had never done that with a man before. It made her wonder. It made her doubt that she was doing the right thing. Was Jon the right man? Lisa had thought about him, alone in her bed. She had imagined what it would be like to be lying with him, naked. She had a picture of him grinning at the camera, wearing his Tilley Longliner baseball uniform. Tanned and strong. His untamed hair, his hazel eyes sparkling. She thought of running across the sands at First Encounter Beach and when he lifted her into his arms and hugged her to him. She remembered his embarrassment all those years ago while she wiped the sand from his feet when he was only wearing his briefs.

At the top of the stairs, she turned to look at him. He was looking down as he came up the stairs. She could see the top of his head, the back of his neck, his broad shoulders, and she was glad. She had surrendered her virginity in another bed years ago. Surrendered it in lust or anger or confusion, but not in love. The mystery of her affection or love for him was about to be unwrapped. Would he be the man of her memories and her imagination? Jon could have done a better job of staying in touch. He could have called more. He could have come to visit. If he really loved her, he should have sent her flowers on her birthday. Did he even know when her birthday was?

Now Jon put down his bag. The two of them stared at each other and then came together and as she felt the strength of his arms, the solid muscles of his body, the stubbled skin of his chin, she stopped thinking. She began unbuttoning his shirt, pulling it frantically out of his waistband.

She felt the strength of his hands as he cradled her head and kissed her lips, tongue greeting tongue. He ran his hand down her neck, down her back, to her waist, and pulled her to him. He helped her pull her dress off over her shoulders and drop it to the floor. They fumbled with his belt and unzipped his fly, and his pants joined her dress on the floor. Now he wore boxer shorts. Now there was no embarrassment. She felt his hands caressing down to the base of her spine. There were no more questions now. Skin on skin. She was sensing every part of his body and her head and her body filled with the joy of the moment.

CHAPTER 2

TILLEY - AUGUST 5, 1984

*J*on awoke to a bright sunny morning alone in Lisa's bed. His first thought was, why in hell hadn't he done this before? Why did he wait to get back together with her? He lay in the bed, watching the sunlight dance across the ceiling, listening—Lisa downstairs, an occasional car moving in the parking lot outside, a gull's call—and he wondered what the day would bring.

He heaved himself over to the side of the bed, pulled on his boxer shorts, headed into the bathroom, and found himself smiling at his reflection in the mirror. He ran his hand back through his hair—the origin of his occasional nickname, "Brillo".

Wow, he thought. Lisa, naked in his arms, was like a soft, refreshing breath of air. Like a new beginning. These thoughts made him swallow hard. His reflection was shaking his head in amazement. And then he thought, *now what?* That question was the chorus to his life. What happens now? Where do we go from here? The festival lasted only until Wednesday.

He walked down to the kitchen, where he was greeted by the wonderful morning smells of frying bacon and fresh coffee, and Lisa, with a spatula in hand, wrapped in a silk kimono.

"Hi," she said. She poured him a cup of coffee. "How do you take it? Milk? Sugar?"

"Black is fine. Straight. No mixer."

She handed it to him. She pushed her glasses up her nose with the thumb and first finger of her left hand, with her little finger pointing up to the ceiling as though the frame was especially delicate.

"Thanks," he said. She smiled.

"Breakfast. Fantastic! I didn't expect this."

"What did you expect?"

"I expected to be sleeping on a cot at ITI and having bean sprouts and fake coffee."

"I don't have any bean sprouts," she said. "Just eggs, bacon, and whole wheat toast."

"Fantastic!" He watched her move the bacon around in the pan. "And I didn't expect you."

That remark must have burst into his brain from dialog in a movie. He didn't feel comfortable with feelings, emotions, gooey sentiment. But they were alone and no one else could hear them. "Last night... were you wearing contacts?"

"Don't you like my glasses?"

"I do, I do. They make you look different, is all." He realized he was venturing into dangerous ground.

"Uh, huh," she replied. "So what is this festival all about? What are you celebrating? Are you going to wear funny hats?"

He grinned. "Marty Robbins asked the same question. I don't know why they call it that. No funny hats, no sacrifices. The Helios is because they're going to talk about solar energy, using the sun to heat houses and water. I'm really interested in the energy efficiency. Can you imagine? What if we could make houses so energy efficient that they actually generated more energy than they used? There would be zero heating bills!"

"Uh, huh?" Lisa buttered the toast, placed the eggs and bacon on two plates, and handed one to him.

"I mean, if we could make homes more energy efficient, we wouldn't be so dependent on foreign oil. And they say that humans are causing global warming—the temperature of the whole earth is rising."

"What does that mean?"

"It means that someday this apartment might be on the beachfront or under water. It's that serious!"

He thought he'd better change the subject. "You haven't told me how it is working for the state police."

"It's good," she said. "I've got a lot to learn. Being a rookie or a 'boots' sucks. And being a boots woman sucks more. I don't get a lot of respect."

He tried to imagine what it would be like. "Is it your father's influence?"

"I like order. I enjoy figuring out how people work. Why they do what they do, particularly when it is stuff they aren't supposed to do." She bit off a piece of her toast and crunched it.

"Ah," he replied. "It wasn't the buff, wide shouldered, ex-marine types in uniform?"

"What do you think?" she asked. "No. I guess there can be some handsome troopers and we're all proud to be wearing the uniform. But, no, it was the law, not the uniforms, that attracted me. More coffee?"

He watched her stride out to the kitchen to grab the pot while he pondered how to answer her question. "Oh, come on!" he said in disbelief. "No one beyond that guy freshman year?"

"What? Oh, come on, what? Yeah, I've had dinner with other men. I've been on dates since you left town. But I don't date men I work with. In fact, I think some troopers think I'm gay and that doesn't help with my boots credentials either."

He wondered how someone as beautiful as her could just ignore all the surrounding testosterone.

"There are some attractive civilians though," she said. "Particularly in the summer. You know the summer money people. Hard bodies. Nice tans. Slick haircuts. Thousand-dollar shoes."

Jon grinned. "You like expensive shoes?"

"When are you going to talk to Ace?" Lisa asked, changing the subject.

Ace was the burly contractor who had housed him and introduced him to the wonders of buildings when Jon had summered in Tilley five years before. That seemed like a different lifetime. He hadn't forgotten Ace or his wife Babs any more than he'd forgotten Lisa or Tilley or baseball or the Salsberg family or their mansion—Casa Grande—the site of the murder the last time he was on the Cape. No, he hadn't forgotten them, but over time other, more immediate obligations and demands just seemed to bury them.

"I've got to get together with him."

Lisa poured them both more coffee. She leaned on the table and rested her chin on her steepled hands, adjusted her glasses again with her little finger pointing up to the ceiling and asked, "So, what's your plan? Am I going to see you again before you head back to Florida? Or was that it?"

"I've got to go to this festival," he said, stalling for time. "I mean, that's why I came. And I want to see Ace and Babs."

"Where are you staying?"

"They have cabins at the institute, and I signed up to stay there."

"Then what?" she pressed.

She's definitely not making this easy, Jon thought. Before he drove up here, he sort of had a plan: he would attend the festival, learn some stuff, chat with Ace about construction, say hello to Lisa, then head back to Fort Lauderdale and sort out his thoughts and his duties there.

But, no! She had knocked that plan into Mrs. Murphy's chowder! She had infiltrated his mind and his heart and compelled him to face a different future, one he hadn't planned for. His instinct was the usual promise, "I'll call you and...." But that wouldn't work. This was an immediate decision, and he was unprepared for it. He found himself saying, "I'll be back!" The words seemed to come out of someone else's mouth. But he smiled.

"I'd like that," she said. "Meanwhile, stay safe. You never know what tree huggers will do."

~

JON FELT DECIDEDLY different as he drove Maybelline down the Cape to the town of Tilley. Lisa had stirred the "What's next" stew in his brain. Before… before yesterday or that morning, maybe, he had the idea of getting into construction, of working with Ace, maybe coming back to the Cape. But Florida wasn't too bad, either. And there was letting his father's company down—failing in the attempt to secure the baseball franchise. That was a challenge his father had laid on his shoulders to help him launch his life. It wasn't something he could ungraciously shrug off like a two-year-old's toy when the interest wains.

Tilley was way down the Cape, a direction branded in nautical terminology that never let go. Sailing to the east along the Cape was sailing with the prevailing wind behind you—down wind. The length of the Cape always surprised Jon. The sixty-five miles from the Canal to Provincetown is never a quick drive. It's surprisingly long with diverse terrains and traffic. The mid-Cape Highway runs down the spine of the peninsula. Buried in vegetation, a visitor could be fooled into thinking that the land was undeveloped. Hardly any houses, developments, or commercial buildings are visible from the highway. There are no gas stations or service areas except the Burger King and gas station at the Route 132 interchange. The Cape seems like an undeveloped and peaceful garden, but there is the sense that the ocean is lurking all around.

He pulled Maybelline off the highway at the Tilley exit and felt a strange sense of déjà vu at the back of his neck. But it wasn't his imagination. He had been there before. The air smelled of grass cuttings and the mugginess of the morning mist. He juggled the printed directions to the International Transmogrify Institute, finally finding the entrance.

In an earlier incarnation, ITI had been one of those motels you see in vacation communities with a collection of cabins surrounding it. It had since become a compound with long motel-like buildings, a farmhouse, and the cabins. Then a flash of sunlight hit Jon in the eye, and he saw a massive, mostly glass or fiberglass-covered structure, which he assumed must be the experimental greenhouse he'd read about, where they raised fish and grew plants while generating heat. It brazenly combined past and future, the quaint and the clinical.

He pulled into the driveway and heard the crunch of shells under Maybelline's wheels. He found a sign that said "Registration" and pulled to a stop. Well, this is different, he thought. He'd half expected to see groups of long-haired, bearded hippies in tie-dyed shirts, shaking tambourines while they chanted Hare Krishna. And in the other direction, overweight tourists in Hawaiian shirts wearing white socks and sandals taking photos with the cameras hanging around their sunburned necks. But it was ominously quiet.

Before he could climb out of Maybelline, a man with spiky hair and Elton John-style glasses came up and greeted him with a loud, "Hi! MG! Midget! Wow! Cool!"

Jon said, "Thanks. Just got here."

"I know," the man said. "I saw you. I'm Brian Nando, but everyone calls me Cheeky."

Jon shook Cheeky's proffered hand and introduced himself.

"Are you here for the festival?"

Jon heard a hint of British warmth in Cheeky's tone. "English?"

"Oh, yes. Just visiting the Colonies." He laughed. "Let me take you to registration. You can relocate your splendid car when we know where you will be sleeping. You are staying with us, aren't you?"

"That was the plan."

"Always good to have a plan," Cheeky said.

"Do you work here?" Jon asked.

"I'm an intern. They kind of imported me and let me learn things. A lot of learning and experimenting is happening here. ITI tries to catalyze the change from a consuming world to a natural world."

"Oh, I see," Jon said, not seeing.

He followed Cheeky down a path lined with what looked like lollipop lights to the main building. Inside, it was very dark in contrast to the bright August sunlight. Once he could see clearly, Jon registered a typical motel lobby with a phone on the counter and travel posters on the walls. "Do people stay here?" Jon asked. "I mean, when festivals are not going on?"

"Oh, yes," Cheeky replied. "We have visitors from all over... like England! Where are you coming from?"

"Florida. Fort Lauderdale."

"Oh, I've heard it's wonderful down there. Disneyland and Cape Kennedy where they send people off to the stars. I haven't had the chance to get there yet, but I hope to."

"It's too warm now. This isn't the best time of year to be there."

Cheeky slid around the end of the counter, pushed up the counter flap like a wing, and then let it drop back into place. He pulled his glasses down his nose, looked at Jon over the top of them, and put on his poshest receptionist accent. "How can I be of assistance, sir?" He paused, then laughed.

"Um..."

"Your name, sir," Cheeky continued.

"Megquire. Jon Megquire."

He scanned a list. "With a 'g' or a 'q'?"

"What?"

"I'm just checking the spelling on our reservation list, sir."

"It has both a 'g' and a 'q'."

"Why? Seems unnecessary, doesn't it?"

Jon looked at Cheeky's face to see if he was kidding.

"Is it pronounced *Meg Quire*? With a kind of stop in the middle?" Cheeky glared at Jon over his glasses.

"No, it's Megquire. I know it's a strange spelling, but that was because of some sloppy work by Sally Megquire, one of my ancestors, on her sewing sampler."

Cheeky looked at him in wonder.

"Never mind. My name is Megquire."

Cheeky gave him one more haughty stare, pushed his glasses back into position, and grinned. "Just taking the mickey!" He did a little dance, offered a grin, and held up "jazz hands".

Jon had no response to any of that.

"Yes, indeed. You're on our list of attendees. If you would be so kind as to sign here and add your name to this badge…. Just your first name, mind you. You will be in cabin 42. Not that there are forty-two cabins. I'll give you a map to help you find your way."

Jon signed the register and used the black marker to write 'Jon' on the card that was printed with, "Hi! I'm--", shoved it in the plastic sleeve, connected it to the lanyard, and hung it around his neck. When he turned back to the desk, Cheeky had disappeared, much like the white rabbit in *Alice in Wonderland*.

Jon pushed back through the screen door into the blazing August sunshine. He wondered if the word "festival" meant weird.

JON SPREAD out the map of ITI on Maybelline's steering wheel and looked for cabin 42. It was one of those two-sided, hand-drawn things with a crude map of the Cape on one side and a more detailed map of ITI on the other. The Cape side had sites of interest, like the windmill in Sandwich, a surfer down near the national seashore in Chatham, and other such graphics. Jon had heard that weekend sailors tried to use restaurant place mats much like this to navigate the waters around the Cape.

ITI was confusing. The property was extensive, but then he realized that this place had existed for a very long time in other forms— from farm to resort motel to institute.

The institute had renamed the cabins. In *The Hitchhiker's Guide to the Galaxy,* 42 was the meaning of life. Other cabins were named after other science fiction notables, like Klingons and Tribbles. The massive greenhouse was labeled the "Mycelium" and the main building or former farmhouse was labelled "Earth." The driveways and lanes and paths meandered between the buildings.

Jon chose what he thought would be the shortest route to cabin 42.

The discipline of the property impressed him. Not that the grass was carefully mowed or the bushes dramatically trimmed; there was just a definite back-to-nature vibe, and yet a subtle sense of order about the place. The cabins were old. No doubt they were thick with lead-based paint. They were simple—one step up from tents. He couldn't imagine that all these buildings had been weatherized, so they probably didn't use the cabins in winter.

At cabin 42, he pulled Maybelline into the sandy drive beside a big blue Buick. He hadn't expected to have a roommate. He pulled his bag out of the trunk and walked up the steps to the front porch, where a man lounged on a chair with a newspaper in front of his face.

"Hi," Jon said.

"Hi there, slim," the man replied, lowering the newspaper. He apparently thought himself shockingly handsome, since he had spent so much time gelling his salt-and-pepper hair topped off by his Irish flat cap. He hadn't shaved his Kirk Douglas cleft chin, and his blue eyes were accentuated by his swarthy skin and almost white eyebrows.

"Hi," Jon repeated. "I'm Jon Megquire. Are you here for the festival?"

"You betcha, slim. Are you staying here, too?"

"This is cabin 42, right?"

"So you're staying here with me? Didn't know I'd be sharing space. Do you snore?" In a John Wayne-like move, he pushed his cap further back and squinted at Jon. He wore a gold cross on a gold chain on his hairy chest, on full display thanks to his open shirt. "Wonderful! Look inside. Not much space. I'm in the room on the right. Good thing we're not staying long. Don't know what this industry has about getting back to nature.

"Kerchini. My name's Chris Kerchini." He lifted the paper up again and readjusted his cap.

Jon pushed through the screen door into the dimness of the cabin. It was basic—creaking pine floors, bare wood-framed walls, thin curtains on the windows, a bare light bulb hanging from a roof beam. He was standing in the living room with a TV, sofa, and a round, pink Formica table with four chairs. The basics of a kitchen with an electric stove, refrigerator, and a couple of cabinets graced one side of the room. Kerchini's bedroom was on the right, a second bedroom on the left, and the bathroom was near the kitchenette. It was as simple as a child's playhouse, tuned for summer vacation fun!

Jon threw his bag on the bed in his bedroom. His room had a bed, a small dresser, and a simple wood chair. He sat on the bed and found it overly soft. The whole place smelled musty and stale, and it encouraged him to not linger.

Back on the porch, he leaned on the railing and peered out at the other buildings in the complex. Kerchini had buried himself in the paper again. "Where are you from, Mr. Kerchini?" Jon asked.

"Waltham," Kerchini replied.

"That's near Boston, right?"

Kerchini lowered the paper to survey Jon. "Yeah. It's near Boston. Always has been. Where're you from, slim?"

"I came up from Florida."

"You drove up from Florida in that thing?" He looked out at Maybelline. "What the hell would you do that for?"

Jon shrugged. "I wanted to learn some stuff. And I know some people here on the Cape. I wanted to visit."

"Learn stuff!" Kerchini laughed. "What stuff did you have in mind to learn at this so-called festival? They should call it a conference instead of trying to force the festival *fun* down our throats."

"Why are you here then, Mr. Kerchini?"

"Call me Chris. Mandated foam insulation training. Easier to do it here than to go down to their factory in New Jersey. Waltham is near Boston, and Boston is closer to Cape Cod than to New freakin' Jersey. I hate New Jersey."

Jon didn't know what to say to that.

"Follow baseball?" Kerchini asked. After giving Jon an appraising look, he said, "You look like you should follow baseball, but then, if you live in Florida, what kind of baseball team would you follow? Do they have anything but spring training down there? What's the closest pro team? Atlanta? That's a stretch."

"That's my job," Jon said.

"What's your job?"

"Getting a pro team established in Fort Lauderdale."

"Really! Now that would make a hell of a lot more sense than a professional hockey team. How's it going?"

Jon looked up at the heart of the complex. He could see the top of the big greenhouse, or whatever it was. He thought back over the past four-plus years he'd spent haggling with code officials, chambers of commerce, and local businesses, and hanging out with egotistical athletes and their model girlfriends. All that money. All that noise and bickering and people stumbling all over each other, grabbing for a piece of a hypothetical pie. The love of money was the driving force down there, not love of the game. "Been at it for a few years now," he said finally. "I don't have high hopes."

"That sucks," Kerchini said, and lifted the paper up in front of his face again. "Red Sox just took two out of three from the Rangers. Kind of mediocre season in general, if you ask me. Did you play? They have quite the minor league thing here in the summer—Cape Cod Baseball League. Maybe you can catch a game while you're here.."

"I know about it," Jon said. "I played in it five years ago."

Kerchini lowered the paper again. "How'd that go for you? There's big money in sports now. That's what I should have done."

Jon sensed Kerchini was missing a piece of the character needed to become a professional athlete. Besides that, he was too pretty—and Kerchini knew it. "They don't make it easy," he said.

"Well, if it was easy, everyone would do it. That's just the point. You were probably too soft to make it. Besides, I think you have to be from Puerto Rico or some other spic place these days. I don't know how many good, red-blooded American boys are getting the big bucks."

It always surprised Jon how prejudiced many sports fans were. He didn't understand what the color of a player's skin, the shape of their eyes, or their theological position had to do with their skills as an athlete. Sports fans felt a vicarious connection to the players—fantasizing that it could have been them if only they had been given the chance—like Kerchini.

Sports fans' hearts and spirits rose and fell with the success or failure of their teams. They felt cheated when a favorite player went over to a deadly rival, and they rooted for the player to fail, to prove that changing teams was a mistake.

Conversations like this proved to Jon that the pro sports world was not where he wanted to spend his life, and for a moment, he returned to the fond memory of Lisa's affections.

"Going to check the place out," he told Kerchini as he stepped off the porch and strode toward the heart of the complex.

~

JON WALKED up the main drive to the center of the compound. Now he was sensing something creepy about the place. It felt like a hippy version of Disney Land—a geeky, energy efficiency amusement park with all the fun and frivolity taken out of it, sort of like a cheeseburger with fake meat and fake cheese accompanied by fake French fries! "Have fun but eat your vegetables!" It gave the place a sense of dystopian doom.

He had no reason to think that way. Maybe it was his conversation with Chris Kerchini. The man clearly didn't want to be there. He wasn't eager to learn about new, energy efficient paths into the future, or how to raise fish in his backyard and use their poop to nourish the vegetable garden.

As he approached the main buildings, he saw other people wandering about with, "Hi! I'm--" badges hanging around their necks.

He found a table with mimeographed copies of the festival's event schedule and free samples of energy and environmental magazines such as *Solar Age, Energy Design Update,* and *Solplan Review.* Another table offered information on electricity and energy efficient lightbulbs.

Behind a third table sat a man with a blond crewcut, a button-down shirt with a paisley tie, a name tag that read "Hi! I'm Lash," and a big grin. In front of him was an Apple II computer with a monitor and keyboard. He looked Jon straight in the eye and said, "Hi, Jon! How are you?"

That was the problem with these name tags. People greeted you as a long-lost friend when they didn't know you at all. "Hi." Jon smiled back.

"Welcome to the festival!"

"Thanks. Are you here as a presenter?"

"Yes! They invited me here to talk about computer modeling."

Jon had been thinking about computers. He'd read about them in *Popular Science*. It was amazing stuff. They were moving from big IBM mainframes on one end to the electronic hobbyists on the other, converging on normal people. They said that it was possible that everyone would have a computer on their desk. The Apple II was a step in that direction. Jon had been fantasizing about getting one.

"Are you... will you show us how to use this thing?"

"That's why I'm here," Lash said, jumping up from behind the card table which shook precariously as he bumped it. "I'm Lash Ashton!" and he thrust his hand out.

"Jon Megquire."

"Have you got a computer?"

"No." Jon laughed. "Not yet, anyway."

"Well, you need one. Everybody needs one."

"Really? You think so?"

"I do. They let you see lots of things that you could never see before."

"What do they have to do with energy efficiency or solar heat?"

"That's what I'm going to be talking about. Got a minute? Can I show you how it works?"

Jon took a seat in the extra chair behind Ashton's display table and watched him tap into a magical world of numbers, words, and questions on his computer's screen.

～

THAT EVENING, on the patio behind the old farmhouse that served as the ITI administration building, Chinese lanterns had been strung, tables set up, and the festival attendees milled about chatting. Jon went to the bar to stand in line for a beer.

Seemed to Jon like there were maybe forty or fifty attendees. Many of the men sported beards and long hair. Several women wore tie-dyed dresses and appeared braless. People looked relaxed and smiled at each other. It was an unusually familial atmosphere, very unlike the high-powered sports and business events he'd attended for the Fort Lauderdale project. Here there was a sense of being united in the cause of "Saving the World."

The smell of the farm—grass and manure, with a twist of marijuana—permeated the warm evening air. Jon could hear laughter, guitar strumming, and a folk song sung with a British accent.

He looked around to find Cheeky Nando playing "Kumbaya."

The kid does everything, Jon thought. Was he also the source of the marijuana smoke?

Jon went over and joined the circle surrounding Cheeky. Other people chimed in, singing the familiar words. And when they got through "Someone's cryin', Lord" and "Someone's singin'" someone began "Someone's laughin'", "Someone's drinkin'," and "Someone's prayin'".

They probably would have continued on to "smokin'" and "tokin'" if another voice hadn't shouted: "Welcome! Welcome all to our little piece of heaven here on Cape Cod!" Cheeky stopped playing and stood up, holding his guitar by the neck. "And just in case you were wondering in this strange year we are living in—1984—Big Brother is not watching us! At least not at the moment! On the other hand, maybe he should be! Ha ha ha."

Jon looked around to find the source of the voice and connected it to a tall, thin, almost emaciated man with a grey ponytail and remarkably large ears standing near the entrance to the patio.

"Good evening!" the man shouted.

Some people repeated, "Good evening," in return.

"No, you can do better than that. GOOD EVENING!"

The group responded with a louder "GOOD EVENING!".

"That's more like it. I want to welcome you. I'm Dr. Elliott Widner, your host and director of ITI. I hope you are all comfortable and ready to learn and… and to teach, might I say. Each of us has lived a life until now. We've had our experiences—our ups and downs. And we can share those experiences with each other and grow as a group. Are you willing to share your lives and your thoughts and your knowledge with us? Together, we will grow. Together, we will change the world!"

Jon had his doubts. He looked around for his roommate. Kerchini wasn't likely to share anything with anybody.

He looked over to smile at the woman standing beside him. "Are you willing to share your life…" he peered down to read her name tag… "Miriam?" She had chestnut hair and brown eyes behind her wire-rimmed glasses, and she reached back to adjust her hair.

"Oh, yes," she said, speaking in a hushed tone. "To a degree, anyway. It's only through the exchange of thoughts and ideas that we grow, don't you think?"

"Sure. Yes," Jon replied. Dressed for a formal cocktail party, she seemed to Jon to be out of place—a business suit at a mud-wrestling challenge. In comparison, Jon felt awkwardly casual in his khaki trousers and his pale blue Lacoste shirt with the little alligator on his left breast.

Widner's welcome was filled with fluff and not much substance. He smiled a lot and waved his arms and reiterated the wonders of ITI and that was that.

"Where are you from?" Jon asked Miriam when Widner had finished.

"Cape Cod," she replied. "Falmouth."

"Oh," Jon said.

"And you are… Jon, right?"

"That's right. Jon Megquire. I'm a rookie at this stuff."

"Where are you from, Jon?"

"Florida. Fort Lauderdale."

"Why?"

"Why am I from Fort Lauderdale?" Jon asked with a smile.

"No. Why are you here? It's a long way from Fort Lauderdale. Of course we get the summer visitors. The Snowbirds, we call them. Fly up here in summer to get out of the tropical heat and then fly back south for the winter. Are you one of those? And why would you be at ITI? It doesn't seem like a tourist attraction."

"Oh, no," Jon laughed. "I'm not a snowbird." He didn't have a good answer to the why he was here question, so he swigged his beer and looked around at the attendees. "Seems like a good turnout."

She looked around the patio. "It's a comparatively small facility, really. And that's good. Not like one of those massive convention centers. This group seems about the right size to be productive. To get something done."

"Do you know any of the speakers?"

"Not personally," she said. "I know of them. Heard their names. Read about them in the trade magazines. Do you read *Solar Age?*"

"No. Honestly, I didn't even know about it until today," he said. "What do you know about Dr. Widner?"

"I read an article in the paper about him when he first got here," she said. "He comes from Saskatchewan with a PhD in something like agriculture or forestry management. He's gotten involved with the Wampanoag here in Mashpee. They want their land back. They've given him trouble about this land."

"Oh," Jon said, trying to put the pieces together, trying to connect Saskatchewan, forestry, the Wampanoag, and buildings.

"Apparently, he was tangled up with the Métis in Saskatchewan when he was there... during what they called 'the October Crisis,' back in 1970. You probably don't remember, but Canada was under martial law because of the crazy French."

"I missed that," Jon said. He was just thirteen in 1970.

"I was pretty young," she said. "I wasn't much interested in geopolitical stuff then," she laughed. "But they wrote about it in the article I read about him. He came to the Cape about a year before I did, and he's been here since this place opened, four years ago."

"And what brings you to this festival?"

"I sell real estate. I want to know more about the buildings I sell. New technologies pop up. New houses aren't the same as old traditional houses and people are buying old houses and trying to make them into new houses.

"I had a house that my husband and I tried to insulate with this foam they are going to be talking about."

"Oh, yeah! I think the foam guy was at the restaurant I ate at last night. His truck was anyway."

"Really? Well, I just want to learn more about it. It can be dangerous for people who don't know what they're doing."

"Isn't that true for just about everything?"

"Well, it's been nice chatting, Jon," she said. "I'm going to call it a day. As Charles Schulz said, 'Don't worry about the world ending today. It is already tomorrow in Australia.'"

Jon thought about that as she walked away.

Meanwhile, Cheeky had started singing "If I Had a Hammer," and the crowd chimed in when he got to the "ding, ding" in the "If I had a bell" verse. The crickets and katydids were singing their own songs. The lollipop lights lit the pathways as the late setting sun faded from the sky. Jon followed a path away from the central courtyard.

He was glad to be back on the Cape. He swam in the memories of Lisa from the night before. He felt her all around him and smiled to himself. She was amazing. She just was. Beautiful and smart and interesting and fun to talk to and fun to be with. And what a smooth, firm body. So how was it going to work out with her?

He stopped walking and tried to get his bearings. The place was dark and confusing away from the central patio—a maze of little cabins, paths, and picnic tables. He heard the creaking of a windmill and saw the shadows of the water tanks. He stepped up beside one and tapped on the fiberglass. The tank flexed a fraction. He wondered if they could raise those flesh-eating piranhas, so you could just throw a body in the tank to get rid of it in seconds! Or sharks. Could they grow sharks in these things? If they grew small sharks, could they throw them into the ocean when they got too big? He stepped away from the tank. They wouldn't grow piranhas. He seemed to remember that those things grew in the tropics. The climate wasn't right. But maybe….

He reached a parking lot where the lights reflected off the vehicles, including the foam truck he'd spotted at the inn the night before. Jon wondered if this was where they were going to do the foam training. He walked through the lot, brooding about his future. In Florida, when he had been considering coming to this festival, what was he thinking that had brought him here? He wasn't an engineer or a builder. He did like houses and Ace had done a marvelous job of instilling the magic of buildings in him. He liked the geeky stuff they wrote about in *Popular Science* and *Popular Mechanics*, and he even waded through the occasional *Scientific American*. And solar energy was in the news. He had been reading about homes heated primarily with solar heat, and how the Pueblo Indians had built adobe walled structures so that they were cool during the day and warm at night. In the Florida heat, he had marveled at the technologies of air condition-ing. It all seemed like practical magic—not fluffy, impractical things, like writing poetry or painting landscapes. It had practical uses—plus you could get paid to do it. These thoughts of energy, nature, and technology had been brewing in his head, and he wanted more clarity. Because who knew what was going to happen next in the world? Who knew what would happen tomorrow?

Walking down the dark drive, he tried to picture the map of the property and remember where cabin 42 was. In the shadows ahead, he spotted a dark form weaving and stumbling toward him. Jon stopped walking and listened. It was a man was humming "Kumbaya".

"Oh, lord, Kumbaya! Mmm. Mmm."

As he got closer, Jon recognized Kerchini. "Chris?"

"What?"

"Mr. Kerchini?"

Kerchini held a beer bottle in his right hand and peered at Jon in the dim light of the nearby streetlamp. "Who's that? I didn't do it."

"I'm Jon Megquire, your cabin mate. We share Cabin 42, remember?"

"Nope. Call me Chris. I'm proud to be a Kerchini, but don't call me that. Out here I am one with the universe!" He looked up at the sky and waved his beer to show the vastness of the night.

"Did you want help to find our cabin?" Jon asked.

"Cabin?"

"Yes, Chris. The cabin you're staying in."

"Do you know that song? That song the British kid was singing? Did he write that? It's pretty stupid. Ever wonder what a 'Kumbaya' is?"

Jon never knew what to do with a drunk. He'd seen plenty—some were privileged people who seemed to assume that the world would take care of them whatever they did. Others just partied too hard. Did you hold them up or let them fall and leave them where they fell? But here he felt obligated to guide his dandy of a roommate back to his bed.

"Kumbayas don't exist, Chris. Hey, I'm headed back to the cabin. We can find it together. I think you're heading the wrong way. Let's go this way," and Jon turned Kerchini around and nudged him back toward the cabin.

CHAPTER 3

FESTIVAL DAY 1–AUGUST 6, 1984

*J*on liked breakfast. Nothing fancy. Just bacon and eggs, toast, orange juice, and coffee. It was predictable and good. He didn't want to make a lot of choices.

That's not what greeted him at the Monday morning buffet. The table featured organic muffins, vegetables, dips, yogurt, and other healthy organic foodstuffs.... There was juice, although it didn't look or taste like orange juice, and there was coffee. He decided he would fill his stomach with the breads—what some establishments called a continental breakfast, which he believed was just a fancy name for "we-didn't-feel-like-spending-the-money-on-a-real-breakfast"—and hope that maybe lunch would be better.

Cheeky was darting around picking up plates, gathering dropped napkins, bringing in more buns. "Jon!" he said, as though surprised by his presence. "What can I get you? The yogurt's made right here, you know. You'll love it!"

Jon smiled weakly. He drifted out to the picnic tables around the patio. Miriam joined him asking, "May I?"

"Sure!" Jon replied. He noticed Miriam had assembled yogurt, buns, and vegetables on a paper plate, and held a paper coffee cup in her left hand.

"So, did you enjoy last night?" he asked.

She looked at him. "Did you?"

"Sure. Cheeky sings well, doesn't he?"

She crunched her celery. "I think I've outgrown the groupie music."

Jon tried to guess her age. Her longish chestnut hair was graying in places. She peered at him in a way that reminded him of a grandmother. She put down her coffee and reached back with both hands to gather in her hair, balled it up as if she was going to secure it, but gave up and let it fall back onto her shoulders.

"You said you live in Falmouth? Been there long?"

"About three years. I used to live up north. Near Boston. And you said Fort Lauderdale? What did you say you do there?"

"I've been trying to establish a major league baseball franchise there. In fact, I used to play baseball, here on the Cape anyway."

"Really?"

"Yeah. I had a shot at the majors, but I blew out my knee playing for the minor league team in Fort Lauderdale—the Suns. You probably haven't heard of them."

"Nope," she said. "I'm not much of a sports fan."

"Players are getting huge salaries these days... if they're good. But that's just it. There's a massive amount of pressure to perform. Competition to get on top and stay on top and that isn't for me."

"The competition?"

"No, the pressure. I don't find pressure fun. When I played here, I had fun. I mean, the Cape Cod Baseball League is very competitive. But it was different, maybe because money wasn't involved. I just enjoyed it. And, I guess, when you enjoy something, it's fun."

"Do you think buildings are fun?" She squinted at him in the morning sun that reflected off her glasses.

Jon laughed. "I don't know. I guess. I haven't decided yet. But more fun than professional sports competition. What about you? Do you think buildings are fun? You sell them, right?"

"You know," she said, balling up her hair again, "I wouldn't call them fun. They interest me. The challenges home buyers face interest me. Homes are a major investment. People used to buy homes for cash, and only poor people took out mortgages.... Not that long ago, you could buy a pleasant house for fifteen thousand dollars. Of course, incomes were a lot lower, too. Now average prices are up around ninety thousand. First-time home buyers think they know what they want and what they want is what they've been reading about in *Better Homes and Gardens, Good Housekeeping,* and *Architectural Digest.* And they're shocked when they see what they can afford. They can't have what they want."

Her enthusiasm for her subject intrigued Jon. She seemed to have been infected by the building affinity disease.

"And with the price of oil going up, they don't even consider what it's going to cost them to maintain a house once they finance it. They don't budget for that. If you can make a home more energy efficient—which is what my husband and I tried to do with our house—you can bring the operating cost down. Which is why I'm here. We better go. Dr. Widner is going to tell us what he wants to tell us in a couple of minutes."

Jon noticed people heading into the main building. He and Miriam gathered up the remains of their meals, dropped it in the trash, and followed the crowd. Maybe he would find the fun.

~

STAFF HAD ARRANGED rows of chairs, transforming the big room in the main house into a compressed auditorium. Bright, sunlit windows were open to the summer Cape Cod air. Several large ceiling fans rotated lazily. The varnished bright yellow pine floors creaked as people walked to their seats.

Jon found a seat and watched as the room filled up. Widner stood at the front, rubbing his hands and smoothing his hair. He was so skinny that he reminded Jon of Washington Irving's Ichabod Crane, in the "Legend of Sleepy Hollow". He strutted. Posed. Looked alternatively nervous and exasperated. Cheeky Nando slid up beside him and handed him a glass of water, which he barely acknowledged.

Kerchini dropped into the chair next to Jon and let out a whoosh of air. The chair complained.

"Hi," Jon said.

Kerchini grunted. Jon wondered if he had a touch of the "wine" flu. There was something about the man that bothered him, but he couldn't put his finger on it. Maybe it was that he was too pretty—with his gelled hair and Elvis sideburns. Some people look and sound like the life and career they are following. And some people are just out of place. For Jon, Kerchini stereotyped as a celebrity-wanna-be—a celebrity without the core—a shell of a star.

Jon hadn't seen him at breakfast. In fact, when Jon left the cabin, Kerchini's door was still closed, as though he intended to sleep in.

"This is so bogus," Kerchini hissed, leaning close to Jon's ear. "Now we're going to be bombarded with 'the beauties of the world' tripe and how we can all work together to save the planet. Blah, blah, blah. That's what pisses me off about this business. They make such a big deal about their altruistic motives. Bottom line: it's the money. Am I right?"

Widner began speaking, so Jon just smiled and turned away.

"Welcome again! I know we met briefly last night, but you are all so welcome—so very welcome—here at ITI on this bright morning."

The murmuring and creaking subsided. Kerchini mumbled, "Bullshit!"

"How did you sleep last night? This is quite a place, isn't it? It's so exciting. You're going to have time to see some things we do here at the International Transmogrify Institute. Just a quick bit of background. Founded just four years ago, ITI's mission is to help to make the world a better place."

Kerchini punched Jon's shoulder. "See!"

"Why 'transmogrify,' you might ask?" Widner said with a laugh. "Transmogrify means to change as if by magic. Nature changes things magically all the time—water into ice or grapes into raisins or oil into heat. Here at the institute we are working to change the world—as if by magic! It's hard work, really. Nature needs help, doesn't it?" He chuckled and got a responding murmur from the audience.

"So who have we got with us today? If you're a builder, please raise your hand."

A scattering of attendees raised their hands.

"Architects?" He looked around the room and one person raised his hand.

"Hmm? Who else? Engineers? Anyone designing solar houses?" He paused. "Great! How about golfers? I mean, these skills are not exclusive, are they? You could be a golfer and a solar designer. You could even be a mountain climber. You could be anything, couldn't you? In this crazy world that we live in, almost anything could happen." Pause. "And probably will.".

"But before I get off track, let me tell you about myself."

"Oh, here we go," Kerchini huffed.

"I grew up in Saskatchewan, Canada. Out on the prairie. I had the honor of working on the R2000 House, which you may be familiar with, but we had a sort of mission disagreement, and I moved to Massachusetts to work with the esteemed Dr. Orville Hawkins at MIT. And Orville is with us today!" Widner started clapping, and the audience joined in. "He has wonderful information that he will share with us, including superinsulation he wrote about in his book.

"And while I'm introducing people, I might as well introduce you to our other speakers and trainers."

He pointed to a very thin, balding man standing at the edge of room. "This is Don Douthwaite, the New Hampshire builder. He pioneered energy conservation and solar home building, and he's also an author of several books, including one on a double-shell solar house design, and his latest on sun to earth connections and superinsulation, which I'm sure he will tell you about."

Don nodded his head, acknowledging the applause.

Widner then indicated a blond-haired woman standing next to Don. She had a pleasant face, Jon thought, but wore an expression of scary intensity.

"This is Gail Barker, who comes to us all the way from Colorado. Gail has lots of stories to tell about farms and forts and the Solar Energy Research Institute.

"And we have Joseph Caruso, who is going to teach us about foam insulation, a technology that we all need to learn more about."

Joe grinned and waved his hand over his head.

Jon felt Kerchini bristle when Widner presented Caruso. "Know him?"

Kerchini tucked his head down as though glaring at his own crotch and emitted a low growl.

"So if you are all comfortable and ready to learn," Widner continued, "I am going to start by getting you to go around the room and introduce yourselves and say a few words about why you're here."

Jon hated these around-the-room introductions. He was okay with saying his name. But then what? What part of his life should he highlight? And could he say he was a sports promoter? Or what? He didn't have a label or a tag. Maybe he should be honest and get a laugh. "Hi. I'm Jon Megquire. And I don't know what the hell I'm doing!"

He turned to see the faces and listened to the voices as they moved around the room. Most people seemed to be connected to construction or energy efficiency. But a few just said they were interested in learning, and that made him feel more comfortable.

When it was Kerchini's turn, in a north-end Boston twang, he said, "I'm Chris Kerchini, from Waltham. I sell aluminum siding and windows. I took on foam insulation because I want to keep people and their cute little puppies warm in the winter." He smiled. "When I started, there wasn't anybody doing it. I had to learn it for myself. My company is fourteen years old now, and I've done a lot to make my community a better place."

"Thank you, Mr. Kerchini," Widner interrupted. "And who's that next to you?"

"Hi, I'm Jon Megquire from Fort Lauderdale. I used to play baseball—here. I guess I'm here to learn. I had a summer job working on houses when I was here five years ago. I'm hoping that I can find out what it's all about."

"It might take you more than three days," Widner said, with a grin. "But we'll do our best."

After all the introductions, Widner stood for a moment, looking around the room. "Before we move on, I want to say a few words about thermodynamics. That is a big scary word, but we can't live without it. Thermodynamics embraces the movement of the stars and the heavens and the magnitude of the universe.

"Thermodynamics is reflected in gatherings of people. The Zeroth Law of thermodynamics states that if two thermodynamic systems are each in thermal equilibrium with a third one, then they are in thermal equilibrium with each other! The key to this festival is to bring all of you together into knowledge equilibrium. All of you have had many life experiences and have deep personal knowledge of life and death. Gathered here, you can share that knowledge, and like adding ice cubes to a warm liquid, the ice would warm and melt and the liquid would cool until the ice and the liquid were in equilibrium —even though the ice would no longer exist! Just like magic. And as all of you learn from each other, you will all get smarter and more knowledgeable together!" He spread his arms wide, simulating a massive group hug.

"The first law is even grander! It is the law of conservation of energy that says that energy can transform from one form to another —like food to human activity—but can be neither created nor destroyed. There is only a certain amount of energy embodied in the universe. There will never be more. We are using it and changing it every single day."

Thermodynamics sounded to Jon like quantum physics or organic chemistry, subjects so impossibly complex that only the elite could understand them and toss the words around like tee shirts or socks.

But Widner was expansive in his joy of his world of knowledge. He raised his hands and said, "Wonderful! So glad all of you are here. I'm so proud of our work here at ITI, and I want to show it to you. Let's go look, shall we? And get out in the famous Cape Cod summer sunshine!"

He swept the crowd out of the meeting hall, and they obediently followed him through the doors and onto the patio, gathering around him.

"This is what we call the plaza," Widner announced, raising the volume of his speech like a tour guide walking through Central Park. "You're familiar with this place if you were here last night. Wasn't that great?"

"That is what we call The Mycelium," he said, pointing to the gigantic greenhouse. The group stood behind him on the hill, gazing. "You might wonder why the roof is a series of four-foot-wide troughs. That provides the maximum solar gain throughout the year with a minimum of reflection. Reflection of sunlight is loss. Although you might not think that if you are looking in a mirror."

He pointed to some small stand-alone solar concentrators. "Those are compound parabolic concentrators. They focus all the sunlight on a single point to create steam. We based the design on the eye of the trilobite, a creature that lived deep in the ocean. The parabolic design of the trilobite eye allowed it to focus what little light there was at those depths. And that connects us to the research being done at the Woods Hole Oceanographic Institute—WHOI. All things are connected. Life is a system."

Widner looked around at the crowd and smiled. "The tanks you see surrounding the Mycelium are tilapia tanks, which are all part of the circle of life. I wish we had time today for me to explain the biological path that the nutrients take, which is miraculous. Simply and extraordinarily miraculous. And we..." he swept his arm around again, "we humans are merely rude pawns."

Rude pawns, Jon thought. Ichabod was becoming Shakespeare.

"We do far more than just grow tomatoes and cucumbers in there. There are eighteen more of the tilapia tanks inside, each one holding over seven hundred gallons of water. Production is so high that we can supply all the local restaurants and markets. And that, of course, produces revenue, which is also part of the circle of life. I know that the people who farmed these lands over the centuries would be amazed and awed by how we have harnessed the natural forces and work with nature in a way they could never have imagined. I like to think they would be pleased by our efforts.

"Oh, if only we had more time. That, my friends, is not something that we can produce. Time is a precious commodity in very limited supply.

"Wander about between our sessions, but please don't disrupt our interns, volunteers, and employees. And don't be tempted to put anything in the tanks. You will be disturbing years of carefully balanced research."

CHAPTER 4

FESTIVAL DAY 1—AUGUST 6, 1984

*J*on didn't think that lunch had redeemed the sketchy breakfast, but what could you put into a cardboard box that would satisfy the food gods?

The tour of ITI was interesting. He didn't think he could see people raising fish in their living rooms, but he was seeing the system thing, kind of reducing a natural life cycle into a compact space. He could also see that a lot of work was involved, and he didn't believe that normal people could manage it. People have trouble keeping house-plants alive. He didn't see them doing well with seven-hundred-gallon water tanks filled with strange-looking fish and covered with floating lettuce. It didn't have quite the same charm as standing in a gushing river among the rocks, swishing a fly line out and wresting a trout or salmon into a net. But then farmers slog out to milk the cows and feed the chickens and slop the pigs every day. A lot about alternative energy appealed to Jon, but grabbing a tilapia was not one of them. He scratched that off his potential new career list.

Next up on the festival schedule was Joe Caruso's demonstration of expanding foam. Everyone migrated to the parking lot Jon had come across the previous night. Caruso had opened the back of his truck and run a heavy-gauge power cord into the building. A couple of fifty-five-gallon drums were visible in the truck, connected to a web of hoses, meters, and valves that were throbbing and pulsing as though alive.

Caruso stepped away from the truck and toward the gathered crowd. "Noisy, isn't it!" he shouted. "But it's alive. This is the latest Grady machine. We've refined it considerably. Although it may look scary, you should have seen the earlier ones." He laughed.

It struck Jon that Caruso didn't look like a foam insulation installer—if there was such a stereotype. He was too short. He was too fat. The tortoise-shell glasses made him look bookish. Although he stepped into the role of trainer, Jon couldn't see him generating respect in a room full of union members.

Caruso explained how the machine carefully blended the two chemicals together, and once exposed to the air, the foam expanded dramatically.

"I've been doing this for a while, and we've come a long way. Used to just do commercial buildings—warehouses and such. Gigantic buildings where you had to get up on lifts. It was ugly and messy, and the stuff would get in your eyes, and I'd come home barely able to breathe. Ruined a whole lot of clothes, which the company never paid for, of course."

The attendees had pulled closer in order to hear better. Jon noticed Miriam, who stood at the front. She seemed mesmerized by what Caruso was saying. Kerchini, on the other hand, appeared not to care. Don Douthwaite, the New Hampshire builder, stood off to one side with his arms folded across his chest. Gail Baker, the woman from Colorado, stood beside him. Jon guessed they considered them-selves the "experts group." They knew all this already and didn't need to take part.

Caruso brought the crowd right up to the back of the truck and pointed out the controls, described required maintenance steps, the delicacy of finessing the chemicals to get the proper mixture, and the importance of keeping the moisture out.

"I used to be independent. Worked here in Massachusetts, in fact. I helped develop some of this equipment. Harvard invited me to do some work." He paused. "This spray nozzle was my idea. The thing must be portable if you're going to work on houses. You have to get into some small places—tight corners, under the eaves. That's what the whip hose is for. I gave Grady the idea for doing that with this smaller nozzle." He held it up. "I should have patented it, but I didn't. I wanted other people to be able to do this. Which is why I'm here. Teaching you." He pushed his glasses up his nose.

Someone asked if the chemicals were dangerous, and if they should all be wearing masks.

"Nah," Caruso replied. "Only if you're in a tight spot. Not too good for the skin, I guess, although I've never had a problem."

ITI had constructed a two-by-four stud bay wall section sheathed with plywood for demonstration. "All right. Let me show you how this works."

He looked at a meter inside the truck. "You have to watch the temperature and relative humidity," he explained. "Foam can react differently on different days."

Caruso cranked up the machine. It clicked and throbbed and hissed.

"Let's look at how urethane foam is produced in...."

Very interesting, Jon thought. How am I supposed to remember all this? Can't I just look in a book?

"... relative volumes of polymeric isocyanate and polyol resin usually referred to as simply A and B components which must be mixed in order to create the specific foam properties the chemical system is formulated to produce."

A and B. Got it, Jon thought.

Caruso pulled a large piece of cardboard out of the truck, shot a small amount of the mixed chemicals onto it, and continued his narration.

Jon noticed Douthwaite start to step forward, as if to comment or intrude on the demonstration—perhaps correct something that Caruso had said. But then he stepped back and crossed his arms again.

"Notice that the mixed materials immediately begin the chemical reaction."

The group gathered closer and peered down at the spot on the cardboard growing explosively.

"The products of this reaction are polyurethane plastic and heat or exotherm, which cause a low-boiling, liquid-blowing agent dissolved in the resin to vaporize and expand. The expanding gas becomes trapped in the polyurethane plastic, causing the liquid to foam up and rise to about thirty times its original thickness."

Thirty times—wow, Jon thought.

"After the complete rise has taken place, the polyurethane plastic, still in its liquid state, forms a solid skin at the outer surface which becomes dry or tack-free to the touch."

Several observers reached out to touch the surface of the foam and held up their fingers.

Caruso smiled at them. "The time required for the tack-free skin to form is called the tack-free time of the foam system."

Was there going to be a quiz? Jon thought. Otherwise, why would you need to remember all these terms? He thought about Lisa's skin.

"A quality foam product will be composed of many uniform small cells which, because of their closed cell structure, will keep the blowing agent gas—which gives polyurethane foam its superior insulating properties." Caruso pulled out a razor knife, sliced down the small pile of foam, and held the piece up to show the audience.

"See how nice and tight that structure is? Besides knowing some of the distinguishing properties of a quality foam, it is helpful to know something about the type of surface or substrate it can be sprayed on. By rule of thumb, any paintable surface is satisfactory. Surfaces containing moisture, oil, scale, or loose dirt would seriously affect bonding of the foam. Human skin would not be a great bonding surface," he said.

Human skin? Jon wondered.

"At temperatures above one hundred degrees Fahrenheit, almost all the exothermic heat of reaction is kept within the foam, which undergoes a normal reaction, giving the most efficient rise. So a warmer surface makes your job easier."

He picked up the whip hose and the gun and dragged it over to the wall section. "The hose can be over two hundred feet long."

He pointed the gun up to the top of the wall section. As he pulled the trigger, the machinery in the truck began to click. And clack. Rhythmically. Click - left. Clack - right. He swept the spray evenly back and forth across the wall cavity. The yellowy orange-edged foam grew as if it was possessed. It reminded Jon of a creature from a horror movie. He imagined the blob of foam sliding out of the wall cavity, creeping across the ground, and swallowing them all.

The audience was mesmerized.

"What's the insulating value?" someone asked.

Joe pointed the gun at the ground. "That's the real beauty of this insulation. It has an R value of almost seven per inch! Fiberglass insulation is less than half that. You could use just an inch of this to two inches of fiberglass insulation."

"What happens if you pile it on quickly?" Miriam asked.

"Remember," Joe replied, "the process generates heat. If you layer it on too quickly, it will get dangerously hot. Anyone want to try spraying it?"

Miriam stepped up. "Right-handed... uh, Miriam?" Joe asked, peering at her nametag. She nodded. Caruso showed her how to gather in the whip hose and bunch it on her left hip.

She pointed the gun at the wall, pulled the trigger and the machine clicked and clacked again for one quick burst in a pile that rapidly blossomed.

"Back and forth," Caruso urged. "Not too fast and not too slow. Just a nice even spread across the surface. That's it. Good job, Miriam. You're a natural. Shall we let someone else try it? We have a small wall section here."

Miriam appeared reluctant to relinquish the gun. Her body was swaying along as she swept it back and forth across the surface, dancing in front of the structure while the machine clicked and clacked behind her.

Caruso took the gun out of Miriam's hand while smiling and repeating, "Good job, Miriam. Good job."

"Anyone else?"

Jon noted Miriam seemed reluctant to let the wand go, and when Kerchini stepped up, she stumbled back as though he repulsed her. "Let me," Kerchini said. "I've got this."

Kerchini yanked on the hose, seized the gun, and shot a burst of foam onto the ground.

"I usually make a test pile before I actually start putting the foam on the surface," he said.

"You've done this before?" Caruso asked.

"Yeah. A lot. You got another piece of that cardboard? I'll show you."

Caruso pulled a piece of cardboard out of the truck. "You don't want to make that pile too thick," he advised. "It could still be hot if you put it in your vehicle when you're cleaning up at the end of the job. I've seen it cause a fire."

"How hot can it get?" someone asked.

Caruso expelled a whoosh of air. "I've been told by the scientists that it can get up to two thousand degrees... sixteen hundred to two thousand degrees Fahrenheit, maybe even more."

"Holy shit!" someone said.

"Yeah. It's hot. So that's when you pile on like twelve inches of the material. If you want greater thickness, layer it on, giving the foam time to cool and set between each layer. You need to be careful and not layer it on too thick. If you spray these test 'buns', like Chris here is doing, you want to take a meat thermometer and measure the temperature in the bun before you throw it in a dumpster or in your truck. It can take as much as four hours for the exothermic heat to reach auto-ignition temperatures within the foam."

Jon shook his head. I should be taking notes, he thought. This is scary stuff. Maybe it had a high insulating value, but was it worth the risk? Kerchini seemed nonchalant about the entire process. After he had built up his little foam bun on the cardboard, he turned to the wall and began slinging the foam back and forth, covering Miriam's original spray until Caruso stopped him.

"We need to let that cool a bit more before you go layering it on there."

Kerchini tossed the gun back to him and dropped the hose with a shrug. "Whatever," he said.

Douthwaite, the New Hampshire builder, cleared his throat, and the crowd looked at him. "It does a great job of insulating."

There was something wrong with Douthwaite's voice. He struggled with the sounds of the words. They tripped up his tongue, and he was almost whispering.

"But it isn't good for the environment," he continued. "I specified it for a house recently, but I couldn't get beyond the polyurethane it puts into the environment."

It surprised Jon that Kerchini stopped moving and put his hands on his hips. "Yeah? I remember you," he said, addressing Douthwaite. "I remember that house. I bought new equipment specially for that job, and then you shot it down. Back to earth—bullshit."

Douthwaite glared at Kerchini. "Not here," he said. "This is not the time nor the place." He paused. "You can't save energy and just sacrifice the earth."

Other people in the crowd looked like they wanted to pursue this further. Caruso interrupted and asked if there were more questions about the foam process.

When nobody spoke up, the group headed back to the main building. Jon noticed Miriam hung behind with Kerchini, but he couldn't hear what they were talking about.

WIDNER DIRECTED everyone to seats in the big room where Orville Hawkins had set up his slides. Jon thought Widner seemed almost nervous in his introduction of the man.

"I had the honor of working with Dr. Hawkins when I was working on the Saskatchewan house. He was kind enough to share his opinions on my thoughts," Widner began. "He believed that..." He turned to Hawkins. "Please correct me if I'm wrong, Doctor. He believed, as I do, that simple design is best. Great insulation and air sealing are most important.

"I don't want to steal his pitch. If you have read none of Dr. Hawkins's books, you might not know that he witnessed the detonation of two twenty-three-kiloton bombs at Bikini Atoll in the South Pacific, or that he holds about twenty patents. He is quoted as famously saying that 'We all believe in progress, but some things just aren't progress.'

"But we're lucky that he has turned his genius to energy efficiency and solar heat, and he is here today to share some work he is doing on innovative solar heating devices, including extracting heat from an attic! But I'll let him tell you about them." He turned and smiled at Hawkins and then stepped away.

Hawkins was a tall, thin man with a wizened face and a quizzical smile. Jon had a hard time associating him with either atomic bombs or construction. He didn't look either part. But as he spoke, Jon put his preconceptions aside; he began to see the connection between the natural forces of energy for blowing things up and those keeping people warm and safe in their homes. Hawkins explained the marvelous natural links between complex physics and mundane home construction. He made clear the systemic bonds between elements that Jon had never noticed before. He talked about how to marry a water-tank storage system to an air-type collector employing hyper-interfacing; about using the excess heat from a triac transistor to drive the electrons through an electronic circuit. Jon felt he was dancing through a wonderland of future possibilities.

By the time the talk was over, Jon's head was spinning, and he needed coffee.

Cheeky had set up the urn on the snack table on the plaza, and Jon grabbed a cup.

Jon drifted over to where Lash Ashton was standing and asked him what he thought of Hawkins's session.

"Oh, yeah," Ashton said. "He's very approachable. He gave me suggestions for the computer modeling I'm doing. He loves the fact that computers connect the world and retrieve information from libraries and newspapers in moments! Do you know he's seventy-five and still going strong?"

"Hope I have that much energy when I'm seventy-five," Jon said. "How many people know all this stuff? Am I just behind?"

"Isn't that why we come to events like this?" Ashton replied. "To learn from smart people?"

"This is really cool stuff! I had no idea. I thought houses were just wood, nails, glass, wires, and pipes. The insulating foam is particularly scary. All that heat!"

Ashton laughed. "Yeah. Isn't that awesome?"

As THE DAY ENDED, the group gathered again on the plaza. The darkening colors of the sky — pink changing to purple, yellow flowing to orange, aqua morphing to dark blue—marked the end of another vacation postcard evening. The lanterns on the wires strung around the plaza swayed in the breeze, making the colors slow-dance on tables and chairs. Cheeky improvised on his guitar in time to the music of the spheres. The occasional clear spice of cool ocean air pierced the warmth emitted from the patio stones and mingled with the smells of the surrounding farmland. At that moment, Jon felt all was right with the world.

It had been a productive day. He was sensing the harmony in the individual pieces of building systems and how they come together to form a systemic unity. He appreciated the festival guests around him —making the world a better place.

The guests chatted in groups—slouching in Adirondack chairs, perched on the picnic table benches, or clustered around the fire pit. Jon noticed Miriam Leathe, who sat so close to the fire that he feared her hair would ignite. She seemed utterly immersed in the dancing flames. Others guzzled beers and sipped wine. Burps of laughter lifted spirits.

Dr. Widner abruptly shattered the harmony by yelling, "You cannot be serious!"

Jon looked up from his reverie and saw Widner face to face with Chris Kerchini.

Kerchini quietly replied, as he massaged the hair of his sideburns, "Don't get all worked up, old man. You'll have a heart attack."

Jon was too far away to hear any more of the exchange, and he was startled when Gail Barker suddenly appeared beside him and murmured, "I wonder what that was all about?"

Jon felt flattered that she was talking to him. It wasn't just that she was an attractive woman; she was a respected authority with an array of credentials, a ton of experience in the industry, and international recognition. He tripped over his tongue, trying to find a clever enough response. Finally, he murmured, "I don't have a clue."

"Gail Barker," she said, introducing herself.

"Yes. I'm looking forward to hearing your session."

"What do you suppose they're bickering about? Kerchini is an ass."

It seemed out of character that someone of her stature would make such a personal remark about a participant. Jon had to wonder if she thought of everyone so critically. "Do you know him?" he asked.

"No... I mean, not really." She paused. "I did a long time ago." She smiled.

Jon smiled back.

"We worked with his company, Foamrite, at the Solar Energy Research Institute—SERI," she said. "We tested the durability and insulating properties of their products in the lab. And we kind of got to know each other."

Another surprise. Barker had been attracted to Kerchini. "Oh," he said.

"And he had some strong opinions. Let's say we disagreed."

Standing side by side, they watched for further interactions between Widner and Kerchini, each lost in their own thoughts.

"I was very surprised to see him here," she said.

"Pleasantly surprised?" Jon asked.

"No. No, I didn't think I'd ever see him again."

"Isn't Foamrite the company Joe Caruso represents?"

"It's a small world," she said. "I should have known better."

"Did I hear my name?" Caruso asked, approaching them.

"Mr. Caruso," Barker said. "I heard your presentation this afternoon. Very scary."

Caruso nodded and tilted his beer bottle into his mouth.

"It really gets up to two thousand degrees?" Jon asked.

"It can," Barker replied. "We saw that in the lab. We covered an apple in six inches of foam. Cooked it." She twisted her face into a challenging expression that dared them to deny her. "So, what's going on with Widner and Kerchini?"

"Widner is convinced that this land was cursed by the Wampanoag, and unless it is treated with respect, bad things will happen," Caruso said. "Kerchini just told him he was full of shit!"

Jon watched Barker's eyes flick back and forth and a nervous smile play on her lips.

"Curse?" she asked.

"Something like that," Caruso replied.

"What about you... Jon?" Barker asked. "How do you feel about curses?"

Jon shrugged. "Makes me think of Snoopy and the Red Baron!"

Barker replied, "So you don't take such things seriously? Do you believe in ghosts?"

Ghosts and curses? Jon figured they would be talking about thermodynamics and convective air flows. But before he could put a reply together, Caruso interrupted.

"How can you take hoodoo voodoo curses seriously?" Caruso asked. "That's just stuff for scary movies."

"Where do you think the stories come from?" Barker asked. "There are millions of tales of curses throughout history. Wars have been fought over them. Murders committed. Scientific discoveries have often been regarded as black magic. It's almost impossible for most people to wrap their heads around a concept as massive as climate change, for example. It's easier to blame failure on a power outside yourself. And sometimes a 'curse' can simply be ignorance."

At that moment, Dr. Hawkins joined them. Jon was excited; now he was in the midst of the festival's brain trust. Years of experience, knowledge, and recognition surrounded him, but he was just a beginner—a 'boots' in state police terms. What could he possibly add to the conversation? He noticed other attendees were looking at them. He picked at the label on his beer bottle.

"There are some sounds that you cannot get out of your mind," Dr. Hawkins said. "Sometimes the earth just screams at you and sometimes it's the silence like before an atomic blast or after you see the lightning. You know it's coming. And you need to hear it. You need the closure like after a person dies. If you don't see the body in the coffin, are they really dead?"

It struck Jon that Hawkins had the face of a dead man—withered, shriveled, and pale. There were a lot of years in those eyes.

Hawkins continued, "Read Bullfinch sometime, if you haven't already. Mythology forms the fundamentals of all curses, and mythology flows from the native people who have developed a harmonious connection to the earth. And," he raised a finger, "and if we don't treat her well, all future human life is doomed.

"You might remember the story of the sachem who had a tree growing in front of his house. The tree harbored a serpent's nest. His servants killed the older serpents, but the sachem insisted on sheltering and nurturing the hatchlings. One day he fell asleep in the tree's shade and awoke to find his ear being licked by the young snakes. At that moment he was astonished to realize that he could understand the words of the birds and creeping things."

"Hell of a risky way to learn a new language!" Barker said.

"During one conflict of that age," Hawkins continued, "the sachem was taken prisoner along with his wife and child and locked up while his captors tried to determine how best to use his skills. Sitting on the dirt floor in the dim light with his back against the wall, he heard the worms in the wall, talking about how the roof beams holding up the chimney were almost eaten through, so the roof and the chimney would soon collapse. The sachem jumped up and pounded on the door of the hut. He shouted and tried to get the attention of his captors to warn them what was about to happen."

Intrigued by Hawkins's tale, Jon didn't notice that Kerchini had joined the group until he said, "My, my, my. You're looking fine this evening, Ms. Barker. The heat of the evening makes your skin glow."

The man's entire demeanor made Jon squirm. His words were inappropriately personal and interrupting Hawkins' story was obnoxious. Jon looked at Gail Barker for any sign of acknowledgement, but saw nothing but contempt.

"I relish those pleasant days we had working together," Kerchini said.

"I remember it differently," Barker replied.

"Aw. Still upset? You really should let such things go. Unpleasant memories can give you ulcers."

"What are you doing here?" Barker asked.

"Just tuning up my skill set," Kerchini replied, stroking his sideburns. "You can never know enough, I always say."

Caruso looked disgusted, but Barker continued. "It was Foamrite that was working with SERI. Not you. Were you even working for Foamrite?"

Kerchini snuffed, "Pfft. Government projects. Companies sucking at the public trough! It's a waste, I say."

Jon shifted his feet and looked down at his beer, wondering if the others found this conversation as uncomfortable as he did.

But Kerchini didn't respond. "You're not all talking about that curse thing, are you? I thought this was supposed to be a scientific, educated group."

"So what happened to the sachem?" Barker asked, turning back to Dr. Hawkins.

"Who?" Kerchini asked. "What did I miss?"

"Did they listen to him?" she asked.

"That was the choice, wasn't it?" Hawkins said. "They could listen to the words of a man who could hear the conversation of worms, or ignore it and assume that their lives would continue along on the predictable paths based on their previous experience."

"What?" Kerchini asked.

"You can't just jump into the middle of a conversation!" Caruso said.

Kerchini laughed and sucked more beer from his bottle. "Horse shit," he said.

Jon sensed—rather than saw—that daylight was finally fading from the sky and the evening was cooling down. Cheeky had put his guitar away. The lights from the colored lanterns caused faces to glow red and green and bodies became less defined, turning into black silhouettes. A few people still stared into the fire pit, while most seemed to drift off to their rooms.

Miriam Leathe left the fire and approached Jon's group.

"Ah, Miriam," Dr. Hawkins said, peering at her name tag. "Did you say your name was Leathe?"

Miriam looked at him and nodded. "Do I know you?"

Hawkins smiled. "I don't think so. Just an old man's curiosity. Where is your family from?"

"England, Scotland. I don't know specifically," she said.

"You probably know this, but since we were just discussing mythology, Lethe is one of the five rivers in Hades—the River of Forgetfulness. Funny about names, isn't it?"

Miriam's mouth had dropped open. "What?"

"Geographically," Hawkins said, "the Underworld was considered to have been surrounded by five rivers: the Acheron—the river of woe, the Cocytus—the river of lamentation, the Phlegethon, the river of fire, the Styx, probably the most famous, and the Lethe, the river of forgetfulness. We all have experiences we want to forget."

"But that's Greek mythology," Barker said. "Not Native American."

"Oh, thanks," Leathe said. "Thanks for that! What are you implying? You don't even know me."

Even in the fading light, Jon saw embarrassment flush the old man's pale face. "I meant no disrespect, Ms. Leathe," he said. "Forgive my rudeness. My wife says she can't take me anywhere!"

Miriam just nodded.

"But you have to tell us what happened to the sachem," Barker told Hawkins.

Although none of this conversation was about him, Kerchini blustered on about how stupid curses were, and the ignorance and myths of heathens.

Miriam didn't speak, but just stared at Kerchini's face for a long moment.

What she did next surprised Jon. She laid a hand on Kerchini's forearm in an almost sensual gesture, and a smile blossomed on her lips and in her eyes. "Let's get another beer," she said. "I need you to tell me more about your work with foam insulation." She led him away.

Dr. Hawkins watched them go and said, "Well! Seems like I've put my foot in it again. As Stan Laurel would say, 'It's a fine mess you've got us into!' or something along those lines. But it's time for me to seek the arms of Morpheus," and he too turned away from the group.

"Good riddance," Caruso said.

"What?" Jon said.

"I meant I've had enough of Kerchini for a lifetime. He's a putz."

"I thought you meant Dr. Hawkins."

"So did I," Barker said with a laugh. "He's getting old, but he's worth listening to."

Caruso muttered, "Good night," and walked away.

Jon looked around at the abandoned patio. "Want another beer?" he asked Gail Barker.

"I want to know what happened to the sachem," she replied.

"We'll have to ask Dr. Hawkins tomorrow." Jon fidgeted. Over the course of what seemed like moments, a series of relationships had developed with this woman—from mentor to conversational companion to woman. He had no designs on her. But they *were* alone. He couldn't avoid the serpent of sensual attraction.

"What about that curse?" Barker asked, tilting her head and pushing back her hair. "Cheeky mentioned something about some unexplained vandalism on the property."

"Really?" Jon asked. "That entire conversation was confusing. Seemed like a lot of anger floating around."

"I guess we'll see tomorrow."

Jon put down his beer, shoved his hands in his pockets, and smiled. "I guess so. Looking forward to your session."

A moment of indecisive silence passed.

"What's it like hanging out with all those stars?" she asked. "In Florida. I mean."

"They're okay," Jon replied. "Different. At least they know they're different. Everyone tells them how special they are."

They sat down to watch the fading fire.

She said she'd never known any celebrities.

He asked her about Colorado and solar energy.

He watched her face in the dim, flickering light. He liked her high cheekbones and the gap between her front teeth.

Then she told him she experimented with rats.

"What?"

"Yeah, you can learn a lot from the behavior of rats. People do. Scientists do. We can't experiment with people, so we substitute rats."

"But rats are not like people."

"No, but Nietzsche pointed out that suffering is the only thing that bestows value on the world. Cows don't anticipate pain the way a man does. Humans anticipate pain and extend the experience beyond the actual event. I wondered if rats anticipate pain."

"You experiment on rats?"

"Rats have personalities. I wondered if a rat's personality would impact their experience of pain—would gentler rats die more easily than wicked rats—or vice versa? I've heard stories like Dr. Hawkins' sachem story before. Myths always have a foundation in truth before they become *mythtified.*" She laughed. "Wouldn't it be amazing if we could hear what creatures were thinking and saying? Then we would know if they anticipate pain. That would blow Nietzsche's theory out of the water!"

Jon's opinion of Gail Barker had shifted once again. Not knowing which personality he was talking to made him distinctly uncomfortable. "I guess I never thought about how rats feel about life," he said, and stood up. "Tomorrow is another day."

"I look forward to hearing the rest of Dr. Hawkins' story," she replied.

"Good night," Jon said and headed off into the darkness of the night.

CHAPTER 5

FESTIVAL DAY 2–AUGUST 7, 1984

*W*hen Jon got up Tuesday morning, the second day of the festival, he was not surprised that Kerchini had not returned to the cabin. He had probably had a few too many of the free beers and was sleeping it off on the grass or in a greenhouse. The breakfast buffet was the same as the day before. He'd been dreaming of bacon and fried eggs but had to make do with yogurt and fruit and muffins. At least there was coffee.

The beautiful warm morning promised a hot day ahead. Edge-of-the-day light was flickering off the trees. The odors of cut grass and wet leaves scented the air.

Ashton stepped up beside him while he studied the food table. "Gonna be a hot one," Ashton commented. "Good morning."

"Morning," Jon replied.

"See what you like?"

"I was hoping for bacon and eggs," Jon said.

"Bad for you. You should try taking a vegetarian path."

"Seriously? I don't think so. Vegetables are all right, I guess, in limited quantities."

"It's the path of the future. It's the gas from cow farts that is killing our ozone layer."

"Cow farts?"

"It's methane."

"I thought it was the stuff they put in hairspray cans."

"Yah, the CFCs. Those, too. We're learning more every day about this stuff. Freakin' scary."

Jon nodded. But he hoped that all this California hippy lifestyle was a fad that would pass.

"Ever heard of CompuServe?" Ashton asked.

Jon shook his head.

"Well, CompuServe is a connection to everything everywhere. I can read newspapers from London or New York on the computer. You really need to get one."

"A computer?" Jon put a croissant on his plate, along with a few pieces of honeydew melon. "Want some breakfast?"

"I ate after I came back from my run. The light is so beautiful at dawn and the air is like crystal clear!"

As Jon looked for a place to sit, Cheeky ran breathlessly into the middle of the plaza.

"Something's happened to the foam machine!" Cheeky shouted. "There's an enormous pile of foam in the parking lot!"

The attendees looked at each other and laughed. "I've got to find Mr. Caruso," Cheeky said.

People got up from their breakfasts and headed over toward the foam demonstration parking lot. Jon grabbed the croissant in one hand, dumped the paper plate in the trash, and carried his coffee with him. Gail Barker, Lisa, sachems, computers dominated his thoughts. When he got to where Joe Caruso's box truck was parked, he saw a massive, manila-colored pile of insulating foam.

"What the hell happened?" someone asked. "The thing must have gone crazy!"

Jon surveyed the scene, seeking the source of a leak or equipment failure, but only the foam itself was out of place. Then he noticed something sticking out near the bottom of the pile. He went a little closer and realized that it was a hand.

"Oh, shit," he whispered. "Oh, shit! There's someone under there. There's someone in there!"

A group gasp echoed under the trees. Someone squatted down to chip out the hand, but the fingers weren't moving. "Leave it!" Jon commanded. "Evidence!"

Dr. Widner came running to the scene, pushing through the attendees. "What a mess! What a god awful mess," he exclaimed. "Where's Caruso? He's going to have to clean all this up. It's his responsibility!"

Jon looked at Widner and pointed to the hand. "There's someone under the foam. There's a person buried in the foam!"

Widner's mouth dropped open. "What?" His mouth tried to form a nervous smile. "What?"

"There's a body under the foam. Probably dead."

"What do you mean 'probably'? Probably a dead body?"

"No," Jon said. "It is definitely a body."

"So why 'probably?'"

Jon looked at him. "It's definitely a body, and it's definitely dead."

"Is it a person's body?"

"Dr. Widner," Jon calmed his voice and looked directly at the program director. "Dr. Widner, there is definitely a dead human body under all this foam."

Widner emitted a stifled scream. "No! No, not during the festival! Not now!"

Cheeky appeared and put his arm around Widner. "I've called the police," he said. "I've called them and they're on their way."

"Oh, my god," Widner said. "Not during the festival. Who is it? Who's under there?"

The individuals in the crowd looked around at each other.

"What the hell's going on?" Caruso asked as he pushed through the crowd. "Who's been messing with my rig?" He stopped and looked at the pile of foam. "That's not right. That's just not right."

"There's somebody under there," Jon explained. "Did you leave this out here? I mean, could anyone have done this accidentally?"

"What?" Caruso almost shouted. "I didn't leave it like this! Of course not! You can't cover yourself in foam accidentally! Jesus!" Jon looked back at Widner, hoping he would take charge of the situation, but the man was babbling.

"Look," Jon said, "this is a crime scene. We need to get out of here. Let's all go back to the patio or courtyard or whatever you call it...."

"Plaza," Cheeky said. "We call it the plaza."

"All right, let's all go back to the plaza and wait for the police."

Muttering to each other, the group headed back to the breakfast area.

"I'm not leaving this," Caruso said. "This is just wrong."

"Did you lock your truck?" Jon asked.

"No," Caruso said. "No, this is Cape Cod! Why would I lock my truck? Who would want to steal foam insulating equipment?"

"Not everyone on Cape Cod is honest," Jon said.

"That's a lot of foam! It's expensive stuff."

"I don't think we have seen the full cost yet," Jon replied. "You and Cheeky should stay here and keep people away. And don't touch your truck," he called when he saw Caruso heading for the cab. "It's a crime scene."

"What do you know about crime scenes?"

Jon shrugged. "I've got a friend in the police."

WHEN JON RETURNED to the plaza, he was disturbed to find nothing seemed to have changed. It still looked like a beautiful day—warm and sunny, with a light breeze. There was a still a slight smell of manure with a dash of sea salt in the air. But a cosmic page had been turned. The harmony of the festival had been fractured. They had passed an inflection point, and life would no longer be the same.

People were milling about. Some were sitting at tables. Others picked at the remains of the breakfast spread. Someone went in search of more coffee.

Jon wondered where Chris Kerchini was. He didn't know the man and didn't like him, but Jon sensed he was involved. And besides, maybe he could have provided some insight about the foam.

Elliott Widner sat alone at a table, his head in his hands, mumbling or moaning—Jon couldn't tell which. Then he spotted Gail Barker was standing by herself, sipping coffee and went to join her.

"Good morning!"

"Oh, hi," Barker replied.

"What do you think happened?"

Barker sipped her coffee and shrugged. "Something went very wrong. The curse, maybe?"

Jon emitted a dry whistle. "You were scheduled to speak this morning, weren't you?"

"I was. Don't know if I am now, of course."

"Yes," Jon said. "This disrupts things, doesn't it?"

They stood in companionable silence for a few moments, watching the attendees mingle and gossip even though they had no facts about what had happened in the parking lot, they suddenly had a lot more to say to each other.

"How did they get you to come all the way from Colorado for this?" Jon said.

"There is an aspect of new technologies that is missionary work," Barker replied. "Are you familiar with our work at SERI?"

"No," Jon said. "But I'm new to all this."

"You drove up from Florida, right?"

"I did, but I've been here before. Here in Tilley. I played in the Cape Cod Baseball League five years ago." That seemed like a lame explanation, so he added, "I worked construction the summer I was here."

"I had summer construction jobs too. It's great, isn't it? You get to be out in the sun and not cooped up inside."

Jon grinned. "What were you going to tell us about?"

"Oh, work I've been doing with passive solar construction. New technologies. New glazing materials. Thermal storage. Have you heard about eutectic salt, phase change materials?"

"I haven't," Jon said. "But that's not surprising. There are a lot of things about this business that I haven't heard of. What do you know about foam?"

"We've done some research. The funny thing about foam is that it's plastic. Remember that great scene from the movie, *The Graduate*? That guy tells Dustin Hoffman that there's a glorious future in plastics. 'Think about it,' he says. 'Will you think about it?'"

Jon wasn't sure if Barker was asking him a question or quoting the movie.

"'Are you listening?' he says," she continued.

"'One word,' the guy says. 'One word: Plastic'.

"'Exactly how do you mean?' Hoffman asks, because he's confused."

Jon forced a laugh.

"Everything is plastic. Plates, cups, relationships, wall insulation. He uses the word to express universality."

"Okay," Jon replied. "He probably wasn't thinking about someone being buried in it!"

"Probably not," Barker replied, grimacing.

Jon looked around. Like the crowd outside the restaurant in Fort Lauderdale after the shooting, everyone here needed answers. He was uncomfortable with the lack of guidance. Widner should take charge, say something. "Excuse me," he said to Barker. "I think Dr. Widner needs to give us some direction."

"He should," Barker agreed.

Jon approached Widner and asked him if he was going to say anything.

Widner lifted his head up and gazed into the distance. "I don't know anything. Don't know what to say,"—and then he put his head down again.

But someone had to say something and although it wasn't his place, Jon said, "All right." Then he walked to the middle of the plaza, raised his arms, and shouted, "Excuse me. Excuse me."

The crowd noise subsided.

"Hi." Jon began. "My name's Jon Megquire. This... accident has come as a shock to Dr. Widner. It's a shock to all of us."

There was an affirmative mumble among the assemblage. "The police will be here momentarily, and they'll want us to stay together.

They'll want to talk to all of us, you know, to get a complete picture about what happened, when it happened, all the details. So it's important that none of us leave."

"What about the festival?" someone shouted.

"Here," Jon pointed to Widner. "I'm sure Dr. Widner will let you know."

Widner heaved himself up and came toward Jon with a watery smile. He looked around and said, "Oh, my. In all my years in this business, this has never happened before. There's nothing in the handbook about what to do if someone is... inadvertently buried in insulating foam. But," he looked up at the sky, "we'll get through it. We will get through it." He took a deep breath before he continued. "Mr. Megquire is quite correct. The police will be here soon, and we should all be available to answer their questions. Please don't wander off. Have some more coffee. Have some more croissants and fruit and yogurt. And make yourselves comfortable while we wait."

"What about the festival?" someone asked. "Will Ms. Barker do her presentation?"

Widner held up his hands as though beseeching heaven or parting the waters. "We'll see what the police want us to do. I'm sure we'll do our best to... keep ourselves amused."

He turned to Jon. "How are they going to move that pile of foam? It's such a mess! Who would do this? Who could do this?"

Jon had no answers. And so they waited.

ONLY TIME SLOWED. The birds still twittered and chirped. Breezes still stirred the leaves and made the paper lanterns dance. And they all waited. Time passed and time, as Dr. Widner had pointed out, is a precious commodity of which we have a limited supply. The crowd got restless. They had come there to learn things. If they weren't going to learn things, they could be in other places, doing other things, back in their normal lives.

It would be a perfect time for a vendor to sell souvenirs, Jon thought, solar energy T-shirts or stickers or caps. But there were no vendors and no souvenirs, so his thoughts returned to the body under the foam. Who was it? Of course, he hadn't met everyone, and this was an extensive campus with cabins spread all over. They'd only been here for two nights and a day. But it seemed strange that he hadn't seen Kerchini yet today. Maybe he was still in their cabin.

Jon returned to cabin 42, but Kerchini wasn't there. Jon brushed his teeth, did a quick pass of his chin with his electric razor, and walked out to the porch. Kerchini's car was still parked next to Maybelline, so he hadn't left the campus. What if he was under all that foam? Jon didn't even know that the body was a man. It could be a woman, but the hand looked to him like a man's hand.

He wondered if Lisa would be part of the police investigation. The thought of seeing her again brought an unfamiliar warmth to his chest, a bubble of joy pushing up in his throat. He had been crazy not to have paid more attention to her all these years. How could he have wasted five years? She was here, waiting. Well, maybe not waiting. He just liked to think she was waiting. Like one of the ethereal women in romance tales who stood on the cliffs overlooking the sea each night, waiting for her lover's ship to appear on the horizon.

Then he remembered that during those years Lisa had been studying to catch bad guys, take them to jail, testify in court, and deal with murder, mayhem, and brutalized bodies. She had not been standing around on cliffs with her hair and scarf blowing in the breeze, waiting for him. But the thought made him smile, anyway.

Just then, a big black Crown Victoria drove past the cabin. Jon recognized the driver as Mark Prence. Prence was Lisa's father and the only police officer in Tilley. Jon mentally slapped himself. Of course it would be Prence. That made sense. When Jon had been in Tilley in 1979, Prence had been driving a Plymouth Fury, and Jon had ridden with him on a wild chase after a bad guy up the Mid-Cape Highway.

Jon pulled the door of the cabin closed, strode off across the campus, and reached the plaza just as Prence was getting out of his car. He had lost a bit more hair and put on a few more pounds that were dropping toward his belly. He still had the brief whisper of a mustache and the big ears.

"Well," he said when he saw Jon. "This is a surprise."

"Good morning, Officer Prence," Jon said, holding out his hand, which Prence shook.

"Chief. I'm the chief now. What are you doing here? You part of this show?"

"Oh, no. Congratulations on the promotion. No, I'm just here to learn."

"How come trouble seems to follow you around? Seems like the last time I saw you, I extracted you from another situation?"

Onlookers were gathering, attracted to this symbol of authority.

Prence asked, "Where's Dr. Widner? He runs this place, doesn't he? Somebody with a British accent called and said there'd been an accident. Something about foam."

Jon studied Prence's face and wondered how Lisa could have come from those genes. She was so beautiful.

"That was Brian Nando... they call him Cheeky. He's with the body."

"Body?"

"Well, it appears to be a body," Jon said. "Can't really tell. It's covered with insulating foam."

Prence gave him a baffled look.

"Show me," he said

At that moment Widner scurried up. "Officer, I'm Dr. Widner."

"Oh, great," Prence said.

"Dr. Elliott Widner. I'm the Executive Director of ITI."

Prence replied, "So you're in charge. This is your responsibility. Have I got that right?"

"Oh!" Widner replied. "Yes."

"Megquire here was just about to show me the... uh, scene."

"Do you two know each other?"

"We've met before."

"But I'm in charge."

"We're clear, doctor."

With Jon following, Widner led Prence down to the parking lot where Caruso's truck was parked and the foam was piled. Prence looked at the truck, the foam, and Caruso and harrumphed. "Anybody touch anything?"

Cheeky volunteered, "No. Nobody. I wouldn't let them. Mr. Caruso wanted to get into his truck, but I stopped him." Cheeky smiled. "No, this is precisely the way it was when I found him, inspector."

"And who are you?" Prence asked.

"I'm Nando... Cheeky Nando."

"You're the one that called?"

"Yes, sir."

Prence walked over to the foam. "That's quite a pile. What is this stuff?"

Caruso stepped up and said, "EPF."

"What?"

"EPF—Expanded Polyurethane Foam. And that's an enormous waste of material."

"And who are you?"

"I'm Joe Caruso. This is my truck. I work for Grady Foamrite."

"So, this is your foam? You do this?"

"What! No way. I would never do this. There's a body under there!"

Prence bent down and looked at the hand protruding from the bottom of the pile. It was a right hand, with the fingers curled as though they were clawing at the pavement. Prence put the back of his own hand on the back of the hand at the edge of the foam. "Who is it?" he asked.

Caruso, Jon, and Cheeky looked at Widner for an answer. "I have no idea," he said. "How would I know?"

Prence stood up. "Anyone missing?"

"Is there anyone missing, Cheeky?" Widner asked, looking at Cheeky.

"Gee, I don't know. We haven't done a roll call or anything."

"Has anyone left?"

"Shouldn't have," Cheeky replied. "Jon told everyone to stick around."

"Jon did?" Prence asked.

Jon said, "It seemed like the right thing to do."

"Gotta call the State Police on this one," Prence said. "It's beyond me." They began moving back toward the plaza when Prence turned back. "Do not touch anything. Don't touch anything. You two—it's Caruso and Nando?—are doing great. Just keep doing it."

"Can I check out my equipment in the truck?" Caruso asked.

"No! Don't touch anything, Mr. Caruso. In fact, why don't the two of you just step away from all this so you won't be tempted to move anything?"

"Can I get a cup of coffee? I haven't had coffee yet."

"I'll get someone to bring you a cup. You?" Prence asked.

"Tea, please," Cheeky replied with a smile.

"Jesus!" Prence mumbled.

"How long do you think this is going to take? I mean, for the State Police?" Widner asked when they got back to the plaza.

"It's about twenty-five minutes between here and Yarmouth. With the lights on... maybe fifteen minutes," Prence replied.

"So what are we supposed to do while we're waiting? And I suppose the State Police have to investigate?"

Prence looked at him as though he were from another planet. "That's why they're coming," he drawled, with infinite patience.

It appeared to Jon that pieces of Widner's brain were disconnecting from other pieces. He was on nervous overload. "Dr. Widner, what if we get the attendee list and assemble everyone here, and... you know, take attendance? That sort of thing," Jon asked.

Widner gulped, nodded, and set off to find the list of participants. Jon made an announcement to gather everyone in the big meeting room. He asked Ashton and Gail Barker if they would set up the chairs and maybe find some coffee. "Cheeky asked for tea," he said. "Do you think we could make that happen? Is there kitchen staff?"

"Must be. I'll find out," Ashton replied.

Some participants had gone back to their rooms after breakfast, were just returning for the morning session and didn't yet know what had happened.

"What are we doing here?" someone asked. "Where's Dr. Widner?"

The sound level and the temperature in the room rose. Someone opened the windows and doors. Widner reappeared with the list of attendees and handed it to Jon, who scanned Cheeky's neat handwriting. "Okay. Do you want to do this?" Jon asked Widner, who shook his head, sat down, and stared at the floor.

Ashton came over. "Hey, I could load all those names into a Multiplan spreadsheet on the computer. We could use it to track all the information we gather about them!"

"That would be great," Jon said.

"What would that do for us?" Widner asked.

"It would help us build a database that we could use to cross-reference all the information about these people."

Jon interrupted Ashton before he could get deeper into the wonders of databases. "That's great, Lash! Why don't you do that while we see who's here?"

He went outside holding the Cheeky's paper list and found Prence sitting in the Crown Vic with the door open.

"You coming in?"

"They're on their way," Prence replied, heaving himself out of the car.

"The folks are getting restless," Jon said.

"No surprise there."

They walked to the front of the room together. Jon turned and held up his hands. "Hello!" he shouted. "Could I have your attention, please? This is Chief Prence from Tilley. The chief would like to find out who's here… and who's not."

"What's happened?" someone asked.

"There's been an accident," Jon replied.

"What kind of accident?"

"The chief will explain. Chief?"

Prence cleared his throat. "Yup," he began. "I'm Chief Prence, and you're in the town of Tilley, my jurisdiction." He looked around the mostly silent room.

"Yup," he said and cleared his throat again. "Megquire here tells me this is some kind of construction conference. There appears to have been an accident with one of the demonstrations. Some kind of foam insulation? And we're going to have to wait for the State Police to check it out. So you need to stay away from that part of the facility."

"What kind of accident?" someone called.

"Someone appears to have gotten foam sprayed on them."

The crowd mumbled. "Is that all? Why would you need the police for that?"

"It is a lot of foam," Prence explained. "Someone is completely covered in foam."

The crowd gasped.

"Buried in foam? Who is it?"

"We don't know because we can't see the person."

"Oh, my God!"

"How do you know it was an accident?" someone asked.

Prence looked at Jon and then at Widner. "That's part of the investigation," he said.

"Could it have been done on purpose?"

"Part of the investigation," Prence repeated.

"Are you saying that there's a murderer here?"

"I can't say anything else. Yup, I know," Prence said. "But we suspect the victim is connected to this event, so Megquire here is going to call out your names—you know, take attendance to see who might be missing. I'm guessing that most of you are strangers. Strangers to each other, I mean."

"That's right," Jon said. He asked the audience if anyone had not returned from his or her room or if they had all reassembled.

"How do you know everyone's here?" Prence asked.

"I don't. But I guess we'll find out who is in the room at least."

Jon read down the list, checking off the names. Most people answered "Here!" or "Present!" when their names were called. There was the occasional comedian who replied, "I think I'm here" with the accompanying nervous laughter. Jon eventually got through them all. Ashton told him the kitchen staff had reported that everyone who was supposed to be there was there.

Several festival participants were missing, including Chris Kerchini.

They had just completed the list when they heard the siren, and flashing blue lights dashed across the walls of the room. The chief went out to meet the State Police officers.

Jon put down the list. He took a deep breath and followed Prence outside. And there she was in a two-tone blue uniform, black leather jump boots, and a black leather Sam Browne belt with all sorts of stuff hanging off it, including a gun. Her beautiful hair was hidden in a tight bun. Jon had never known a state trooper before, and he had certainly never slept with one. She didn't acknowledge Jon, although she smiled briefly at her father.

She was accompanied by a tall, thin trooper with more insignia and an angry expression. He had high cheekbones, sallow complexion, and a crew cut. He introduced himself as Sergeant Smith, and then he asked, "Where's the body?"

"Are we going to just hang around here?" someone asked. "We didn't come here for that."

Dr. Widner asked the participants, "Maybe you could give us some time?"

Jon sensed the crowd was worse than a bunch of restless six-year-olds. They had come to the festival with a purpose and expected their hours to be filled with information. They did not expect to have to entertain themselves when something derailed that process. Jon supposed that a similar group of six-year-olds would simply find something to play with and entertain themselves. These adults didn't want to do that. They wanted someone to entertain them.

Jon followed the police away from the building toward the scene of the crime and left Dr. Widner to take care of the participants.

CHAPTER 6

FESTIVAL DAY 2–AUGUST 7, 1984

*L*isa had worked with Sergeant Smith long enough to know that he was a by-the-book officer. She also knew he had seen an array of crime scenes, but she doubted he'd ever seen anything quite like what greeted them in the parking lot. She had been told repeatedly in her training to avoid jumping to conclusions, but this was not a subtle crime scene. The victim was encapsulated in foam! They were going to have to find the face to identify the body. And it was unlikely that the perpetrator was some random vagrant who just came across the victim and covered them in expandable foam. It had to be someone with knowledge of the stuff, and the most likely suspects were all here—including Jon. That was something else they had taught her: suspect everyone, don't rule anyone or anything out without evidence. But she had a hard time suspecting Jon. Of course, she had missed the last five years of his life. Maybe there were things about him she didn't know. Maybe there was a lot about him she didn't know. That made her pause.

They stood and stared at the pile of foam. It still emanated a wet dog smell. "Shit," Sergeant Smith said.

"Looks a bit like that, doesn't it?" Caruso said, walking up to them.

"Who are you?" Smith asked.

Caruso introduced himself and shook both troopers' hands.

"Nobody's touched anything," Cheeky said, joining them. "I'm Brian Nando. That's N-a-n-d-o. I'm from England."

"We could tell," Smith replied. "What are you doing here?"

"Working," Cheeky said.

"Yeah? What's that mean?"

"Oh, I'm an intern."

Lisa pulled out her notebook. "We'll need a permanent address, Mr. Nando. You too, Mr. Caruso."

"Who's under there?" Smith asked.

They all looked at each other. Cheeky said, "Can't see, can we? Not even quite sure where his head is. It's just a gigantic pile!"

"How do you know it's a 'he' and not a 'she'?" Smith asked.

Again, they all looked at each other. "We're supposing it from the hand," Cheeky replied.

Smith knelt and examined the hand without touching it and snorted. Then he stood and said to Lisa, "Get the tech guys here. Don't want to mess with this pile of shit without pictures."

Lisa stepped away, contacted the barracks on her radio, and told them to send a crime scene team. Without the visible hand, it could just have been a pile of expanded foam. The shape of the body was not obvious. The victim was completely engulfed. They couldn't start chipping away at the foam. She wondered if they would have to lift the whole mess into a truck and take it back to the lab. Seemed like it was lying face down from the position of the hand. How would the foam affect determining the time of death? It would have insulated him. And what about the fact that the weather was warm? And cause of death? There were several ways that could have happened. What was the victim doing here, and then the fundamental question: who did it to him or her?

When Lisa stepped back to the others, Smith said, "Let's get this roped off."

She walked up the hill to the cruiser, pulled out a roll of crime scene tape and brought it back to the site. "I'll give you a hand," her father said.

Lisa thought, this is weird. It wasn't a game she was playing with her dad, but it felt like it—decorating with flashy yellow tape, as though it were a birthday party. No. There was an obvious and distinct difference between this and a birthday party.

She started unrolling the tape and stretching it around the parking lot, wrapping it around trees and lollipop lights to hold it up.

"It should be bigger, wider," her father said. "You want to enclose more of the area. There will be footprints."

She stopped and looked at him. "Dad, I know what I'm doing."

"You just want to make sure that you're cordoning off the entire relevant area."

"I know. Look, this is our jurisdiction now."

"Yeah. I called you, remember? This your first?"

"No," Lisa said. "Well, sort of. We practiced."

"Not like this, I'll bet."

"No, not like this. Bet you haven't seen one like this either."

"Can't say that I have," the chief said with a shake of his head. "And I hope I never do."

They finished stringing up the tape. "Don't know what rain would do to this stuff," Lisa said. "Have you heard any weather forecasts? I bet Jon would know."

"What's with Jon?" her father asked. "Why is he here?"

"The festival is what he said."

"Did you know he was here?"

"He stopped at my place on Saturday."

Her father rumbled. "What's he got to do with this place? It's got a strange reputation, you know. The town doesn't know what to make of it. Drugs? Is it a commune? I've kept my eye on it. Never know what will happen when a bunch of tree huggers live together. Know what I mean?"

"Cripes, Dad. It's not like that." She pushed her glasses up her nose.

"I thought Jon was doing baseball stuff in Florida or somewhere. Why's he here? What's he got to do with back-to-the-earth... crap?"

"He said," Lisa patiently explained, "he was fed up with the professional sports world. The money and the phoniness and the pressure. I don't know. He enjoyed the sports and talking to famous athletes but the promoters were too much for him. Ultimately, he didn't see the point because generating the biggest bluster was the way to win. Most of it seemed like lies to him—not something he's good at."

"Well, that's a good thing," her father said.

"He had a memorable dinner with a client from Ohio who talked about wanting a house on Cape Cod and getting Jon to build it for him. Jon told him about this conference and the guy told him he should go."

"Seems like you had quite the conversation. I'd thought he was out of your life."

"Guess not," she replied. "We've got to get back to Sergeant Smith."

"You know that you have to consider him a suspect?"

They stopped walking, and Lisa looked at her father. "Like the others," she stated.

"That's right," he said. "Like the others. He could have done this. You've got to keep an open mind. He's a good guy and you like him and all, but you have to put that out of your mind."

"But why? I understand I have to treat him like the others, but why would he do this?"

"Well, that's what you have to find out—the motive. What's he been doing all this time? Does he have any connections to these people, to this person, whoever he is?"

"Or she is," Lisa interrupted.

"Exactly. This is a pretty vicious way to kill someone. There had to be a lot of hate behind it. This wasn't just a freak accident."

"Cripes, Dad, I know all this. I took classes—lots of classes. I have the paper to prove it."

"And I don't," he mumbled.

"That's not what I'm saying. You have experience. I'm not discounting your instincts here. But you know Jon, too. I mean, the last time he was here, he helped you catch that Scoles creep after he killed his mother-in-law with the carbon monoxide and all. He was a hero. He saved people's lives, and he helped you figure out what happened and chase down the killer. I don't think you could have done it without him."

"That's the thing," her father said. "There's more to Jon than meets the eye."

~

WHEN THEY RETURNED to the plaza, Lisa reported to Smith that the crime scene was secured. She saw that the festival attendees were still milling about in groups. One of them was likely to be a murderer. Someone needed to organize and engage the entire group.

"Is there a list of these people?" she asked Smith.

"I've got it," he said. "Let's get them all back together. Inside."

When everyone was settled back in the meeting room, Widner stood up and started a monologue about how sorry he was about the delay in the program, and how it wasn't ITI's fault. It was simply an unfortunate event.

Unfortunate, Lisa thought. Unfortunate indeed for the sorry person buried out there. Wasn't that a bit of an understatement, Doctor Who. She was not impressed with Widner or with the International Transmogrify Institute. She would have to research what they actually did here.

Smith walked over and interrupted Widner. "Yes. It's an inconvenience. Sorry about that." He flicked Widner a smile. "I'm sure the doctor will get things back on track, but we're going to need to get statements from all of you."

Lisa scanned the faces, looking for anomalies in their expressions.

"So who's missing?" Smith asked, scanning the list of names. There were several people who hadn't checked in yet when they'd taken attendance earlier. Sergeant Smith called out those names. The only one who still hadn't shown up was Chris Kerchini.

"Anybody know where this Kerchini might be?" the sergeant asked. "He was staying in Cabin 42 according to this list."

"That's right," Cheeky chimed in. "He was staying with Mr. Megquire. The guy with the cute MG."

"Megquire! Do you know where this Kerchini is?"

Lisa flinched. She struggled to believe that Jon could have done this. The leather of her Sam Browne belt creaked as she inhaled. Her training demanded she keep an open mind. Her instincts told her to override that training. Cop instinct, or maybe desire?—simply the way she wanted it to be. She couldn't look at him.

She heard Jon say, "No, I have no idea. I haven't seen him."

There was an expectant moment of silence as the crowd seemed to contemplate Jon's association with the apparent victim.

"Of course, we know nothing yet," Smith continued. "The tech guys are still on their way."

"What about lunch?" someone asked. "I don't mean to be insensitive, but we missed the morning session, and now we're hungry."

"Of course," Widner said. He looked at Cheeky, who hurried off to the kitchen. "And I'm sure that we can move on with the program, can't we? Buildings go on through stormy weather, and so can we!" He raised his chin and patted his chest.

Widner guided the troopers to a separate room and, with Chief Prence's help, they divided the attendees up to interview them.

Lisa could see there was going to be a mountain of paperwork on this one. Lots of interviews. Lots of tangled and twisted connections among the attendees. Lots of dead ends. Lots of words, prevarications, body language and facial expressions to catalog mentally. She slapped herself for making more assumptions. To assume, she had been told, was to make "an *ass* of *u* and *me*." And it often did. But if you couldn't assume anything, how could you rule anything out? They couldn't go back in time to witness the event.

Jon approached her and asked if there was anything he could do to help.

She hadn't settled her thoughts about his involvement.

"No," she said. "Stay out of it. This is an official investigation."

He looked surprised at the abruptness of her tone. He stepped back, and she could feel him distancing himself. "Oh. Right. I understand." And he held up his hand in a stopping motion and moved away.

No, he didn't understand, Lisa thought. Her energy had to be focused on deciphering what had happened here and arresting a murderer.

As they were setting up for the interviews, she asked Smith, "We can assume this was murder, can't we?"

"What are the options?"

"Could it have been an accident?"

"There had to have been two people involved. If it was an accident and the victim was dead, how did he put the equipment away?"

"Right," Lisa said. "No accident. And that would rule out suicide as well."

"So if it wasn't suicide, and it wasn't an accident, what do you have left? An act of God?"

Lisa snorted. "I guess we can rule out insurrection or armed conflict as well!"

"So that leaves us with murder—one person killing another—the murderer and the victim. We have the victim. We just need to find the murderer. Right?"

Lisa didn't need a college degree to figure that out. She was pleased that *assuming* worked in this situation.

"And if we can determine 'why' the murder was committed, that would lead us to the murderer," Smith continued.

The skill came in knowing how to find the why.

"So what kind of murder do we have here?" Smith asked. "Crime of passion? Murder for hire? Implied malice or extreme neglect? An irresistible impulse? Murder while under duress?"

"You think someone hired someone to do that?"

"Maybe not that particularly bizarre way," Smith said. "The employer rarely specifies the method of killing. Just the result. And did something happen here prior to the murder? Something so horrific that it would have resulted in murder? Could someone have been so passionate about building a house that they would have killed for it? Seems unlikely."

"So I guess we can rule out murder for hire."

"To me, it seems like this may have been an impulse-driven

murder. It could have resulted from something that happened in the past, and it was just coincidence that the two parties came together in the same place at the same time. I hate coincidences. Don't believe in them."

"But they happen."

"Yeah. So what is it between you and this Megquire person? Is that a coincidence? I mean, you're seriously involved in what happened here between Megquire and your father being the local chief. Can you treat this case dispassionately?"

"I can, sergeant. I wouldn't have accepted this assignment if I couldn't."

"Did you know Megquire was going to be here?"

"I saw him on Saturday and he told me he was coming here."

"What's he do? Why's he here?"

Lisa hesitated. Jon was on a quest to find his future, and apparently, he still hadn't found what he was looking for. The connection between sports promotion and construction seemed indirect, but she was pleased that he had followed the path back to Tilley and building. "He did construction work here in Tilley. He worked for a local contractor. They developed a bond, I guess. Jon talked about... I don't know. Houses? Energy efficiency? Science?"

"Do you have a personal relationship with him? I've got to know because that could cloud your judgment here."

Lisa's hand curled and her little finger pointed toward the ceiling as she tweaked the position of her glasses again. "I do," she said. "But I can set that aside. I already told him to back off when he offered his help."

"He offered to help?"

"He did. But I said no."

"'Just say no.'" Smith quoted. "That'll have to do for now. Let's get them in here. We should start with Widner."

"Dr. Widner?"

"Yeah. What's he a doctor of, anyway?"

"I guess we'll find out," Lisa said. "I know it's not medicine."

~

"Got a minute?" the Lisa asked Widner, slipping up beside him, startling him.

"I don't know that I can leave all these people to their own devices," Widner said.

Lisa looked around the room. People were gathered in small groups, chatting and eating lunch. "Seems like they're doing okay," she said. "We just need to ask you some questions." She gave him her affiliative smile, compressing her lips, and dimpling her cheeks.

He followed her into the interview room, where Smith was waiting.

"Have a seat," he said. "I'm Sergeant Smith and I think you've met Trooper Prence."

Widner smiled, shrugged his shoulders, and sat in the proffered chair.

"We're going to be recording this, if you don't mind," Smith said.

"I don't mind," Widner replied, "but what if I did?"

Smith smiled and continued. "So you're Dr. Elliott Widner, is that correct?"

"I am. Dr. Elliott Armstrong Widner, if you want my complete name. I can give you my post-nominal initials as well, if you like."

"What are you a doctor of, doctor?"

"I hold a doctorate of Natural Science from the University of Saskatchewan. That's in Canada."

"Ah," Smith said, making a note in his notebook.

"Saskatchewan is one of the western Canadian provinces, you know. The university is in Saskatoon. It's known as USask. It's on Treaty 6 territory and homeland of the Métis."

"Is that right?" Smith commented, glancing at Lisa, who was seated across the room. "Very interesting. I know little about our northern neighbors. Heard stories about the Mounties and how they always get their man." He laughed.

"Most Americans know virtually nothing about Canada. Nor do they care."

"Are you Canadian, then?"

"I'm an American citizen now. This is my home. Cape Cod has been nasty to the Wampanoag. Like the Canadians have not been respectful of the Métis. This land really belongs to the Indigenous people, doesn't it?"

"So you run this place?"

"I do. I've been in charge for three years now. Almost since the beginning. I didn't found it, but I certainly have married into the founders' way of thinking. Connecting with the earth. It's a state of mind, really. A state of mind that we all should.... "

Smith interrupted. "That's great, Doc. But we need to know what happened here today?"

"Oh. I don't really know. I wasn't there."

"You mean you didn't bury the guy in foam?"

Widner funneled his lips as though he were going to kiss a horse. "Of course not!" he said. "I would never do such a thing. What motivation would I have to perform such a heinous act?"

"I don't know," Smith said. "You tell us."

Widner funneled his lips again. Lisa noted his discomfort. Men of authority and reputation could stand up on a stage and deliver a speech to hundreds of people with confidence, but as soon as they sat in a chair for one-on-one questions about a personal subject, they got flustered and babbled. Police interviews could do that to most anyone except professional criminals—who would fall apart if you put them on a stage in front of twenty people! Sometimes.

"What were you doing out there in Saskatoon?" Smith asked. "Before you came here?"

Widner straightened. "I had the distinct honor of working with the Canadian Homebuilders Association and led the development of the design of what they called the R2000 House. It was revolutionary."

"Yeah? Was it insulated?"

"Of course! Extremely well insulated."

"So you would know about foam insulation, wouldn't you?"

"We didn't use foam. The technology wasn't available for residential use. I don't know if we would have even if it were available. It would have been experimental, and not commonly accessible. We were creating a prototype that could be employed everywhere across Canada."

"Ever been in trouble with the police before?" Smith asked abruptly.

Widner looked around the room in sudden alarm. "What? Are you saying that you're about to arrest me?"

Smith gave a laugh. "No, no, no."

Whoops, Lisa thought. There must be something there. Something in Widner's past, something that brought an interaction with authorities. Could it be related to what happened here? Widner was literally squirming in his chair—shuffling his feet, dry-washing his hands.

"You just seem uncomfortable, Dr. Widner," Smith said. "Sometimes police uniforms can make people uncomfortable."

"Of course."

"And sometimes... and I'm just saying sometimes, that indicates some sort of previous disruption in their lives with authority. Know what I mean?"

"Where did you go to school, inspector?" Widner asked, looking up. "What degrees do you have? Would I be able to read any of your articles in reputable journals?"

Smith ignored the diversion. "Do I make you uncomfortable, Dr. Widner?"

Widner sniggered. "Hardly!" he said. "But I know exactly what you mean." Widner squirmed on the hard chair. "The Mounties tried that."

"Tried what, Dr. Widner?"

"They tried to accuse me of starting the riot."

Lisa watched Smith zero in on the professor's face. Movement stopped. She felt the room tighten and heard the murmur of distant voices.

Finally he asked, "Riot?"

"Well, that's what they called it. But it wasn't a riot. It was merely the passive resistance of the Indigenous people to defend their rights to the land. They needed to stand their ground, but they didn't use violence to accomplish their mission as the government did. I was proud to be a part of that resistance."

Widner smiled and massaged his graying ponytail.

"Can you explain to me what relevance that has to the situation here?" Smith asked.

"You asked if I had had interaction with authority in the past."

"Is there an outstanding warrant for your arrest by the Mounties?

"No! Of course there isn't."

"So why did you tell me about your so-called riot? I'm sympathetic to the plight of the Indigenous people. Especially here on the Cape. We're all sympathetic. Was the guy under that foam some old agitator who looked at you sideways? Are you telling me this was revenge for something that happened... what, fourteen years ago in Saskatoon?"

"No. You're misconstruing my words."

"But you would know how to use that foam machine, wouldn't you?"

"Of course," Widner said. "But we were teaching people how to do that yesterday. It's part of the training at the festival."

"Ah," said Smith. "Are you saying that anyone could have done it?"

"No, not anyone. Not all the attendees were present for the demonstration."

"Who was? Can you give us a list?"

"I'll ask Cheeky."

"Cheeky?"

"Yes. That's Brian Nando's nickname. Actually, that's what he calls himself."

"Then we'll have to get Mr. Nando to give us that list then."

"Well, I don't know if he has a list."

"What do you mean?"

"We don't take formal attendance at the sessions. It's a small group and there's only one session running at a time. People pay to come to the festival, and then they do what they like."

"Ah," said Smith. "Where's Nando now?"

"I assigned him to watch the scene."

Lisa watched Smith heave himself up, but Widner didn't move. He leaned back in his chair as if to get more comfortable and stared at the sergeant.

"So that's it then?" Widner asked.

"For now," the sergeant replied with a smile.

"Well, use this room as long as you like." Widner stood slowly, gave both officers his best arrogant glare, and left.

CHAPTER 7

FESTIVAL DAY 2–AUGUST 7, 1984

At lunch time, Jon lusted for a cheeseburger, but gathered up what he could bear to eat amid the bean and alfalfa sprouts at the buffet table, poured Sprite into a plastic cup, and found a place to sit and think.

This situation was extremely strange. Lisa was here in her official capacity. So was her father. The last time Jon had seen him was five years before, when they were racing up the Mid-Cape highway in that Plymouth Fury, chasing a murderer. Now here were the Prences and him and another murder—although that had not yet been officially established. How could someone have done something so brutal? And was it Kerchini under all that foam?

While he munched on greens and whole grain bread, his curiosity about the crime grew. Building science was fascinating stuff, but a lecture about R values and thermal mass seemed very tame compared to a body lying under a pile of expanded foam. He knew for a fact that Chief Prence would not understand the principles behind thermodynamics. And even if Sergeant Smith had a lot of experience in crime solving and Lisa had taken numerous courses in human psychology and interrogation, they would not understand the motives behind the people who came to this festival. They understood the legal system, but they wouldn't appreciate a passion for the laws of thermodynamics. Jon was confident that he could help them by adding that dimension.

Lisa would not appreciate it if he messed up her investigation. But policing was new to her, and he could help, and he was confident that she would welcome it. He would be expressing an interest in her work. As though they were married!

Wait—what was he thinking?

He finished the final edible bits on his plate, dumped it into a trash can, and decided the first thing he should establish was whether Chris Kerchini was under the foam. He set off to find Cheeky for updates on the participants.

∾

Jon found Cheeky in the parking lot. Police techs had arrived and were walking around the pile of foam with cameras and tape measures. Jon stood with Cheeky, watching the techs at their work. Going with the assumption that the victim was lying face down on the pavement, there was less foam where the feet must be and more around the head area. The surface of the foam was uneven and globbed in mounds and swirls. Jon wondered if the victim had writhed about while the extreme heat of the exothermic reaction burned his skin and cut off his breathing until he could no longer move.

Jon wondered if they were going to need a forklift to hoist the mass onto a truck to haul it back to the crime lab.

But they needed to know who was under there. He asked Cheeky if he knew how they were going to identify the body.

"They took fingerprints from the hand." Cheeky shivered a bit.

"Really? Wow. That might take a while."

"No. They said they have computer analysis now. There's a vast computer database of fingerprints."

"Why would this guy's fingerprints be in that system?"

Cheeky shrugged and turned away.

"Is that why they are being so careful with the foam? You can get great fingerprint impressions on foam." Jon paused and looked at Cheeky. "You seem pale. Are you okay?"

Cheeky gulped. "Dead bodies give me the creeps."

"Have you seen a lot of dead bodies?"

Cheeky laughed nervously. "No, no. Just my gran in her coffin. Hope I don't have to see any more."

"This is a pretty tame dead body," Jon said. "It's more like a dead hand."

Cheeky shuddered.

"By the way, do you have that list of all the people who are here or would have been here last night?"

"I gave it to that nice lady trooper."

"Lisa," Jon said.

Cheeky looked at him. "You know Trooper Prence."

"I do," said Jon.

"Is she related to the other one from the town? Chief Prence? "

"He's her father," Jon said.

"Oh, wow," Cheeky said, smiling.

They watched the police technicians working around the insulation pile, trying not to disturb anything. Periodically, they would squat down and touch the surface, perhaps to check the solidity.

"Do you remember how many people are at the festival?" Jon asked.

"Forty, including the speakers… including myself and Dr. Widner. Do we count?"

Joe Caruso came up beside them. "Think there's more coffee?" he asked Cheeky.

"I'm sure, sir," Cheeky replied. "Do you mind, Mr. Megquire?"

"What?" Jon asked.

"Do you mind if I just run back and get this gentleman more coffee?"

"Oh, not at all," Jon said. "We're just waiting, right?"

"That's right," Cheeky replied. "Cream? Sugar," he asked.

"Regular," Caruso replied.

"Getcha a fresh cup," he nodded at Caruso, and set off toward the main building.

Jon and Caruso stood together to watch the technicians at their work. "Think this results from that curse Dr. Hawkins was talking about?" Jon asked.

"Curse, schmurse," Caruso replied with a snort.

The man had stubby fingers and grimy nails. He was short. Jon towered over him. He could look down into Caruso's hair and see his scalp among the greasy follicles. Jon wondered if he were big enough to lug the drums of insulating foam around.

Jon was confident that Cheeky wasn't a murderer. But he wasn't at all sure about Caruso. Spraying foam was what the man did for a living. He owned this rig, and he taught people how to use it. Who better to encapsulate the victim in the parking lot?

"I heard you were a baseball player, right? And the lady trooper is your girlfriend."

"Who told you that?" Jon asked.

Caruso grinned. "Oh, word gets around. Don't get me wrong. I don't blame you. Tight little body there."

Jon watched him. How could you identify a murderer? Murderers should look like a black-and-white wanted poster, a mug shot. But there had to be something about a person that would cause them to kill. But this guy was just... stubby. Not intimidating at all. Maybe Lisa could see some telltale characteristic with her trained eye that Jon couldn't.

"Major waste of foam." Caruso shook his head. "That's expensive."

"Besides, there being a dead body under it," Jon said.

"Yeah. That too."

"Do you do a lot of teaching, Joe?"

"Yeah. Pretty much. That's what the company hired me to do. They want to get into the residential arena in a big way. The industry primarily uses foam for commercial applications—massive warehouses and stuff. But with the oil prices climbing, Foamrite sees an enormous market in homes."

"An... uh... accident like this will not help much."

Caruso looked at him.

"I mean, this is not exactly good publicity," Jon said. "Didn't you warn us in your class yesterday about the heat? Have there been any fires? That could impact your business."

"Clearly, this is not an accident," Caruso said. "You don't have an 'accident' like this and then put the tools away afterward. And, no. There haven't been a lot of fires."

"Know of any fires when somebody got hurt?"

"What are you going on about? I just said there haven't been fires."

"Actually, you said there haven't been a *lot* of fires. That means there have to have been some," Jon said.

"No. No fires."

"None?"

"Look. Accidents happen from time to time, right? It's new stuff. People make mistakes."

"How about you, Joe? Any mistakes? Were the police involved? Did it make it into the papers?"

Caruso moved toward his truck.

"Were you involved?" Jon asked.

Caruso stopped, turned back, looked up, and glared into Jon's eyes. "Yeah, there were police! People died! And the papers were all over it and they got the story all wrong, as they always do." He came back to stand right in front of Jon—almost on his toes, challenging him.

"I imagine that wasn't too good for your business."

"I had a talented lawyer," Caruso replied, moving away again. "Kept my identity quiet. As I say, it wasn't my fault. Lucky that Foamrite hired me to work for them directly. They've been good to me. Got me to move to New Jersey."

Caruso moved away again, and Jon followed him.

"I've got to ask: why would you leave your truck unlocked?"

"Nothing in there except foam dispensing equipment. Who's going to steal that?"

Still, it seemed careless to Jon. "Aren't you afraid that you're going to be blamed for this?"

Caruso stopped moving again, and it suddenly seemed to Jon as though it was one of those moments where the invisible audience of the world was holding its communal breath. He could hear the techs scuffing around the parking lot in their booties. The breeze ruffled the leaves in the trees. A red-tailed hawk whistled its hunting call. Then silence.

Caruso pivoted and shouted, "I'M SICK OF THIS SHIT! I'M SICK OF IT. You can keep your opinions to yourself. I'm sick of getting blamed for things I didn't do. The finger gets pointed in my face. WHY would I do this? Who the hell is that under there? Who? Why would I come out here in the middle of the night and randomly waste a shitload of foam on some random person in a parking lot? You think I'm some sort of psycho?"

"No," Jon protested. "But you had access to what was apparently the weapon in this case."

"Foam is not a weapon!"

"It was here, wasn't it? Just like a 'gun'. And it's your 'gun'."

"But anyone could have done it. The truck was unlocked. I taught a bunch of people how to use it yesterday, and I wouldn't be surprised if some of them knew how to dispense foam before they came here. Like that Kerchini person."

"And that comes back around to the question of why you would leave the truck unlocked. Isn't that like leaving a loaded gun on the table?"

"Jesus, man. You're crazy. It's insulating foam, for Christ's sake. Insulating foam! Used to insulate buildings, not kill people!"

"We use a candlestick for holding a candle until Colonel Mustard whacks someone over the head with it in the library."

"What?"

Cheeky returned with Caruso's coffee. "They want to talk to you, Mr. Megquire," he said.

Jon thought about what Caruso had said as he walked toward the main buildings. If Caruso didn't have something to hide, his reaction to being accused seemed unnecessarily extreme. Jon would have to relay that information to Lisa later.

Then, off to the side of the path between the roots of a tree, he saw a white shape in the grass that looked like a paper plate, but when he bent over to pick it up, he recognized Kerchini's flat cap.

~

INTERVIEWING Jon was going to be weird, Lisa thought as she waited in the interview room.

"You have a relationship with this guy, right?" Smith asked.

"I do."

"I said it before, but you shouldn't be here then. Can you be unbiased? Completely? We have to treat him as a suspect, just like all the others."

"I'll just sit back against the wall," Lisa said. "Won't say a thing. I can do this, Sarge. He lives his life. I live mine." She shrugged.

"I don't like it. But I'm willing to try it. You've got to learn."

They had just completed interviewing Gail Barker, one of the festival's featured speakers. Bright woman. Maybe a bit troubled about life, but hard to read. She was cool and controlled, and fielded their questions like a pro, someone who had faced congressional committees and put them in their place. And she was an attractive woman and perhaps you could hide behind the science in an ivory tower to avoid relationships. A technical whiz, no doubt. Jon could learn a lot from her. Barker admitted she was familiar with foam technology but denied previous knowledge of the attendees. Denial certainly didn't make her statements true. Maybe she was one of those chameleon characters who appeared lovey-dovey on the surface but was really a viper underneath. A calm and cool scientist was a perfect cover, Lisa thought.

It was wrong, but initially Lisa had a hard time imagining a woman killing in such a vicious way. Barker had been at the reception, but she hadn't had a lot to say about it.

Protocol said that they had to interview everyone who could have been involved with the victim because the connections in a group of strangers like this were not obvious. The psychology of criminals—and especially killers—fascinated Lisa. Although TV shows told stories about murder every week, murder didn't happen frequently in small towns, and most of the time the cause was completely obvious, like domestic abuse or a drunken argument outside a bar over a football game.

When Jon entered the room, Lisa tried to keep her face neutral—to be the interrogating officer and not the lover. That was tough. She did, in fact, love this man and had loved him since she had first seen him five years before. She had watched him struggle to find his direction in life, and finally he had come back to her—both emotionally and physically.

What if she didn't really know him? People had dark sides, secrets that they didn't want anyone to know. Plus, one night does not reveal all the missing days. She hadn't been with him during all that time in Florida. What had occupied all those days and nights beneath the surface of his explanations? There were a lot of criminal connections with sports and drugs. Did Jon have some ulterior motive for coming back to Cape Cod for this festival? She didn't want to believe it, but there was a great deal she didn't know about this man. Time passes, and she hadn't been at Jon's side to see all the days, hours, minutes, and people passing through his life.

"Good afternoon, Mr. Megquire," Smith said, indicating that Jon should take the chair across the table. "I believe you know Trooper Prence."

"I do," Jon said, smiling at her.

"I'll just sit over here," Lisa said as she settled into a molded plastic chair against the wall behind Smith, so she could watch Jon's face. She noticed her palms were sweating.

"We'll be recording this," Smith said. "Just routine. For the record."

"Okay," Jon said with a smile. Then he dropped Kerchini's flat cap on the table. "By the way, that's Chris Kerchini's hat. Thought you might be interested."

Sergeant Smith pushed back from the table in surprise.

"It was in the grass by a tree. Kind of hidden. I nearly missed it. Guess the techs did too. So I guess that confirms that it's Kerchini under all that foam."

"How do you know it's Kerchini's?" Smith asked.

"He was wearing it when I met him. He never took it off."

"Bag it, trooper," Smith instructed Lisa. "That's evidence. You shouldn't have moved it, Mr. Megquire. You interfered with evidence, you know that?"

"Just thought you'd like to know before someone stepped on it. It looked like trash. I was just trying to help."

"Don't help," Smith said. "Let us do our jobs."

Lisa thought there was something different about Jon, but she didn't know what it was. Maybe it was just in her mind—seeing him in this context as a potentially violent murderer. She shook it off.

Smith rattled through the preliminaries—identifying who Jon was, his permanent address in Florida, his occupation.

"I'm a promoter," Jon said, to Lisa's surprise. "A sports promoter working for a consortium to establish a new major league baseball franchise in Fort Lauderdale."

"Really? So why are you at this event? Is this connected to sports promotion somehow?"

"No, it's not," Jon said. "I'm here because I'm interested in energy efficiency."

"Oh, yeah? Why?"

Lisa watched Jon run his hands over the surface of the table between him and Smith as though he were cleaning it. Did that mean he was about to tell a lie? That wasn't good. She had taken classes in human tells like micro expressions, voice stress analysis, and body language. She'd studied the use of so-called lie detectors or polygraphs, but they were only about fifty percent accurate, about the same as flipping a coin. How people positioned their feet, where they looked, the movement of their hands were much better clues about the veracity of the suspect's answers.

She didn't want to associate "suspect" with Jon. He was just here to fill in facts.

"You know," Jon insisted. "You know. Everyone should be interested in energy efficiency. There is an international energy crisis. We're messing up the planet."

"Oh, yeah?" Smith said. "So you're here to fix the planet. Is that what you were doing last night?"

"Excuse me?" Jon asked.

"What were you doing last night?" Smith repeated. Jon looked at Lisa.

"I was sleeping."

"Before that?" Smith asked. "Did you take part in the party on the patio? Out there?" Smith nodded toward the plaza.

"Yeah, sure," Jon said. "Everyone did."

"Tell me about it?"

"About what?"

"About what you were doing last night at the party. Did you talk to anyone?"

"Well, I didn't just stand around mutely!"

Lisa watched the sergeant pushing Jon off balance.

"Of course I talked to people," Jon continued. "I had a pleasant conversation with Gail Barker. It was great to have a personal conversation with authorities in the field. The personal interactions are a great thing about conferences like this."

"Yeah?" Smith said. "Who else? What about your roommate? Kerchini? Did you talk to him?"

Lisa watched Jon look around the room. It was strange that Kerchini was the victim and that he was Jon's roommate. She wondered if Jon had asked to share the cabin with Kerchini, or was that just coincidental? She made a note to check on how the housing assignments had been made for the festival.

"We were talking. I mean, I was talking with Gail and Dr. Hawkins and a couple of others."

Gail? Lisa thought.

"How about Kerchini?" the sergeant asked.

"Maybe for a minute. Dr. Hawkins was talking about some sort of curse and Kerchini interrupted."

"What did you know about him before you got here?"

"Nothing! I'd never met him before."

"Don't you think that is strange?"

"What? That I hadn't met him before? There are millions of people I haven't met before."

"Mm, hmm," Smith mused. "Turns out that he also had a sports connection. Betting. Sports betting."

"Really?"

"You didn't know that, Mr. Megquire? You're sure?"

"Of course I'm sure. I never met the man before I arrived here on Sunday afternoon."

"And now he's dead and you're sitting here talking to me. I find that interesting, don't you? I don't much like coincidences. Know what I mean?"

Lisa didn't like coincidences either. Could she just accept that Jon had returned to the Cape because of this conference? And that was the only reason? She liked to think that she had something to do with his thinking, but it was suspicious. She was glad to see him, but they had trained her to be suspicious, to doubt the truth of what people said, whether friend or stranger. She didn't want to doubt Jon. It was a curse to look for the evil side of everyone and everything.

"Have you ever used a foam machine before last night?" Smith asked.

"I didn't use the foam machine last night!"

"Sorry. What I meant was, have you used a foam machine before you came here?"

"No."

"Did you question why Mr. Kerchini didn't come back to your cabin last night?"

"Jesus," Jon said. "I don't know. He's… was a grown man. He could go to sleep in a tree for all I cared."

Lisa adjusted her glasses. She didn't like to see Jon uncomfortable. He wasn't under attack. This was merely questioning. She heard the sergeant shift his tone of voice to the next question. It got softer, more persuasive.

"Mr. Megquire, if you want to help us, maybe you saw who Mr. Kerchini was talking to last night?"

"I didn't," Jon replied. "I was enjoying chatting with a couple of people and getting to understand more about thermodynamics."

"Thermodynamics!" Smith laughed. "Really? That would have engaged me too! But did you notice any unusual conversations going on? I mean, other than thermodynamics. Any conversations that might have been... well, heated? Like an argument? This was a vicious crime. Try to picture the event in your mind. You're a smart guy. You probably saw things you don't even remember you saw."

Lisa watched Jon look up at the ceiling and laugh. It didn't seem like the right time to laugh. Why did he do that, she wondered? Was he nervous? Had he seen something or done something that he would be nervous about?

"Nope," Jon said. "It's one of those quiet, scientific crowds. Some people raised their voices, sure, but it was because of their passion for their subject. These people believe in what they are doing and why they are doing it. They want to impact the future of this world."

"Okay. I get it," Smith said.

"No, what I mean is that people get passionate about making a difference. People like Dr. Widner and Mr. Douthwaite—he's one of the speakers—have had many experiences they feel strongly about. So, yes. There were some raised voices. And besides, we were all drinking. You can't blame us."

"I can blame someone for killing Mr. Kerchini, now that you've confirmed that it was Kerchini," Smith waved his fingers in the air, "by 'finding' his hat! What happened was torture. Not something one human being casually does to another human being. It takes a sick mind to do that."

Lisa watched the sergeant study Jon's face, looking for signs that he was lying or hiding something.

"Wait a second," Jon said. "There was a moment when Dr. Widner seemed upset with Kerchini."

"How so?" the sergeant asked.

"Apparently, it was something to do with that curse that I mentioned. That's what Gail said, anyway."

Gail again, Lisa thought.

"Well, she didn't know the story, but Dr. Hawkins said that it was something about a sachem who could hear worms in the walls. Kerchini said that was bullshit."

"So what happened? To the worm-hearing sachem, I mean?" Smith asked.

"Dr. Hawkins made some remark about Miriam Leathe's name—about it being connected to Hades. That upset her. So we didn't hear the end of the story. I think Dr. Hawkins was embarrassed."

"That doesn't seem very explosive," the sergeant laughed.

"No. But there didn't seem to be a lot of love lost for Kerchini. Gail didn't like him. Caruso didn't like him, but Marion seemed to be fascinated."

Sergeant Smith looked around at Lisa. "Okay. Worms talking. Sachems. Thermodynamics. Wish I'd been there!" he said.

"I guess," Jon said.

"Well, thank you, Mr. Megquire. Appreciate your help. You will stick around?" Smith said.

"Sure," Jon said, standing up. "I'll be here." He looked at Lisa and she looked away.

After he'd left the room, Sergeant Smith asked her, "What do you think? You know him. Did he have anything to do with it?"

"No," she said emphatically. "No, he was just here."

"Why is he here? He could have known that Kerchini was going to be here before the event. He could have come for the specific purpose of settling an old score. No one leaves the glamor of professional sports to learn about thermodynamics and expandable foam! Did he ever play pro ball?"

"He had an opportunity to play with the Angels, but that was years ago."

"Look, I know you like him, but you can't let that cloud your judgement. He's a potential suspect like they all are until we know for certain that it was someone else. That truck was unlocked." He paused. "Do you think we could get some coffee?"

Lisa moved toward the door. "Sure," she said.

"He knows more than he's saying, that's all," Smith said.

～

NO WAY, Jon thought. No way they think I did this! He stood still for a moment outside the interrogation room, readjusting his reality. He felt as though they had chewed him up and spat him out. Did they think he'd planted the hat and conveniently turned it in? How could Lisa just sit there and listen while that sergeant grilled him? She knew he wasn't guilty of burying someone. She knew it! It had crossed his mind to ask her to marry him. How could you marry someone who would even, for one second, think you were capable of something like this? Even if it was their job! How could someone go through life with a job that made them doubt everyone's honesty? That would be like being married to a proctologist—someone who spends their lives examining assholes! How sexy would that be?

No. He could find the actual murderer and prove it, so Lisa could see how wrong she was to even begin to suspect him. And how was he going to do that? Including the ITI staff and the trainers, there were way too many people here—even eliminating himself and Chris Kerchini. He couldn't investigate the way the police could investigate. He couldn't interrogate anyone. His big advantage was that he was one of them. He was a suspect, just as they were. They would trust him, tell him things that they might not tell the police.

He might be wrong, but he was going to rule out the staff. This was murder. The killer seemed to have had an intense grudge against the victim. And the killer must have been very persuasive—able to lure Kerchini out to the truck, incapacitate him, and then kill him. Did that mean it was a woman? He couldn't rule out Widner or Cheeky. He suspected they might be gay; maybe this was some sort of sexual revenge crime. He'd heard that crimes by gay men could be exceptionally violent. What about Hawkins? No, he was just too old, and nothing about his knowledge of atomic bombs or myths and curses would entice Kerchini. Then there was Gail Barker. She was certainly appealing, and she'd made it clear she couldn't stand Kerchini.

Ruling out the staff dropped about twelve people out of the picture. He could also discount the few members of the press in attendance. A story about the misuse of foam insulation wouldn't be good for the industry, and *Solar Age* was hardly a sensational tabloid. Then there were all the attendees. He wouldn't have time in the next day or so to question all of them. Another evening reception was scheduled for the plaza. He was going to have to talk to as many people as he could and be observant—seeking odd associations and interactions. How would a murderer behave once the murder had been committed? Wouldn't they try to disappear? Unless they were so sure that they couldn't possibly be identified? Or they were insane and had blanked out what they had done. Should he be looking for someone wandering about with a blank look on his or her face? That would include several people at this festival.

∼

"So you know the trooper?" Cheeky said, sliding up beside Jon.

Cheeky's comment startled Jon. He had been spacing out, lost in his thoughts of uncovering a murderer. "I do," he replied.

"Tough cookie," Cheeky said.

"Yeah. Surprising interrogation! I didn't expect to be given the third degree."

"'No one expects the Spanish Inquisition,'" Cheeky replied, quoting Monty Python. "'Our chief weapon is surprise... surprise and fear... and ruthless efficiency!'"

"Yeah. It was like that." Jon laughed.

"I always liked the 'ruthless efficiency' part. But they didn't torture you with the 'comfy chair', did they?" Cheeky chuckled. "Have they discovered anything? Do they know who did it? Do they know who it is... or was, I guess?"

"It's Chris Kerchini. I found his hat."

Cheeky stepped back and covered his mouth. "Ahh. That's really strange, isn't it?"

"Why strange, Cheeky?"

"Well, you know. Here today. Gone in a fortnight."

Jon looked at him with a distinct lack of clarity.

"Well, I found it odd to see Mr. Kerchini here at all."

"Did you know him?"

Cheeky swung his gaze around the patio and up to the sky before he answered. "I met him once. There was no question that he was a handsome man. Manly, some might say."

"So tell me, where did you meet him?"

"At the bar in Atlantic City. And you're going to ask me why I was in a bar in Atlantic City. Doing a bit of sleuthing yourself, are you?"

"Just curious is all. That is a curious coincidental connection to Kerchini."

"It was just a bit of a side trip before I indentured myself here."

"What did you talk about?" Jon asked.

"Oh, this and that, you know. Just trying to get to know the man, if you catch my drift."

"Just a friendly chat?"

"You could say that. He asked me about England. You know that always happens when people hear how I speak. They want to know where, and you have to tell them about London no matter what the actual answer is."

Jon laughed. "I know. It's like telling people you're from New York and they say, 'I know someone from New York' as though you know everyone in New York!"

Cheeky laughed.

"But what was he doing in Atlantic City?"

"What do people do in Atlantic City? He was gambling. Sports. Baseball. I know nothing about baseball. I know nothing about sports, really."

"Did he ask why you were in the States?"

"Sure. And I told him about signing up as an intern for ITI and about this conference."

"Oh," Jon said. "Maybe that's how he found out about it. Did you know he sold insulating foam?"

"To be honest with you, I knew nothing about insulating foam! So we didn't get that far in the conversation."

"Have you told the police about this?"

"They haven't talked to me yet."

"Got anything to hide?" Jon asked with a smile.

Cheeky looked down at his shoes and then up at Jon's face. "There are always skeletons in the closet."

"Really??"

"Well, I wouldn't call them exactly skeletons, but the police can twist things any way they want, can't they? Make things look evil when they're really not evil at all."

"Mmm hmm," Jon agreed.

"Tell me about these skeletons," Jon asked.

Cheeky shuffled his feet. "Things were tough back home, so I skipped out."

"Tough how?"

"Well, there was the miners' strike last March."

"You weren't a miner, were you?"

"No way." Cheeky snorted. "But it was almost impossible to find a job. The Iron Lady—that's Thatcher to you—is a bitch, and there was a bit of rioting. Students looting, that sort of thing."

"Was that you?"

"Not on my own. But it's a bit of fun, isn't it? Scary but thrilling at the same time. Being someplace you're not supposed to be. Doing something you're not supposed to do. Gives you a kind of tickle in the balls. And you're there with your mates, and they're all laughing and shouting and singing. It's just a bit of shits and giggles."

"Singing?" Jon asked. "You were singing while you were breaking into places?"

"Oh, protest songs like 'Coal not Dole.' Stuff that Maggie Thatcher wouldn't like."

"Did you get arrested?"

"Slipped away in the nick of time. Mum and dad couldn't afford me, could they? I was what they call a luxury."

"Was your father a miner?"

"Nah, but they shuttered the factories. It was like the Middle Ages! Thatcher was putting the squeeze on all of us working-class people."

Jon wondered if any of that would make Lisa suspicious of

Cheeky's history, anything that would connect him to this place. She would be more interested in his connection to Kerchini, but where did that go? "Let's go back to your meeting with Kerchini. Anything happen there that might make you want to kill him?"

Cheeky looked surprised. "What? No! Of course not!"

"Why did you put us in the same cabin?"

"Alphabetical chance," Cheeky replied. "'K' comes just before 'M'. We didn't have any 'L's."

"Oh," Jon said. "Well, somebody must have really hated the man. Killing someone with insulating foam is not a spontaneous spur-of-the-moment activity for, as you say, 'shits and giggles'. Did you notice anything odd about any of the attendees that might identify them as a killer?"

"Can't say that I did," Cheeky replied, frowning. "But it certainly wasn't me."

"Sorry, Cheeky. I had to ask. Hey listen, I have to make a phone call. Thanks for chatting with me."

"Cheers," Cheeky replied.

JON SUPPOSED every attendee would have some sort of backstory. No one was totally squeaky clean. You would have to live in a bubble to be without sin. That might be the wrong word. He wondered how Lisa would sort the bad stuff from the terrible stuff. That Cheeky had taken part in looting during difficult economic times didn't mean that he was capable of murder. That Kerchini and Cheeky had met previously was more interesting. It made Jon wonder who else at the festival might have crossed paths with Kerchini in the past.

This was not an obvious premeditated killing. There were quicker, safer ways to kill someone than to bury them in expanding foam. How could you plan something like that? You don't say to yourself, "I'm going to make sure I'm alone in a place with the person I want dead with an expanding foam machine nearby." Jon shook his head in perplexity.

He returned to the lobby of the institute where he'd noticed an old phone booth. It was wood paneled with a folding, sliding door. The pay phone was mounted on the wall, and a small kidney-shaped plastic slab served as a seat. When he pulled the door closed, an over-head light and exhaust fan turned on. Jon pulled out his wallet and extracted a piece of paper with Ace Wentzell's phone number. He dropped a quarter into the phone's slot, listened for the dial tone, and dialed.

On the fifth ring, he heard a woman answer, "Hello?"

"Mrs. Wentzell?" Jon said.

"Yes?" Babs replied.

"Hi, this is Jon. Jon Megquire."

"Oh, Jon! How wonderful to hear you!" Her voice faded as she held the phone away to call: "Ace! It's Jon."

He heard Ace bark, "Who?"

"Jon Megquire."

"How are you, Mrs. Wentzell?" Jon asked.

"You can call me Babs, if you like. That's the modern thing to do, isn't it?"

"Oh, okay," Jon said. Jon had been brought up to show respect to people older than himself. Calling them by their first names felt awkward.

"I'm right as rain, Jon," she laughed. "And you? We haven't heard from you in a while."

"I'm fine, thank you. And how's Ace holding up?"

Babs lowered her voice. "He actually seems pretty tired. But how's Florida?"

"I'm actually not in Florida at the moment. I'm in Tilley."

"Here in Tilley?"

"Yes, they're having a festival at the institute here in Tilley. I'm here to learn about energy-efficient building techniques."

"Really?" She held the phone away while she shouted to Ace. "Jon's in Tilley."

Jon heard Ace say, "Now?"

"Yes, now, He's at that institute place. You know, at the old Bed Right Inn."

"Of course, I know where that is," Jon heard Ace reply. "Let me talk to him."

The Wentzell house had been Jon's home away from home five years before, when Jon came to play for the Tilley Longliners in the Cape Cod Baseball League. His summer job had been working for Ace's construction business. Ace had infected Jon with a love for buildings, wood, joinery, light, and structure.

"So what the hell is going on out there now?" Ace boomed over the phone.

"They're having a festival!"

"What kind of festival? Like a music festival? Not like that Woodstock thing."

"No, no, it's a building festival. Like how to build better, more energy-efficient buildings. You should be here."

"Psst!" Ace hissed. "That's all the rage now, isn't it? That place is weird. I've wondered what they do out there. Are there a bunch of hippy, LSD space trippers out there?"

Jon laughed. "Not that I've seen."

"And they're trying to grow vegetables with fish poop. I heard that."

"Could be. But I'm learning interesting stuff about building techniques. They have some excellent speakers. Maybe you know Don Douthwaite? He's a builder from New Hampshire."

"Never heard of him."

"He builds houses that are coupled to the warmth of the earth. Wicks the heat up in the walls and wraps it around the people."

"Sounds creepy," Ace replied.

"Thing is, the program is on hold at the moment because someone got murdered."

Ace assimilated the word. "Murdered? Really? Why? Was it something they said?"

"Well, it probably wasn't an accident. It's hard to kill someone *accidentally* with expanding foam. Do you use expanding foam?"

"Why? Wasn't a gun available? I've heard about that foam stuff," Ace said. "Don't they make it out of piss and dead frogs or something?"

Jon laughed. "I think you're thinking about urea formaldehyde."

"Yeah. That's the stuff."

"I don't think that's really made of urine!"

Ace coughed. "Well, people don't stand around and piss in a pot to make it these days, but some Dutch scientist discovered it back in the 1700s. That stuff stinks. It really is urine."

Jon had forgotten that Ace had studied engineering.

"I hope they didn't really bury someone in that," Ace said.

"No. It was a polyurethane foam."

"At least there's that. But I guess that put a damper on the party, didn't it?"

Despite the fan, it was getting so hot and stuffy in the phone booth that Jon pulled the door open slightly.

"Do they think you had anything to do with it?" Ace asked.

"That's another funny thing. Do you know who's investigating this for the State Police?"

"They brought in the staties?"

"It's Lisa Prence. So both Lisa and her father are investigating!"

"That's your girlfriend. At least she used to be your girlfriend, didn't she?"

Jon watched people wandering through the lobby. The light had gone out when he opened the door and he felt odd sitting in the dark. "Well, I thought she was a friend, but they interrogated me, too. No mercy!"

"Chief Prence and Lisa?"

"No. Lisa and the sergeant. Tough guy. Sergeant Smith."

"Don't know him. How come you keep getting tangled up in murders? There was all that fuss with Faith Salsberg and carbon monoxide when you were here five years ago. Tilley is peaceful until you show up."

Faith Salsberg had been a summer resident of Tilley, killed by her son-in-law, who wanted the family business for himself. He simply disconnected the flue from the water heater and let the carbon monoxide silently kill her. At first the authorities blamed Ace because he had built the house, but Jon proved Ace had nothing to do with it.

Jon laughed, although the thought struck him as a strange coincidence.

"Still playing ball?" Ace asked.

"Only for fun."

"And how about your sister? Has she gone to the moon yet?"

It surprised Jon that Ace remembered that Jon's sister, Cornelia, worked for NASA. "She has a shuttle launch she's working on that's supposed to go at the end of this month. I think it's amazing that they think they can get that big plane up into space and bring it back down again in one piece."

"She is some smart cookie," Ace said. "So tell me. What are you doing with this building science stuff? I thought you were a jock."

Jon needed a concise answer to that question. Why did he have to explain his motives? Did he have to have a plan? Or did he have a plan that he didn't acknowledge to himself? Cornelia had a plan. She had gone directly there and look at her now.

Before he met Ace, Jon hadn't cared about buildings. He had built forts under tables, in a pile of leaves, in a pile of snow, and he'd put a few boards up in a tree to make a tree house. But until Ace taught him the structural elements of houses, how craftsmen notched the beams, set the studs, and linked the floor joists together, Jon had only thought of houses as places to live. But if he had fallen in love with buildings, why had he gone off to Florida to promote baseball? Why was he so fearful that he would miss what might be the most important turn on the road of his life if he stayed in one place? And now, why had he signed up for this conference, which had nothing to do with promoting sports?

"Jon? You still there?" Ace asked.

"I am."

"Thought I lost you for a moment."

"No. It's a good question, Mr. Wentzell... I mean, Ace."

"I hate that expression," Ace replied. "It means that you don't have an answer."

"No. I really like houses. You showed me how amazing they are."

"Don't go blaming me. You like Lisa Prence and you needed an excuse to get up here and see her, but you didn't need to subject yourself to a pile of mumbo-jumbo about 'building science' to accomplish that! You could have just come up."

Jon spotted Widner and Cheeky having a whispered conversation a few feet away. He pulled the door to the phone booth almost closed, but not enough to turn the light back on.

"I'd like to get over to see you," he murmured into the phone.

"I can barely hear you," Ace replied.

Jon repeated his words a bit more loudly.

"Babs would love that," Ace boomed. "Listen, Jon, you're welcome anytime. You don't have to make an appointment. Maybe you can figure out why you're here."

Jon could feel Ace smiling on the other end of the phone. "Maybe tomorrow night?" he suggested.

Ace agreed and broke the connection.

Jon then sat in the booth with his left hand on the phone and his right on the handle of the folding door, trying to make out the words Widner was spitting at Cheeky.

"These people have paid to be here!" he hissed. "My reputation is on the line!"

"It's the police," Cheeky replied. "There's a murderer among us!"

"Don't you think I know that? I know what's going on. This isn't my first rodeo."

"I think nothing of the sort, Elliott," Cheeky mumbled back.

"Maybe you should go. Go! I mean… leave… depart."

Jon's view of the pair was not clear. The angled glass of the door distorted the two men. Jon was trying hard to hold it still, but the spring-loaded hinges were trying to pull it all the way open.

"What, now?"

"It might be for the best. Before this goes any further."

"Are you sacking me?" Cheeky asked.

That was the last that Jon could hear of the conversation before the pair moved away. He needed air, so he let the door spring open and stepped out.

ITI remained a mystery to him. Jon needed to understand how the place worked if he was going to understand why Kerchini had been murdered.

~

THAT EVENING, Jon returned to the plaza and looked around. Lisa, Smith, and Prence had left, and the crowd seemed thinner than it had the night before. Maybe it just felt that way, as if participants were avoiding each other. After all, it was a crowd of strangers. People didn't come to these things as couples. It was rare for a husband and wife to enjoy the thrill of thermodynamics together, the challenge of the "R" value, the titillation of polyisocyanurate insulation. They might have come together, and while one of them went to the festival, the other went to the beach. But they weren't likely to be hanging out at a reception where people were deeply engaged in discussing thermal mass or the transmissivity of glass.

Tonight's group felt nervous, standing in isolated clusters, quietly murmuring, clutching beers, nibbling the snacks like mice in a science experiment. A gentle sea-scented breeze rippled the leaves of the trees and jiggled the festive strings of lights that stretched from one side of the plaza to the other.

Cheeky strummed his guitar and sang his usual repertoire, though few voices chimed in. Jon detected the distinct smell of marijuana mixed with the scent of pine and warm, wet sand.

He was tempted to ignore the murder question and seek Ashton to talk about computers, or Gail Barker to talk about the feelings of rats or living in Colorado. but he forced himself to find someone who seemed *least* likely to be a murderer that he could rule out of his investigation. He settled on Miriam Leathe.

She was sitting by herself, staring into the fire pit. She seemed drawn to what she saw in the flames. Jon grabbed a beer and stepped over beside her. For a moment, he shared her vision of the dancing light. The fire wasn't necessary on such a warm August night. He wondered how she could tolerate the heat.

"Nice fire," he said. Miriam didn't respond.

Jon gulped his beer. The flames crackled, and the wood hissed. The smoke seemed intent on blowing in his face, no matter where he positioned himself. "Hardly need the heat, do we?"

Miriam stayed silent. She seemed to have picked the perfect spot, a spot the smoke avoided for some thermodynamic reason.

"Can I get you anything? Miriam," he asked. "Aren't you getting hot?"

Miriam looked up, then returned her gaze to the fire that flashed before her.

"It's too bad that we weren't able to hear all the sessions today," Jon said. "I had hopes I would learn a lot here."

Miriam mumbled, "So did I."

"I came all the way up from Florida for this," he said. The heat of the fire was making him very uncomfortable, and the smoke made his eyes water. The woman seemed to be in a sort of hypnotic state.

"Terrible thing that happened today," he said.

"Yes," she replied. "Unless he deserved it."

"What do you mean?"

"The man who died. Maybe he deserved it."

"How can you say that?" Jon asked. "Aren't you hot sitting this close to this fire? The human skin is incredibly efficient at absorbing radiant energy. Dr. Hawkins told us that."

Miriam looked back at the fire. "I'm fine."

"But I have to ask again, how can you say that the victim deserved what he got? That must have been a terrible way to die. It must have been almost like being burned alive."

"Yes," she agreed. "It must have been."

Jon's eyes were watering, and his nose was running. He tried moving around to a more protected spot.

It just didn't seem to bother Miriam. Maybe because she was sitting, and the smoke was flowing over her head. He had heard of the ceremonies of Indigenous people where the shaman sat beside the fire, sucking in the smoke, getting lost in the flames, prophesying the future, seeking the truth. It might work for a trained shaman, but it sure wasn't working for him.

"Did you know Chris Kerchini? He lived around here too, didn't he?"

Miriam looked at him across the fire. The flickering light reflected in her watery eyes.

"I didn't know him," she said. "I knew of him."

Jon tried to test the theory that Miriam was the murderer based on the evidence. Just because she was strange didn't mean that she was a murderer, right? She was nowhere near big enough to force Kerchini into a compromising position, and she would have had to persuade him to follow her into the darkness. She certainly didn't seem very persuasive at the moment. And what motive did she have?

"We shared a cabin," Jon said. Miriam didn't reply. "But we didn't talk much."

Jon wondered what she had meant by she didn't know him, but she knew of him. Did Kerchini have some kind of reputation?

"You sell houses, don't you?" Jon asked. "Did Kerchini ever insulate any of them with foam?"

She looked across the fire at him. Tears were running down her cheeks.

"Jesus!" he said. "I'm sorry. I didn't mean to upset you."

"It's the smoke, you ass," she said, wiping her eyes with the back of her hand. "Sorry. No, I've never sold a house insulated with foam."

"Can I get you anything?" he asked again. "You must be boiling."

"I don't want to talk about this," she said. "You seem like a nice young man, but I don't want to talk about this anymore."

The "leave me alone" was implicit.

Jon said, "Right," and turned away. She didn't fit his vision of a murderer anyway. Hunched over her knees, glaring at the flames, she looked like a crone. But he wouldn't rule her out yet. She was just too odd.

~

JON WANDERED BACK to the refreshment table, where he found Joe Caruso fumbling around in the icy water at the bottom of the beer cooler, mumbling to himself. His glasses had slipped down to the end of his nose, and his face was covered in sweat.

It felt cooler away from the fire, but only by contrast. "Looking for something in particular?" Jon asked.

"There's only the crappy beer left. Just need a Bud, but I'd settle for a Busch. I'd go buy a couple of cases, but I can't move my truck because of the crime stuff."

"We could ask Cheeky if there is any more of what you've been drinking. I'm surprised that they've run out."

"I'm not," Caruso replied. "Not in this tight-assed place."

"We could take my car if you want," Jon suggested.

"Great. Know any place around here?"

"Plenty of liquor stores on the Cape."

"Let's go."

Jon was glad that Caruso wouldn't be driving. The way he was walking suggested he may have been the one to drink all the beer. As they walked toward cabin 42, Caruso took out his cigarettes. He offered one to Jon, who declined.

When Caruso pulled out his lighter, the flame illuminated his face and reflected off his glasses. *This is more like what a murderer looks like,* Jon thought. Stubby, sweaty, with greasy black hair, with his head wreathed by cigarette smoke. Jon wondered how the guy could work with flammable foam and smoke cigarettes.

"Where are we going?" Caruso asked..

"Cabin 42. I guess the person who named these things was a science fiction fan. Forty-two is the meaning of life in a *Hitchhiker's Guide to the Galaxy.* Do you like science fiction?"

"I don't have time to read," Caruso replied. "I don't like fiction."

"Did you say you were from around here?"

"Hingham. Long time ago."

"Now you live in New Jersey?"

"That's where the factory is. Jesus, if I'd known your car was this far away, I would have grabbed one of those other beers for the road."

"Not much farther," Jon said. "I guess they want to give people some privacy in these cabins. People come here to relax, play tennis, golf, go to the beach...."

"I don't have time for golf," Caruso said. "And I definitely don't have time to lie around on the sand. Don't mind the beach babes though." When he tried to laugh, he coughed.

"So what do you think happened with your truck last night?"

"Some wacko. They're everywhere these days. Yeah, maybe I should have locked my truck. But that lady cop didn't have to be rude about it."

They arrived at Jon's cabin. Kerchini's Buick and Maybelline were parked side by side.

"Which one's yours?" Caruso asked. "No, let me guess; that little foreign thing, right? I'm not going to fit in there."

"Bigger men than you have been in Maybelline."

"Maybelline? You named your car? Oh, man, this really is hippy heaven."

"The Buick belongs to Chris Kerchini. I'm surprised they haven't taken it away yet. We were sharing this cabin, but I hardly got to talk to him."

"Yeah. He probably had little to talk about, anyway. *Chooch!*"

"You didn't like him?"

"There wasn't much to like. The man gave insulating foam a bad name. That statie bitch will probably turn him into a martyr. You got good taste, by the way—she has a splendid set of tits."

Jon took a step closer to the little man. Caruso's cologne did little to mask his body odor.

"Kerchini was an asshole," Caruso said, who couldn't see the flash of irritation on Jon's face.

"Yeah?"

"Yeah. He defined the word. Refused to get trained until the company forced him to. That's why he was here, you know. They wouldn't let him sell any more foam until he got properly trained. I could have helped him, but he didn't want to be helped. He was helpless."

He lit another cigarette. "Hey, are we going to just stand here or are we going to get some more beer? Let me drive. I'll show you how a stick shift should be driven." He held out his hand for the keys.

"No way," Jon said. "You're half in the bag. I'm surprised you can walk and talk. And I don't want you smoking in my car."

"You scared, kid? Come on. Let's have those keys. I'm dying of thirst here!" He poked Jon with the index finger of his chubby right fist.

"No way," Jon said again, taking a step back. He regretted his suggestion to secure more alcohol. His suspicion of Caruso as the murderer grew. Kerchini was competition, and Caruso thought he was an asshole. Caruso appeared to have what might arise as an uncontrollable anger issue. He could operate the foam machine. Jon could easily imagine the two of them out in the dark—drunk, arguing, pushing each other around. And now Jon might be alone, arguing with a killer.

"Tell you what, Joe, why don't you park yourself up there on the porch, and I'll go get the beer. You can take a nap. Just don't set the place on fire."

"No way," Caruso said, mocking Jon's tone. "You'll go out and get some sort of hoity-toity horse piss. Got any money? I've got money. Or maybe you won't come back. Just leave me sitting here on my ass waiting for a bus that never comes."

The man's logic was impeccable... for a toddler.

Caruso threw his cigarette down on the drive and yelled, "GIVE ME THE FUCKING KEYS!" He stepped close to Jon and pushed him.

Jon stumbled, but regained his balance. "No way you're driving Maybelline."

Caruso tried to sing: "Maybelline. Why can't you be true? Oh, Maybelline! Do what you do. Hoo hoo hoo."

"What's it like dating a cop?" Caruso asked. "Do you play cops and robbers before you screw? There's a fantasy I can get behind! Come to think of it, she has a nice behind too! You got it coming and going." He tried laughing, but coughed again.

Jon stepped up to the little greaseball. "Knock it off," he said.

"Knock what off? Hey, she's a piece of ass, you lucky shit."

"Knock it off," Jon repeated. "Have some respect."

"Respect for what?" Caruso started trying to sing again, "R E S P E C T! Sock it to me. Sock it to me. Sock it to me."

"Shut up, Caruso! Did you kill Kerchini last night?"

Caruso stepped back. "What?"

"Did you kill Kerchini? How could you hate him that much? What the hell did he do to you? Rape your wife? Ruin your business? You called him an asshole." Jon's blood was boiling. He longed to knock the man down, tie his hands behind his back, march him back up to the main building, and present him to Lisa or her father as a trophy. Caruso was such a weasel—such a worthless, insulting piece of shit that it would have given Jon pleasure to smash his face in, although he was wearing glasses and Jon had been told to never hit someone with glasses. There was also the minor problem that Lisa, the sergeant, and the chief had gone home for the night. And that he would have had to improvise rope or something else to tie Caruso with.

"No! Why would I do that?"

"Because you could. You're the most likely suspect."

"What are you, a cop now? Did the cop-ness from your girlfriend rub off on you? Is that something you can catch in bed?"

"So why did you kill Kerchini? I don't understand how you can hate someone that much!"

"Maybe I should kill you, too," Caruso shouted. "I got a gun in the truck! I thought you people were peaceful tree huggers. Didn't think I needed to carry my gun on my person. But you never know, do you? Jesus, I could use another beer. Talking to assholes makes me thirsty as hell."

"What?"

"If I killed Kerchini, aren't you afraid I'm an out-of-control maniac? Maybe I should eliminate you, too. Did you see me kill

Kerchini? What evidence do you have that I'm a killer? Did you see me do it?" Caruso stepped back and kicked Maybelline's fender.

"Hey!" Jon said. He grabbed Caruso and pushed him against the Buick. "Knock it off! That's enough."

"I'm a killer," Caruso said. "You said so yourself. Better be careful. Maybe I have my gun. New Jersey people always carry guns."

Jon threw Caruso down on the ground, face first. The man expelled a whoosh like a flattened cushion.

"Hey!" Caruso said. "You can't do that."

Jon knelt on his back to hold him down. The man didn't have any place to hide a gun. He was wearing Bermuda shorts and a black T-shirt. Jon felt nothing under his knee. He wasn't about to pat down his ass.

"Apologize for what you said about Trooper Prence, or I will have her lock you up and put you away for a million years for being a murderer."

"I didn't do anything! Let me up. You're pushing the air out of my lungs! Ow!"

"If you're carrying a gun in that truck, you are in big trouble, asshole. You can't carry a concealed weapon like that across state lines."

"I think I'm going to puke!"

"And I'm sure you killed Kerchini. Don't know what your motive was, but you sure as hell had the opportunity and the skills to handle the weapon. That was just a plain sadistic way to kill someone. Now admit it!"

"I didn't do anything," Caruso whined.

Without his glasses, which had skittered across the asphalt when Jon dropped him, he looked pathetic—like part of his face was missing.

Jon leaned harder. He weighed over two hundred pounds. He transferred most of it to his right knee on Caruso's back.

Caruso coughed out, "Jesus, stop. All right. I apologize about your girlfriend. Now get the hell off my back!"

Jon stood up and stepped back.

Caruso struggled to his feet. "I should sue you, *stronzo!*" He coughed twice and hawked a loogie on the driveway at Jon's feet. He leaned over and picked up his glasses, pulled out his pack of cigarettes, and lit one. "You're a jerk," he said. "Anyone ever tell you that before? I bet they have. Bet you hear it all the time!"

"Get the hell out of here," Jon said, and booted Caruso in the ass, pushing him in the direction of the plaza. Caruso staggered away.

Jon found he was sweating profusely. He went inside the cabin, angled his mouth under the bathroom sink, and gulped the water. He came back out to the porch and leaned against the post.

It really was possible, he thought, that Caruso had killed Kerchini. If that was the case, and Jon had just told him what he thought, then wouldn't he get in his truck tonight and drive away? What would keep him here? Some yellow crime scene tape? Jon decided he'd better call Lisa and let her know about Caruso's anger issues. But first, just to spite Caruso, he jumped into Maybelline and headed into Tilley to find beer.

ALONE IN THE CAR, he yelled expletives at the windshield and pounded his hands on the steering wheel. Jon needed to drive and clear his head. Gradually Maybelline's familiarity soothed his mind and slowed his throbbing pulse with friendly reassurance as her headlights picked out the curves. He restrained himself from roaring out of the ITI complex, and he let his body sway as he dove into the corners, downshifting into the curves and upshifting out. He was used to the vagaries of her drifting back end. They were a team. They had been through some interesting times together in rain and snow, carburetor troubles and flat tires. She'd never been quite the same after some idiot forced his car into her front end, making a parking space near the beach in Fort Lauderdale. That was how Jon learned never to leave Maybelline in gear when he parked. He had to drive for six months with no first gear before getting the gear box fixed. Despite all the issues, she got him where he wanted to go when he wanted to go there—regularly, if not reliably.

By the time he reached downtown Tilley, he'd decided he didn't want more beer. What he wanted was a burger. He looped back around and headed up the Mid-Cape highway toward Sandwich. It was a haul for a burger, but he knew where it was, knew it would be open, knew he could get gas there, and knew he would find a phone so he could call Lisa.

He turned on the radio and tuned in WCIB in Falmouth. The DJ, Robert Bobbert, was playing Stevie Wonder's "I Just Called to Say I Love You." The murder of Chris Kerchini took top billing in Jon's mind. What was he like? Did he have a family? What had he done that would cause Caruso to hate him so much he felt he had to kill him?

Jon kicked himself for losing his own temper with Caruso. He should have gotten him more beer and then been more persuasive at extracting the motive out of Caruso's past. Jon was sure it was there. Jon tried to put himself in the murderer's shoes. Money? Religion? Violence to a family member? He had missed an opportunity to see into the mind of a murderer.

What about Caruso's past? Why did he abandon his business in Massachusetts and take a job in New Jersey? Maybe Kerchini knew something about that and Caruso had to silence him?

Jon's blood began simmering again, turning that rock over. But then Widner popped into his mind. The guy was a dork. Could a dork be a murderer? Jon would have to talk to him one on one and rule him out.

What about Gail Barker? She said she had dealings with Kerchini when they were doing research. She was an attractive woman and Kerchini might have made the moves on her. She was totally out of his league, and maybe she didn't like it. But that hardly seemed an intense enough motive. Jon could imagine her shooting him, but not burying him in foam. Unless it was an experiment? Admittedly, she had a foam connection. It was such a unique weapon. In any case, he wouldn't mind talking to her again.

Then there was Widner's connection with Cheeky. What was that all about? The whispering in the lobby? They seemed to have a private thing going on. Why would someone come all the way from England to work without getting paid? Did Cheeky see a career path through the back-to-the-earth movement? Did he view Widner as some sort of Christ-like savior figure—or as something more intimate?

Bobbert had moved on to Tina Turner and "What's Love Got to Do with It?" Another serious question, which brought Miriam Leathe to mind. What was her role in all this? What was she doing at this thing? Her motives for attending the festival seemed as vague as Jon's. Was she really here because she was so concerned about her clients and wanted to learn about the safety of new building techniques? That sounded awfully altruistic. Altruistic was an interesting word. It was related to benevolence. Jon wondered how he had ever come across it. Maybe he had paid more attention in his English Lit classes than he'd realized.

How about Lash Ashton? Jon tried to fit him into the picture. Ashton was a computer nerd. They fit everywhere these days. They said that it wouldn't be long before everyone had his or her own computer. There was some law of computer development that said the power of computers would grow exponentially until the world of Dick Tracy's wrist phone would become a reality! Ashton was right on top of it already. It was impossible for Jon to imagine any reason he might step outside his world of ones and zeros and bury some guy in expanding foam.

Sade and "Smooth Operator" were playing on the radio as Jon turned off the Mid-Cape, crossed Route 132, and pulled into the Burger King parking lot. He sat listening until the song ended before he shut off Maybelline. The burger beckoned.

～

As Jon crossed the parking lot, he could smell the frying food mixed with the gasoline fumes from the attached Mobil gas station. "Eat here. Get gas!" His mouth was watering, anticipating something other than bean sprouts and whole grain muffins.

The big overhead lights inside the restaurant were blazing. Jon waited briefly in line, ordered a Whopper® meal with a Coke, and took his tray to a small table. He unwrapped the burger and took a massive bite, wiping the juice off his chin with a napkin. He couldn't remember a burger ever tasting that good. Not that it was an epicurean delight, but it harmonized with Jimmy Buffett's "Cheeseburger in Paradise." Somehow, healthy food didn't hit Jon's pleasure sensors the same way. The old adage that if something tasted good, it probably was bad for you was probably true. The thought made Jon shudder.

He savored each French fry, enjoying the salt and the crunch. When they were all gone, he took his tray to one of the trash cans and set off to find a phone.

There was a bank of phones outside the men's room. He dialed Lisa's number. She picked up on the third ring.

"Lisa? It's me. Jon."

"Oh, this is unexpected."

Cheeky's comment about the Spanish Inquisition leapt into his mind. "Were you expecting someone else?"

"You're not going to ask me about the case, are you? Because you know I can't talk about it."

"No, I know that, but I have to tell you about Joe Caruso. We got into a fight."

"Shit. Are you okay?"

"Oh, yeah, of course. The man's a doofus. I don't think he could punch his way out of a spider web."

"Did you hurt him? Am I going to have to arrest you?"

"No, of course not. But you might have to arrest him." Jon told her about his confrontation with Caruso and his worry that the man might run off.

"It's late, Jon."

"I know," he said. "But I can be there in about half an hour."

"What?"

"Yeah. I'm at the Burger King at 132."

"What the hell are you doing there?"

"I needed a burger. That health food is like eating grass and leaves."

She laughed. "But seriously, we can't talk."

"That's okay with me."

"Hey," she said. "All right then, but bring me a Whopper. And you have to be out of here early. Real early. Before they have breakfast over there. Sergeant Smith wouldn't be happy about me sleeping with a suspect."

"I'm not really a suspect, am I?"

"I can't talk about it. Of course you are. In his eyes anyway, everyone's a suspect."

"You can't believe that I would do anything like that, can you?"

Jon didn't like the pause she took before answering. It should have been an immediate and emphatic NO! A guy in a plaid shirt with a bandana wrapped around his head looked at Jon as he turned into the men's room.

"No, of course not. That was a vicious way to kill someone."

"Do you think I could have done it if it had been a less vicious method? Like, say, taping a plastic bag over his head so he suffocated?"

"Oh, come on, Jon. You're being stupid."

"No, I'm just asking. Do you suspect everyone of being a criminal now? Does that come with the uniform?"

"I'm going to hang up now," she said. "Just get the Whopper and get over here before I change my mind."

"Yes, dear," he mumbled as he heard the phone click, breaking the connection.

CHAPTER 8

FESTIVAL DAY 3–AUGUST 8, 1984

*T*he morning sky had sucked the blue out of the eyes of an angel. The temperature hovered in the low seventies. A hint of a breeze blew in the smell of the warming earth and the distant sea. A perfect Cape Cod vacation day, a day that did not match Elliott's mood in the slightest! Somehow, the beautiful days in Saskatchewan had seemed harsher, more replete with the fighting spirit that he needed to take on the authorities and overcome the obstacles. Those were hard days, but good days and thinking of them made Elliott smile. Cape Cod summer days felt like candy that was so sweet it made his teeth hurt.

Oh my god! Elliott Widner thought, how the hell am I going to keep this together? What's going to happen if all these people ask for their money back? We can't afford that! I don't want to go back to the trustees and tell them that this event was a failure. They'll blame me. Maybe they'll fire me. Then what will I do? And it will be because of something I had no control over. I wasn't even there. I took all the reasonable safety precautions. Didn't I? He wondered.

He abruptly thought of that old standard, "There's No Business Like Show Business." The show must go on. Behind the scenes, show business was all about adversity—overcoming the obstacles to make it happen. When things started coming apart, you didn't stand back and let it happen! No, you reached down and pulled yourself up without help and kept going. He was a firm believer in self-determination. He'd done it before. He would do it again.

Cheeky appeared and stood looking up at him. "Yes?" he asked.

"Septic system is backing up again."

"I don't have time for that right now."

"It doesn't much matter how you feel about it," Cheeky replied. "It's happening. What would you like to do about it? The meeting room stinks."

"You deal with it, Cheeky. Can't you solve a single problem on your own? Do I have to do everything?"

"I thought you sacked me." Cheeky put his hands on his hips and glared at him.

Widner gave him his best ingratiating smile, tilted his head to one side, and laid a hand on his shoulder. "Oh, no, Cheeky," he said. "That was just bluster! I didn't mean that. Really!"

Cheeky shrugged. "The kitchen's okay, and we've got breakfast out on the plaza. But people are wondering if the festival is going to continue. Some of them want to leave. They're afraid for their lives."

"Really? Do they think this so-called murderer is going to bury someone else in foam? That's ridiculous."

"I'm just telling you what I've heard."

"Can you get the plumber? What's his name? Russ something."

"I can ring him up."

"Do that and bring me a cup of coffee, will you?"

"Certainly, sir."

"Oh, don't do that! Like you're some kind of lackey. I hate it when you do the bowing and scraping bit."

"Namaste, master," Cheeky said, pressing his hands together and backing away, bowing.

It's so hard to find good help these days, Widner thought.

If the meeting room smelled, maybe they would hold the sessions outside. Maybe they could catch up on yesterday's sessions. He would ask Gail Barker to compress her presentation. And the builder from

New Hampshire, Don Douthwaite, could follow on after her. Since people were already gathered on the plaza for breakfast, maybe they should just stay there. They could rearrange the chairs, and gather around Douthwaite. Maybe it would appear they'd planned it! Arranging the chairs would take their minds off... other issues. Mr. Douthwaite had that speech issue that might make it difficult for people to hear him outside, but that couldn't be helped. His information was so intense. Yes! Widner thought. They could do this! And then he set off to get some breakfast and coffee.

After eating, Widner enlisted the help of Lash Ashton and Jon Megquire to arrange chairs. He was about to go in search of Douthwaite when the state police arrived. That sergeant certainly filled out his bright blue uniform. He kind of creaked when he strutted. And why did they have to wear those boots? They weren't like the Canadian Mounties, who one suspected of always having a horse tethered somewhere close by. The buzz-cut hair seemed to round out the man's face, adding an intensity to his lips.

"Morning," Smith said. "We need these people to stay here until we finish talking to them."

"That might be difficult, sergeant. Today's the last day of the festival and everyone's scheduled to go home. And they're not happy with what has gone on here. This... murder thing. People are afraid it's going to happen again. They're afraid for their lives! Until you catch him."

The lady trooper was standing back. Widner thought she was trying to look equally tough. Butch, maybe?

"You must tell them they have to stay here," the sergeant said.

"What am I supposed to do, officer? Wrestle them to the ground? Take away their car keys? What you're asking is impossible! If they want to leave, they're going to leave. Especially since our septic system just backed up, and it smells in the meeting room."

"I'm not going to argue with you, sir. Just make it happen." The sergeant turned and walked away.

Officious bastard, Widner thought. You give people a mere taste of authority, and they become petty dictators.

He told Barker about the smell situation but found that she was eager to talk about her research. "The smell in the meeting room is pretty bad," she said. "Much better to be outside."

He found Douthwaite getting coffee and explained the situation. His speech impediment made him a challenge to follow, and Widner was seriously concerned that the audience would struggle to understand him, especially without the support of slides or projected overheads. Widner knew he had led an exceptional life, standing up for his beliefs as a conscientious objector, getting arrested for refusing to pay federal income taxes to support the military industrial complex. But his New Hampshire building company had garnered awards for their energy efficient construction, and Douthwaite had a compelling message to convey to those who would make the world a better place.

The audience appeared to relish being outside listening to Gail Barker. It reminded Widner of those rare days in University when the professor took the class out to the lawn and they sat on the grass and soaked up the sunshine along with the pedagogical message.

When Barker had finished, the audience sought coffee and asked about using the bathrooms, and then they resumed their places on the plaza flagstones and surrounding grass. The air was calm, and even the birds seemed to have stopped their singing. Widner introduced Douthwaite with the briefest biographical sketch. Then he stepped back and let the magic begin.

Luckily, this audience knew Douthwaite's reputation and skills. He talked with the inspiration and enthusiasm of Daniel Webster facing the devil. His vocal challenges simply disappeared, while his words took the audience through the harmonies of passive solar design, of how to integrate buildings with the earth and the sun.

"Heat," he told them, "is simply the energy of molecular activity, driven always from warmer to cooler, towards uniformity and molecular rest."

He talked about the Indigenous settlements designed to channel the winter winds between the buildings to blow away snow, of the thermal mass of Pueblo adobe walls to naturally temper the internal swings of temperature. He talked about the mass of the stone in

Notre-Dame Cathedral, keeping the interior cool through a natural thermal flywheel. And he talked about the light passing through the glass, changing from photons to phonons—light to heat—as if by magic.

Widner knew he should find Cheeky and the plumber, see what the police were doing, deal with the million details of keeping the festival running, but he found himself enthralled. These were the ideas he had been working with for so many years, yet somehow, Douthwaite was forming them into a harmony of understanding he'd never felt before.

He looked around at the audience. They were all leaning forward, seeing what Douthwaite was saying. Who would have believed that words could paint the brilliance of thermodynamics in such radiant colors?

When he finished, Douthwaite became one with the audience, fielding their questions, asking his own, the learning and teaching going on in both directions with no barriers: the clear transfer of knowledge.

Widner tore himself away and set off to find Cheeky and the plumber.

∿

As Lisa drove Sergeant Smith from the barracks to the festival that morning, she tried to describe Jon's confrontation with Caruso to Sergeant Smith.

"Did you actually spend the night with him last night? Jesus, Prence! He's a suspect. You keep that firmly in mind or you have to step away from this investigation. A romantic connection to a suspect in an active murder investigation is unacceptably unprofessional."

Lisa wanted to say, "I didn't mean to. It just happened. I have to have a life outside of this uniform!" But she didn't. She would not jeopardize her job. So she said, "Yes, sir."

"You understand, don't you?"

"Yes, sir," she repeated. "I understand he's a suspect, but it's pretty remote, isn't it?"

"Why is he any less likely than any of the others? Because you have a history with him? He was there, he's trained on the equipment, and he's big enough and athletic enough to overpower Kerchini. Maybe they argued."

"Oh, come on, sir. Jon's not a cold-blooded killer. He doesn't have that kind of... I don't know... profile."

"How much do you know about his past? How much do you know about what he's been doing in Florida? Sports figures have drug connections and maybe this was a drug deal gone wrong."

Lisa could not imagine Jon as a drug dealer. She thought of him more like a Dudley Do-Right—one of the good ones. Was that just the image she was forcing on herself—the way she wanted him to be? That was something that they had warned about at UMass. Keeping an open mind, uncluttered with personal prejudices and reactions, was impossible. There was simply too much input. The human brain is compelled to make assumptions and take shortcuts, as much as one might want to avoid unconscious bias. Except for the killer, no one knew what had actually happened during the crime. They would have to construct a picture, a movie, from what they were told. The blank screen they started with would gradually get filled in. She understood it was impossible to start with a purely blank screen, and there were always prejudices and personal experiences that danced through the dots of events before they asked questions. But the fewer of those, the cleaner the final picture would be. But Jon was like a brilliant splat of red paint on the canvas that her eye kept being attracted to.

"Now explain to me again about Joe Caruso?" Smith asked.

"Well, Megquire attested,"... she was going to take a step back and make this formal... "that Caruso stepped out of line last night. Apparently, he was drunk and he and Megquire got into a tussle."

"A tussle?"

"Yeah. Caruso kicked Megquire's car."

The sergeant laughed. "Well, there's a criminal offense. I guess we have our murderer."

"Yeah, well, Megquire's pretty particular about that car."

"Anything else?"

"That's why he called me last night. He thought Caruso might take off and take all the evidence with him."

"What evidence?"

"The truck. The foam machine is the murder weapon, and it is on that truck."

"Did Megquire think there was more evidence in the truck?"

"Caruso told him he had a gun in the truck. He threatened Megquire with it."

"Megquire saw the weapon?"

"No. Caruso just told Megquire he had a gun, and, if Jon didn't back off, he would deal with him. Jon... Megquire... said that Caruso maintained that all people from New Jersey carry guns."

"So you're telling me they got into a fight because Caruso kicked Megquire's car, not because Caruso threatened to kill him?"

Lisa laughed. "As I say, Megquire's pretty particular about that car."

"I guess," the sergeant replied. "Let's get Caruso in here first."

~

A FAINT SEWAGE smell scented the room they had been doing interviews in.

"What's that smell?" the sergeant asked.

"Widner mentioned they were having a problem with the septic system this morning," Lisa said.

"Just great. Maybe we can get a window open. And see if you can find us some coffee."

Lisa hesitated.

"And get Caruso in here before he skips town."

Lisa set off in search of Caruso and coffee. She saw the attendees were gathered outside on the plaza and appeared to be mesmerized by Gail Barker's session. Jon was sitting up front, taking notes, like a kid in school. When he saw her looking at him, he smiled and then nodded his head at the speaker as if to say, "Isn't this great?"

Lisa couldn't see Caruso in the audience, and for a moment she wondered if he had indeed taken off. She found Cheeky in the front office. She asked him to see whether Caruso was in his cabin, and if he was, to send him to the interview room. Cheeky set off running.

Lisa walked back to the parking lot and was relieved to find the truck still sitting there. She told the tech guys to put a boot on one wheel to make sure Caruso couldn't drive it away.

The pile of foam and the body had been removed, but the stain on the asphalt would probably remain for years. Lisa thought about the pain the man must have been subjected to. Even if he were drunk, the searing heat must have pierced his consciousness. The agony would have seemed endless. Although death—from suffocation? Burns?— took place within minutes, he must have struggled against the immobilizing foam. How did the murderer hold him down? They needed to be sure to check the hands of everyone they interviewed for foam traces, but many people had been at the training event. By now, most traces of foam had washed away.

~

WHEN LISA GOT BACK to the main building, Caruso was slouched in the interviewee chair. The sewer smell assailed her.

"Shit," she muttered.

"Yeah," Smith replied. "You get used to it. This is Mr. Caruso. We've just been doing the pleasantries."

Lisa nodded to Caruso. "We've met," she said and took her place behind the sergeant.

Caruso straightened up. He looked worse for wear, but he didn't seem to have a black eye or any other obvious sign of bruising. Jon told her he hadn't hit him. Just shaken him up a bit. He looked like a pile of oleaginous shit to her. So maybe he was the killer. It would be great to get it resolved. This seemed an uncomfortably messy crime.

"So, Mr. Caruso, where are you from?" Smith asked.

"New Jersey. Weehawken."

"And did you say you used to live around here?"

"I didn't say, but I did."

"Where?"

"Hingham."

"And when was that?"

"About three years ago," Caruso said.

"And what are you doing here?" Smith asked.

Caruso cleared his throat. Lisa half expected him to spit on the floor. He ran his hand back through his uncombed hair.

"My company sent me here to teach foam insulation installation techniques."

"What's your company?"

"Grady Foamrite."

"Uh-huh. And where are they located?"

"They're in New Jersey. Trenton. You need more than that? I can give you an address. I can give you the phone number. I have a card in the truck. They want people to know how to use the equipment and do the job right."

"I'm sure. We'll get all that information from you later when you can get into your truck."

"When will that be? My stuff is in there. Personal stuff, you know."

"What personal stuff, Mr. Caruso?"

"Oh… stuff… you know, things that don't belong to the company."

"You wouldn't have a weapon in the truck, would you, Mr. Caruso?"

Caruso looked surprised. "What?"

"You wouldn't have a gun in the truck?"

"No!" Caruso tried to laugh, but it came out more of an explosion of spit. "Who told you I had a gun?"

"Of course, if you have a gun in the truck, we'll find it. So it would be good if you let us know now. That would help us believe what you tell us."

Caruso squirmed and looked out of the corner of his eye up toward the ceiling.

The sergeant let him stew, and Lisa felt the silence penetrate Caruso's brain. She noticed that the air didn't seem to stink any more. Jon had told her that after a short time, nose-blindness or odor fatigue sets in. It's important to note significant smells when you first walk into the room, although she thought she could still detect Caruso's sweat. She pushed Jon to the back of her mind.

"All right," Caruso said finally, "there's a Colt 1911 under the driver's seat. It's for my protection!"

"Can I see your permit, Mr. Caruso?"

Caruso looked back and forth between the sergeant and Lisa. "It's in the truck, sir. I think it's in the truck. I leave my wallet in there with my driver's license and all the other stuff."

"Uh-huh," said the sergeant. "Why would you carry a weapon, Joe?"

Caruso's eyes roamed the ceiling of the room again. "'Cause. You know. There are a lot of nasty people out there. They see a truck like mine, and they think there's something valuable in there. I mean, you're a cop, right? You must see this stuff every single day, right?"

"Did you threaten Mr. Kerchini with your gun, Joe? Is that how you got him down to your foam truck?"

"What? No! Who's Mr. Kerchini?"

"Are you saying you didn't know Mr. Kerchini?"

"Kerchini's the dead guy, right?"

"Did you know him before you came here? Weren't you supposed to train him on how to use the equipment? Didn't your company tell you he was going to be here?"

Caruso looked over at Lisa. He began rubbing his palms on his thighs, and he had locked his ankles around the front legs of his chair. Caruso was trying to wash his hands of the situation. It was satisfying when she recognized they got the right stuff into the textbooks.

"I guess." Caruso said with a laugh. "There wasn't anything… you know… formal about it. It was supposed to be his responsibility."

"Uh, huh. But you knew nothing about him? Anything at all?"

"Well, I'd heard his name, I guess. We got a list of all the people who would be here. It's a selling thing, you know, so that we could follow up later to sell stuff to the people who are here. I read through the list, sure, but that's all. That's not a crime, is it? Sharing names?"

"You had no history with him?"

"No! Pfft!" Caruso dismissed the concept.

"So why did you kill him, Joe?"

The sergeant let the question sit there on the table like rotting meat.

"You think I killed him? Why would I do that? I just told you I'd seen his name on a list. That's all. Period."

"You tell us, Joe. You tell us and let us all go home."

"You're crazy! What reason would I have for doing such a thing?"

The sergeant stared at him. "Do you have anger management issues, Joe?"

"What?"

"How was your evening last night?"

"What? What are you talking about?"

"I heard you attacked a car."

Caruso glared at Lisa and crossed his arms across his chest. "Oh, I get it. She's been talking to her boyfriend. I get it now. That Megquire kid has been telling tales between the sheets. I get it."

The sergeant's control impressed Lisa. He leaned onto his elbows on the table between him and Caruso, pushing his body and face toward the man.

"Where were you on Monday night?" he asked.

Caruso leaned back in his chair with his arms still crossed. "I was here. Where would I be?"

"Specifically? Were you in your truck?"

"No. After that get-together on the patio, I went to my cabin and went to bed."

"Were you drinking on Monday night?" the sergeant asked.

"Of course! Everybody was. That's how it gets to be social. I mean, that kid on the guitar was playing shit like 'Kumbaya'. I mean, this is a real hippy group." He laughed. "Some people joined in… singing, swaying. Weird shit."

"Did you talk to anyone there on Monday night?"

"Jesus, I don't know. I can't remember. Probably. No one jumps to mind. It wasn't like I was going to get friendly with anyone. There were hardly any women here. I've heard the stories about these hippy women in these back-to-the-earth places, but the days of free love are over now. AIDS put an end to all that, didn't it? You've got to get a complete lover profile before you can even kiss a girl these days. Not that I'm gay or anything."

The mere presence of the man made Lisa feel dirty. If he hadn't killed Kerchini, he should be locked up for something else.

"Tell me something," the sergeant said, leaning back in his chair, "tell me about foam insulation."

"What?"

"It's pretty new stuff, isn't it?"

Caruso straightened up, uncrossed his arms, and pulled his chair up to the table. "It's not that new. We've been using it in commercial buildings, warehouses, and stuff for a long time. It's pretty new to houses. They've been perfecting the formulas and equipment. It's complicated to get it right. Handling the chemicals so that they mix properly—so they set up properly."

"How many companies make the stuff?" Smith asked.

"Oh, I don't know. Not many."

"Are there many people selling it?"

"No. As I say, you've got to know what you're doing."

"And how long have you been doing it, Joe?"

"I guess you could say that I'm one of the old-timers. A pioneer."

"So it's a small industry. I don't know, I'm a policeman, not a businessman, but in a small industry, doesn't everyone know everyone? You would know that better than I, of course."

"I guess."

"And there have been some problems, haven't there?"

"Early on. With people who didn't know what they were doing."

"And people like that give the industry a bad name, don't they? Make it harder to sell. Harder for you to do your job."

"What are you getting at?" Caruso asked.

"Was Kerchini one of those problems? Isn't that why your company wanted you to give him special training?"

"What?"

"Was Kerchini one of those problems that needed to be removed? Didn't you know that before you came here?"

Caruso leaned back in his chair and crossed his arms again. "No. I told you. I didn't know the guy."

"Uh-huh." The sergeant looked back at Lisa.

"I didn't know him!"

"Did he use Grady equipment?"

"I don't know. I never saw his equipment."

"Did the two of you go to your truck on Monday night for a private lesson and things got out of hand with your demonstration? That can happen, can't it? I've been there. I've taught a few classes in my time. When you're trying to teach someone something and they just don't get it and they don't even seem to care. I mean, it can be really frustrating, can't it? And maybe you started spraying the foam, and it started as a joke... but then it got out of hand. Kind of an accident, maybe? Is that what happened, Joe? I mean, you <u>do</u> have anger issues?"

Caruso's mouth was open. "What? No!"

"Was it just an accident, Joe?" the sergeant asked. "I can understand that. Teaching can be hard and frustrating."

"What? No!" Caruso repeated. "That's not what happened! I had nothing to do with killing him."

"Who did, then?" the sergeant asked with a smile.

"How the hell should I know?"

The sergeant looked at Lisa, as though seeking an answer.

"Can you give us a better explanation, Joe?" the sergeant asked.

Caruso said, "I don't know who did it. That's your job. All I know is that I didn't do it. It's a waste of foam."

The sergeant flopped back in his chair and sighed. "Right. Hey, can we get you some coffee... a Coke, water? I guess I could use a refill. Would you mind, Trooper?" He held up his cup.

It surprised Lisa how quickly Caruso regained his composure. "Yeah. Coffee would be great. Regular." He looked up at Lisa, who had gotten up and was now standing beside the interview desk, reaching for Smith's cup.

Twenty years of schooling... she thought. Bob Dylan was right about that. "Yup," she said. "Massachusetts regular or New Jersey regular."

"What?" Caruso asked.

"Regular!"

"Light, sweet, dark, decaffeinated?"

"Just regular coffee. Cream and sugar."

"One sugar or two??"

"Look, sweetheart, I just want a cup of regular coffee! Okay?" Lisa gave him a look. The sweetheart moniker did not sit well. She slammed the door on the way out.

She had to wonder if Smith had a reason for her to be out of the room. Why else would he send her off in search of coffee?

Outside, Widner was talking to several people and when he saw Lisa, he asked her to explain why people couldn't leave yet. "Our guests want to know why they have to stay here when the festival ends today?"

"The sergeant will give you an update," she said.

"But why do we all have to stay here?" someone asked. "Have you found out who did this?"

"It's an ongoing investigation, sir, and I can't talk about it."

Cheeky came over and took the sergeant's cup. "More coffee?" he whispered.

"Yup," Lisa replied. "And a 'regular' for Caruso." Cheeky looked at her questioningly.

"Cream and two sugars," she said.

"We don't have cream. Will milk suffice?"

"Sure. Whatever."

"What *can* you talk about?" someone else asked her.

"We would like all of you to remain available," Lisa said. "We understand that this disrupts your lives. Murder does that."

"So you're saying it was murder?"

Lisa wanted to slap the idiot. Did he think the vic had sprayed foam all over himself? Sort of like a Buddhist monk setting himself on fire?

"Look, just help us out here," she said. "Stick around. Talk to each other. Learn stuff. We'll get to you as soon as we can, all right?"

Cheeky returned, and she took the two cups of coffee and turned to go back into the interview room when Jon stopped her.

"How's it going?" he asked.

"I can't talk."

"I know, but I just want to make sure that you're all right."

"I'm fine. We can't talk now."

"Right, I understand," and he smiled at her.

Back in the interview room, she gave Smith his cup and plunked Caruso's cup on the table in front of him, slopping some over the edge.

"Thanks," he muttered sarcastically.

"Mr. Caruso was just telling me he needs to be back in New Jersey."

"Oh?"

"And I told him that wouldn't be possible at the moment."

"Am I under arrest?" Caruso asked.

"Did you do it?"

"I already told you I didn't."

"So what did your company tell you to do about Mr. Kerchini? I just find it hard to believe that you knew nothing about Chris Kerchini until you got here. Don't you find that strange, Trooper?"

Lisa nodded.

"It's a small world, Joe. Not many people are in it. You're a pioneer. Been at it for a long time, right? That's what you told us. How many companies are selling foam machines? That's what they're called, right? Foam machines?"

Caruso grunted.

"Yeah, so how many, do you think? Three? Five? Twenty?"

"Not as many as twenty. Less than ten."

"Really? And how many customers do they have? Ten each? So maybe a hundred total customers?"

Caruso sipped his coffee. "Maybe. I don't know."

"So, explain to me what your company asked you to do. What's it called? Roger's or Roy's?"

"Grady's!" Caruso said.

"Yeah. I knew that," the sergeant said with a laugh. "Must be getting old. Was he out of line? Did they want you to discipline him? Straighten him out?"

"How many times do I have to tell you? I didn't know the man!"

"See, the thing is, Joe, I don't believe you." The sergeant leaned back in his chair, swallowed some coffee, and let the silence build.

Caruso squirmed. "Listen. That's too bad, sergeant. But I've got to take a leak. Are we through here?" He stood up.

"Fine," the sergeant said, leaning forward on the table. "But you should know that we are not the hicks you New Jersey people think we are when you come up here for vacation. But the thing is we have resources, too. I'm going to have a look-see about your past here in Massachusetts. Think I'll find anything, Joe? Are you just a squeaky-clean hombre?"

Caruso didn't reply.

"Don't leave town," the sergeant said.

CHAPTER 9

FESTIVAL DAY 3–AUGUST 8, 1984

*A*t lunchtime, Jon stepped into the lobby phone booth and called Ace to set up a time to get together. When Babs answered, she was out of breath. "Jon, I'm so glad you called. I didn't know how to get in touch with you. Ace had a heart attack last night."

"What?!"

"Oh, Jon. You know Ace. He just won't give in. It was all I could do to get him to go to the hospital."

"Are you okay?"

"I'm worried sick, of course. He's not young anymore, and he refuses to give up smoking that damn pipe."

"So what happened?"

"Well, he's been feeling a bit more tired than usual, and then last night he said he woke up and thought it was indigestion, thought maybe it was just gas, you know. We keep ginger ale for when he gets indigestion, and he drank one of those and said he hoped he could just… burp. Then he turned on the TV and sat there and hoped the pain would go away."

"But it didn't."

"No. It didn't. He said he didn't want to bother me. The pain wasn't that bad. Wanted me to keep sleeping. He didn't want the medical bills."

"Stubborn bugger."

"He said he started feeling steady pain at about midnight. He was trying to find a comfortable position in the bed, and he couldn't do it." Babs gasped. "So he got up and took one of those gas pills—you know, the ones you chew up for indigestion—and then tried to go back to bed, but got up again.

"He said the pain was relentless. Not like anything he had ever felt before, and he's had a lot of pains over the years."

"I bet."

Babs paused. "Do you have time for this, Jon? I know you're busy, and I'm sure you didn't call to hear about our troubles."

The seat in the phone booth was hard, and the air was hot and heavy, but Jon's discomfort came from his feelings for Babs and Ace and what they were going through. He knew Ace was not likely to complain about pain unless it was intense.

"He said that the pain was a continuous pressure in the middle of his chest without a break. Just one continuous never-ending strike of a hammer."

"He told you all this?"

"Oh, you know how he is. I called the ambulance. My first thought was to drive him."

"I'm glad you didn't, Babs. The ambulance people are professionals."

"I know, Jon, but I can't believe that Ace worried about the money. I mean, he's always worried about money. Making sure his suppliers and his crew get paid. He told me today in the hospital that he actually considered not waking me, and letting himself die so that I could have his life insurance to pay off our bills!"

Jon heard her gasp down a sob.

"Why would he think such a thing? Why would he think I would want him... dead?"

Jon couldn't conceive of thinking that death was the best option. He thought of Ace as a gruff Santa Claus of a man without the beard.

Big shoulders, enormous belly with his suspenders stretched to the limit, clean shaven, intense eyes, sharp as a razor knife, with an encyclopedic knowledge of construction, and the skills to match. Jon thought of him sitting in his kitchen in Tilley, reading the "New York Times", grumbling about the Red Sox and the Yankees, and smoking his pipe. Jon didn't think of him as old or wizened or overburdened with debt and troubles. Ace was an immutable force of nature who would be there forever.

That thought brought Jon back to buildings, and he envisioned Babs standing in the hallway of her house, phone to her ear, waiting for Jon to respond to something she'd said.

"What?" he blurted. "Oh, no. How could he ever think something like that? He's too good."

"Oh, you're kind, Jon."

"Is he back at home?"

"No, he's still in the hospital. They did something called a PTCA —*percutaneous* something or other—I think, and they don't want him moving around."

"I have to ask: are things really tough, economically I mean? You certainly don't have to tell me if you don't want to."

"No, it's all right. Ace doesn't talk about it much. He keeps it all inside. But you know he's a perfectionist, Jon. He likes to work on the big old houses the most. He hasn't signed on to these computer-designed, modern things, so he doesn't do a good job of selling himself to the young families who want to commute to Boston. I keep telling him we should update the books and the billing. I've decided I'm going to take a course at the community college."

"Really? That's great."

"I don't think Ace thinks so. He hasn't exactly encouraged it. He says that's something else for him to worry about!"

"Can I see him?"

"Oh, sure. He would love to see you. Cape Cod Hospital. They've been wonderful there. Ace loves to flirt with the nurses."

Jon told her he would get to the hospital as soon as he could and hung up. Babs and Ace had been married for a long time. They had lost their son in the swamps of Vietnam during the war. Jon couldn't imagine Babs' sense of loneliness and fear right now.

But Ace would return. He was tough and Babs was tougher.

Jon wanted to help them both.

∿

THE INTERVIEW with Orville Hawkins was a formality. Lisa knew without a doubt that a man with his credentials and ethics would never murder anyone. Not that someone with Harvard degrees couldn't kill someone and wouldn't find an interesting way to do it, but Hawkins had worked on the atomic bomb with the Manhattan Project, opposed supersonic passenger planes, and wrote many books on passive solar buildings and superinsulation. Murder did not fit his character.

Lisa had asked him about the Native American curse story that Jon had mentioned Widner getting upset with Kerchini about. Hawkins told them about the captured sachem who heard the worms talking in the walls and the failing roof beams.

"His captors wouldn't release him or his family," Hawkins said. "And eventually the chimney collapsed, and the house burned. The story is that as he died, the sachem cursed the settlers and the land."

"Wow! Quite the tale," Lisa said. "Did that happen here?"

Hawkins smiled. "Who knows? Of course, it's just a myth. The Cape is an old place. The source of a lot of tales."

"What does it have to do with Dr. Widner?"

"From what I understand, Widner has a lot of connections with Indigenous people. Maybe he has a guilty conscience."

Interviewing Miriam Leathe differed from interviewing Dr. Hawkins, although she didn't look like a murderer either. Lisa felt her age to be indeterminate—not young but not old either—a touch of gray in her hair and wrinkles on her chin. Lisa's first impression was that she was a grandmotherly type—like she might make cookies for the crossing guard at the corner. She had a toughness, but she did a good job of hiding that toughness under a kind-old-lady shell. Evil old ladies make good horror story villains. But there was a difference between an old lady poisoning someone with elderberry tea and someone who could physically manipulate a spray foam machine and bury a man.

Lisa noticed Sergeant Smith was excessively polite with Leathe. Almost gentle.

"Thank you for coming and talking with us, Ms. Leathe. I'm Sergeant Smith and this is Trooper Prence."

Miriam nodded and took the seat across from the sergeant.

"You live on the Cape, don't you, Ms. Leathe?"

"I do," she said. "Falmouth."

"Oh, okay. Not far. We're based in Yarmouth. Are you staying here at the institute for the festival?"

"Yes," she said.

"That's easier, isn't it?" Smith asked. "Means you don't have to leave early to beat the traffic. You can take part in the evening socializing, right?"

"Yes," she said.

"You don't have to be nervous, Ms. Leathe. These are just routine questions. We're trying to figure out what happened here on Monday night."

"I'm not nervous."

She sure seemed nervous to Lisa. Leathe appeared to be wound tighter than an overstretched guitar string. But maybe she was always that way. Already she was working her hands in her lap, twisting and stroking them, one against the other like they were cats.

"What brought you to the festival?"

"I want to know more about how houses work."

"Really? That's interesting. Why?"

"I sell real estate, sergeant."

Smith looked confused. "Explain that to me."

"Look," she said, "if I understand how houses work, I'll be better at my job. You have to understand the product you are selling."

"Oh, that's admirable," Smith said, smiling. "Wish I'd had you for my real estate agent when I bought my house. I don't think my agent knew anything except granite counter tops and sunken living rooms!"

Leathe didn't respond.

"How long have you been selling real estate?"

"Three years," she said.

"Have you always lived in Falmouth?"

"No," she said.

"Are you married, Ms. Leathe?"

That seemed like a softball question, but there was an obvious change in Leathe's body language. Her hands stopped moving. She straightened her back and glared at Smith. Then she reached back to smooth her hair, pulled out her hair tie, rearranged her hair into a new knot, and redid the tie.

Whoa, Lisa thought. *Hit a nerve!*

"I was," Leathe said.

"Divorced?" Smith asked with a smile to soften the word.

"Dead," Leathe replied with finality.

"Oh. I'm so sorry for your loss."

"Thank you," Leathe said.

Lisa waited for the sergeant to ask when he died, or how. Could such information possibly be relevant?

But Smith leaned back in his chair, clasped his hands behind his head, and changed the subject. "So tell us about Monday night."

"What do you want to know?" Leathe asked.

"Did you enjoy the food?"

"What?"

"I was just wondering if you enjoy the natural foods they offer here. From their own gardens, I understand."

"I have a garden," she said.

"Do you grow your own food, too? I have a black thumb," the sergeant laughed. "You know, everything I try to grow dies!"

"I have an extensive garden. I grow so much that I have a farm stand and sell the extras."

"I really admire that," the sergeant said. "Do you grow stuff, trooper?" He turned to Lisa and smiled.

"Don't really have the space for it, sir. My apartment doesn't come with a yard."

"Does it take a lot of time, Ms. Leathe?"

"No," she said. "You just have to set a routine, be consistent, and pay attention. It helps to know what you're doing. I've been growing a garden for years."

"Even before you came to the Cape?"

"Oh, yes. I had quite the garden at our house in Hingham. We always ended up with too many zucchini and summer squash and had to give them away to neighbors. Don't know if they loved us or hated us!"

"Did your husband help with the garden? Was he into gardening as well?"

"My son helped too," she said, running her hand through her hair again.

"Does he help you now?" the sergeant asked.

Leathe began to cry, leaning over, clutching her face in her hands. "No," she blurted out between sobs. "He can't. He's dead, too."

"Oh, I'm so sorry. That's awful."

Lisa expected the sergeant to console Leathe, but for a few minutes he sat watching her sob. He finally leaned forward, pulled a handkerchief out of his back pocket, and passed it to her.

"Sorry," she said. "Thank you," and she dabbed the square on her nose and eyes without unfolding it.

Lisa wondered if handkerchiefs were standard trooper gear she hadn't been told about. The room was tense, and so quiet that she could hear laughter out on the patio. Finally, Smith leaned back in his chair and it squeaked again.

Leathe looked up and tried to hand the handkerchief back. "Keep it," Smith said.

Then he asked, "How did your son pass away?"

Lisa held her breath, waiting for the answer. She couldn't fathom the pain of losing a child.

She watched the woman gather herself, sit up straighter in her chair, run her hand back around the knot in her hair, and say, "He died in the fire when our house burned." Leathe glared at the sergeant as though it was his fault. "Can I go now? My son has nothing to do with this."

That information sent Lisa's head spinning. It surprised her when Smith didn't follow up.

"Can you tell us anything about what happened on Monday night? Did you see anything? Hear anything that would help us?"

"No," she replied. "I don't remember anything else. I have nothing else to tell you."

"Don't you think it's a strange way to kill someone?"

"Of course."

The sergeant waited for her to elaborate. But she didn't. "Did everybody know how to use that machine? Isn't it hard to do? Do you know how to turn it on?"

"That Mr. Caruso taught us. He taught everyone."

"He must be an excellent teacher. Boy, that thing looks complicated to me. Don't think I'd know how to spray foam all over the place. Is it fun?"

Leathe didn't reply.

The sergeant looked at Lisa. Did he want her to chime in? Was he setting a trap in order to get Leathe to reveal things she didn't want to reveal? Lisa didn't see it so she kept her mouth shut. Pressuring Leathe made Lisa uncomfortable. There was something slightly off about the woman. Was she even physically big enough to be a murderer? She certainly didn't seem mean enough. She was a real estate broker and a gardener who was trying to learn more so she could do a better job of selling houses, and she'd experienced a terrible tragedy in her life. What would she have to gain by killing a foam salesman?

Lisa looked back at Smith and almost imperceptibly shrugged.

"Okay, Ms. Leathe. Thank you for talking to us. Maybe we can talk some more later, hmm?" He guided her to the door.

~

AFTER HIS PHONE conversation with Babs, Jon ran down to his cabin to get Maybelline. He jumped into the driver's seat, turned the key, but Maybelline refused to start.

"Oh, not now. Come on!" he said, thumping the steering wheel. "Really? You have to do this now? Shit!"

He jumped out, pulled open the hood, and looked at the engine in disbelief. The feeling of mechanical inadequacy swept over him. Why couldn't he have been one of those people who could look at a car engine, twiddle this or fiddle with that, and the car would jump to life like they did in the movies? This wasn't the first time he had stared blankly at Maybelline's engine. She was fun to drive, but she wasn't the most reliable vehicle on the road.

He reached in and shook the spark plug wires and tapped the carburetor—he knew that much, but no more. Then he got back in the driver's seat, turned the key, and the engine turned over and over like a goat with a terrible cough. He banged the steering wheel again.

"Damn," he said. Now what? The alternatives were few: hitchhike, get a ride from someone, call a taxi. The hitchhiking and the taxi were not good options. Maybe he could get a ride from Cheeky. He jogged back to the main building and found Cheeky in the kitchen.

"Hey, got a minute?"

Cheeky was carrying bread out to the tables on the plaza. "Sure," he said. "What's up?"

Jon briefly explained about Ace and his heart attack. "Oh, shit, man. That's terrible."

"I know. I've got to get over to the Cape Cod Hospital to check him out."

"Good idea," Cheeky said.

"There's just one problem. Maybelline."

"All right. Who's Maybelline?"

"My car. The Midget. I call her Maybelline."

Cheeky smiled. "Of course you do! What's the problem?"

"She's refusing to start."

"Just like a woman," he said.

Jon looked at him, hoping for a follow-up, but none was forthcoming. Cheeky just stood there with his bread tray. "Can you give me a ride?"

"Love to, man, but as you can see, I'm in the middle of lunch."

"Does the institute have a utility vehicle or truck or something? I'm kind of desperate here."

Cheeky set the tray down. "Sorry, Jon. No such luck."

Jon looked around at the attendees. They had cars. They were simply hanging around, waiting to be set free by the police. He couldn't ask Lisa to give him a ride in the police car. He felt like jumping up on a table and shouting, "Anyone want to give me a ride to Cape Cod Hospital to see my dying friend?"

But before he could act upon that impulse, Lash Ashton appeared and plucked a roll off Cheeky's tray. "Hey, Jon," he said. "I've got something I want to show you. I think you're going to be interested."

"Not right now, Lash. You've got a car, right?"

"I do."

"Want to give me a ride to Cape Cod Hospital? I've got a friend who's had a heart attack and my car won't start."

"When do you want to go?"

"Uh, how about now?"

Lash looked around the room. "Yah, sure. We can do that. Police said they want to talk to me, but I guess they can do that when we get back. How far is it?"

"Maybe twenty minutes if the traffic's not bad. It shouldn't be bad now. It's the middle of the week, and it's not raining. People will be at the beach."

So they headed off to Ashton's car, with Ashton talking animatedly about computers, RAMs and ROMs, floppy disks, and BAUD rates— none of which penetrated Jon's brain, now focused entirely on Ace and Babs.

～

THEY ARRIVED AT THE HOSPITAL—A sprawling building with arched windows and a massive parking lot. Jon didn't want to inconvenience

Ashton by making him wait. He would need a ride back to the festival, but he didn't know how long he was going to be, and he always underestimated how much time something would take.

"Can you give me half an hour?"

"Sure. Take your time. Maybe I'll go check out Hyannis. See if there are any computer stores. I think there's an Apple store. Actually, they're selling Apples at Sears. I'll see what I can find."

"Great," Jon said, and set off to find Ace.

Signs and arrows directed him down hallways and up stairs. The antiseptic smells of cleaning fluids mixed with floor polish, assailed his nostrils. His shoes squeaked. It became increasingly obvious that this would take more than a half hour. It would take that long just to find his way back out of the building!

Turning the last corner, he came upon a nursing station, populated by nurses sitting behind desks, studying monitors. Behind them, other nurses referred to clipboards, and a couple of doctors with stethoscope necklaces leaned on the chest-high counter, chatting.

One nurse looked up as Jon approached. He told her he was looking for Asaph Wentzell. She gave him a room number and pointed down the hall.

He barely recognized the man in the bed as Ace. He lay flat on his back, staring at the ceiling, and he looked sallow and diminished under the sheets.

"Ace?" he mumbled. "It's Jon.."

The man in the bed tried to lift his head. "Jon?"

"Yeah, it's Jon. What happened?"

"Doc doesn't want me to sit up. Gotta pee into a cup lying on my back. Jesus, that's hard."

Jon laughed. "So, tell me about it?"

"Nothing," Ace said. "Pain in the chest turned out to be a pain in the ass! Babs wouldn't let me get away with it."

"Well, she was right. You look terrible."

"Thanks a bunch, kid. Good to see you, too." Ace said he'd felt a few chest pains a couple of weeks before. "I got out of breath hauling shingles around, you know, but I just thought it was old age and being out of shape. It's been too hot to go jogging."

Jon looked stunned. "You're kidding. You never went jogging in your life!"

A sound that reminded Jon of someone moving a cart full of rocks emerged from Ace, and Jon realized he was trying to laugh.

"So where the hell have you been?" Ace asked.

Jon wondered if Ace had forgotten their phone conversation. "Florida. That's where I'm living."

"I know that! I mean now. Where did you just come from?"

"Oh, the festival at ITI."

"Festival, my ass." Ace choked. "Are they dancing around and waving flags and blowing horns? Don't make me laugh. It hurts. You know, they showed me an ultrasound of my heart. I never thought I would see my own heart. There it was—ba-bump, ba-bump, ba-bump. And it's been doing that for sixty-four years. Twenty-four hours a day. Three hundred and sixty-five days a year. It just keeps going. It's an incredible machine, isn't it? Ever know a man-made machine that was that reliable?"

"No, sir."

"Speaking of reliable, how's that little bucket of bolts you called a car? Still got it?"

"I do," Jon said, "but at the moment, she's not that reliable. I couldn't get her to start to come see you, so I had to get a ride."

"You should get a real car. A truck maybe."

"What would I do with a truck?" Jon asked.

"Well, you told me you're studying building science stuff. Want to be a builder?"

Ace looking at the ceiling, so Jon couldn't see his eyes. Jon wondered if that was an invitation. Working with Ace on Cape Cod wouldn't be the worst thing in the world. The Eagles' song "Desperado" floated into his mind.

"Been thinking about it."

"I got to tell you, it's not the easiest job on the table. You might think it's just hammering nails and sawing wood. But it's all the paperwork that'll kill you. I can't keep up with the changes in pricing. And all the taxes that the government makes you keep track of—withholding, unemployment benefits, dependencies or whatever they're called. You have to be a mother to people. They come whining to you if you don't wipe their noses. And the insurance! I hate insurance, but after I nearly lost my shirt in that lawsuit years ago, I got insurance. So now I lose my shirt every year with some sort of 'errors and omissions' insurance. I don't even know what that means. I thought seriously about just cashing it all in this time."

Jon blinked.

"Yeah, I mean, this heart attack might have been my ticket out of here. Babs could have gotten my life insurance, paid off the bills, and moved on with her life. If I hadn't told her what was going on, I might have just shuffled off—passed on, you know?"

"No!" Jon said. "You can't think that way."

"I can and I did. I'm old enough now to think any way I want to." He turned his head away to face the curtain separating his bed from the one beside him.

Then he turned back. "Now, don't you go telling Babs any of this. It's between us men. It didn't happen. I guess I decided that wasn't the best solution, but hospital bills can be killers. I hear about people going bankrupt just because they went to see a doctor or went to a hospital. They have to live under a pile of bills for something that happened years ago, and it never ends. I don't want that to happen to Babs. And it just happens. It's out of your control. So I thought about it. Thought about just rolling over in bed, putting up with the pain, until it just—stopped."

"No," Jon said. There was no answer, no response that he could make. He wasn't a priest or a psychiatrist, so he had no experience turning to a God whom Ace didn't already have a connection with. He had no training to guide Ace away from the edge of death. In his family, discussion of feelings was inappropriate—at any time. He struggled to find words. "How can I help?" he asked finally.

Ace turned to face him. "You can tell me about this murder."

"Oh," Jon said—glad to change the subject. "People are crazy, aren't they? The police haven't figured out who did it yet. They don't even know why."

"And your girlfriend is investigating?"

Ace had the uncanny knack of pushing all of Jon's buttons. Jon's first reaction was to deny that Lisa was his girlfriend. But if she wasn't his girlfriend, what was she? Friend, for sure. Woman? Well, that was for sure as well. Woman friend sounded terrible. Jon remembered that someone had once told him that Inuits had something like a hundred words for snow. And we only have one word for… girlfriend? How about beloved? Truelove? Sweetheart? Paramour? Sounded like a greeting card. No matter what word he used… no matter what the word… it would require a commitment.

"Jon?" Ace asked. "You still there? My view here is not the best. The things on the ceiling haven't changed much in the hundred years I've been lying here. Stick your face in."

"Lisa? Yeah, she's working on it."

"She any good?"

Jon processed that question in multiple ways. "Yeah," he said. "She seems to know what she's doing."

"Let me guess," Ace said, "you're poking around, too. Just like you did when you teamed up with her father. What was it… five years ago? Frankly, between you and me, I thought Prence was kind of just cruising in his job."

"No, Lisa's good. She interrogated me!"

"Really?"

"Well, she didn't do the questioning. It was the sergeant. But she was there."

"She really thinks you might have done it?"

Jon laughed. "Nah. I'm sure she doesn't, but they've got to talk to everyone. Rule people out. Prence was there too. He came by first, you know, to check out the body. I mean, that was pretty horrible. To see this enormous pile of expanded foam and find a body underneath it. I mean, there was a hand sticking out, and we couldn't see any of the rest of the body. The state police had to use the fingerprints and the guy's hat to figure out who it was. Couldn't see his face at all, but that might have been a good thing because that foam can get up to sixteen hundred degrees! It's the temperature of napalm."

"I don't believe it," Ace said.

"Yeah. That's what our instructor told us. Sixteen hundred to two thousand degrees, as it's curing. That's why it can cause fires if you layer it on too thickly. The layers kind of concentrate the heat. I can't imagine what that poor guy's face looked like!"

"Damn. I don't think I want to use that stuff. Talk about liability. Hell of a way to die."

At that point, Babs came into the room. She stood still for a moment as she recognized Jon. "Oh, my word!" she said. "Jon!"

"Hi, Babs," Jon said, grinning.

"You came!" she said.

"Couldn't keep me away."

She put her bag down on the table that slid over the bed. "Oh, my." She reached out her arms and Jon found himself folded into the familiar, warm-cookie and clean laundry smells of the Wentzells' kitchen. He lingered for a moment before pulling away, and he noticed Babs wipe a tear from her eye.

"How are you?" she asked.

"Better than your husband," Jon said with a laugh. "What did he do to himself?"

"Going too hard. Trying to do too much."

"Just getting it done," Ace said, glaring at the ceiling.

From the hallway, Jon heard the wheel shrieks of food carts, the squeaks of rubber-soled shoes on polished linoleum floors, and the dings of some automatic monitor.

"How long is he supposed to lie here?"

"I don't know," Babs said. "They want a couple of days for the arteries to heal, they told us."

"That sounds pleasant, doesn't it?" Ace asked. "I thought that EMT in the ambulance was going to be carsick on the way over here. I mean, there are no windows back there. That thing swaying around the corners. It's not a limo, you know? Who's going to pick up that bill?"

"We have insurance, Ace. We're going to be all right."

"Did you check, or are you just saying that?"

"No, no. I checked." She looked at Jon.

Jon made a mental note to talk with Babs about that later. He could check with his father and see if there was anything supplemental. He was in the industry, after all. There was no reason Ace should consider dying, because he couldn't pay a medical bill. His cardiac event wasn't a choice, like a vacation in the Bahamas or new TV.

"How's the festival?" Babs asked.

"Oh, it's good," Jon said. "But this murder has disrupted things."

Babs clicked her tongue. "Imagine that. Murder. Ace and I have said for years that place was up to no good. It's out of place in Tilley. Imagine raising fish to eat in big water tanks and using their poop to grow vegetables. I don't think I'd want to eat those vegetables."

"You have," Ace said. "I've bought vegetables at their farm stand."

She shuddered. "I suppose," Babs replied.

Jon looked at his watch. "I've got to get back to my ride."

"You still have that sporty little car?" Babs asked.

"I do, but she wouldn't start, so I got a friend from the festival to drive me over. I told him it would be about half an hour, and I think it's going to take me that long to find my way out of here."

Babs stepped to the side of the bed and picked up Ace's hand. "Will we see you again?"

"Oh, sure. I'm not going straight back to Florida after the festival is over. I've got to see Ace upright again." He grinned.

Ashton wasn't there when Jon reached the hospital entrance. *Now what?* Jon couldn't call him to find out where he was. Jon wished Maybelline was more reliable. Maybe it was time to think about replacing her. She wasn't practical. He needed a ride that reliably got him where he needed to go and would carry the things and the people that he needed to carry. But he couldn't see himself driving some sort of boxy family sedan. The thought made him shudder. Ashton drove a white AMC Gremlin. Jon was relieved when it appeared, and drove under the entrance overhang.

"Sorry," Ashton said as Jon opened the door. "There is so much out there in the electronic jungle that you can just wander along from place to place."

Jon settled into the seat.

"How was your friend?" Ashton asked.

"Better, I guess," Jon replied. "It's just weird seeing him lying there flat on his back. It's not normal."

"Heart attacks are definitely not normal," Ashton laughed. "And thank god for that! When was the last time you saw him?"

"Five years ago. He looks a lot older."

"What's he been doing?"

"Building. He's a builder. Has been for a very long time. He worked on those houses on Long Island—Levittown—where they built hundreds of houses for the soldiers coming back from World War II. He told me they were all the same. It was hard to tell one from the other. They built them like an assembly line in a factory. I worked for him for a summer when I played in the Cape Cod Baseball League."

"You were a ballplayer?"

"I was. Seems like decades ago."

"Is that why you're here?"

"Is what why I'm here?" Jon repeated.

Ashton maneuvered the Gremlin into the traffic on Route 6. "The construction stuff? You want to build houses in Florida?"

"Nah," Jon replied. "I don't want to live in Florida. A wise man once said, 'Florida is the capital of unintended consequences.' I'm not sure I know what that means, but it sounds good."

"But if you listen to the experts at this festival, they make building sound exciting."

"I suppose people will laugh if you tell them that energy efficient houses are exciting!" Jon laughed.

They drove without talking for a while, listening to the radio—it was Kenny Loggins with "Footloose"—lost in their own thoughts. The highway was populated with cars full of families off to the beaches and the summer cottages interspersed with the local workforce trying to get to their jobs, pick up their deliveries, or find their way back to work before they got fired. It was the middle of the week, after all. Not the day when all the summer rentals changed hands. It was as close to a normal traffic day as possible in the first week of August in 1984.

"Hey, you ever read *1984?*" Jon asked.

"What?"

"You know, the book by George Orwell, *1984?*"

"Nope."

"It's one of those world-of-the-future stories when everything has gone to shit and everyone is being controlled. When we read it in school, we got spooked imagining actually living into 1984. But here we are, and it doesn't seem as bad as Orwell imagined."

"How do you know?" Ashton asked. "Maybe it's just not obvious. There are a lot of very rich people who seem to work together to pull the strings of us little people. Like magicians. They get you to look over there while they do something nasty over here." Ashton turned his head from one side of the road to the other as he said this.

"I don't buy into the conspiracy theories," Jon said. "I'm sure those guys landed on the moon and the holocaust really happened."

"Yah, but you should see what I can see on my computer. That's why I was late picking you up, because Sears let me try out their new computers. These things are getting faster and faster. You know, TCP/IP was adopted as a defense standard in 1980. That enabled Defense to share in the DARPA Internet technology base, and then they partitioned the military and non-military communities. Just last year, a significant number of defense R and D and operational organizations used ARPANET. The transition of ARPANET from NCP to TCP/IP permitted it to be split into a MILNET supporting operational requirements and an ARPANET supporting research."

"What?" Jon asked. He wasn't sure if Ashton was kidding.

"No, seriously," Ashton continued. "They call it the Internet! And it's fantastic. You can connect to places all over the world. It's being used by geeky communities for daily computer communications. But it's going to go way beyond that. You can already use electronic mail across communities, with different systems, but interconnection between different mail systems shows the utility of broad-based electronic communications between people. CompuServe was the first service to offer electronic mail capabilities and technical support to personal computer users. They were the first to even offer real-time chat!"

Jon didn't understand a word, and he hoped Ashton wouldn't simply drive off the road in his enthusiasm. He realized that Ashton in a computer store was like Jimi Hendrix in a guitar store or Rachmaninoff in a piano store: savoring the instruments.

They arrived back at the ITI compound, parked the Gremlin, and walked back to the main building, with Ashton still talking.

Miriam was sitting by herself on the plaza, and Jon asked her if the festival was still going on. "We've just been visiting a friend of mine in the hospital. He had a heart attack."

"Think so. Think it's still going on. I just needed some air," she replied.

Jon and Lash dropped onto a picnic table bench.

"You're probably wondering why I'm telling you all this," Ashton said. "CompuServe is connected to the Associated Press, and I might be able to get into the *Boston Globe* archives and check out house fires caused by insulating foam back in 1981!"

"You can see newspapers on your computer?" Jon asked.

"Some of them. Maybe I could check out if that expanding foam could actually set a house on fire."

"Caruso warned us about that when he was demonstrating it," Jon said.

"But he didn't say that it had actually happened," Lash said.

"Or, if it did, that it happened to him."

"Nope." Lash lowered his voice. "But you told me that your girlfriend, Trooper Prence, said that Miriam Leathe's husband and son died in a house fire! I was just wondering…."

CHAPTER 10

FESTIVAL DAY 3–AUGUST 8, 1984

*L*isa didn't know what to make of Brian Nando. He was surprising looking; short, with spiky blond hair and large glasses with colorful frames. Then there was that British accent. Then there was the goofy nickname.

Sergeant Smith welcomed him into the interview room. "Your name is Brian Nando, is that right?"

"That's right."

"And you're from England?"

"London, actually."

"Oh, London. That is London, England. Not New London, Connecticut or Londonderry, New Hampshire?"

"That's right, inspector.."

"It's sergeant," Smith said.

"Oh, right. Sergeant, sir."

"The 'sir' is unnecessary, Mr. Nando."

"And you can call me Cheeky, if you like."

"'Cheeky,'" Smith repeated.

"That's what people call me. Cheeky."

"Okay, Cheeky. Have you got a passport?"

"Of course. Do you want me to get it?"

"Maybe later. So, what are you doing here, Cheeky?"

Cheeky looked surprised. "You asked me to come and talk with you."

Smith snorted. "What I mean is, what are you doing in the States? You are a British citizen, aren't you?"

"Oh, yes," Cheeky said with a smile. "Answering only to her Royal Majesty, the Queen. The family kind of kicked me out."

"Trouble? Sowing some wild oats over there?"

"Not really. Life in England is rocky at the moment, with the miners' strike and all. The Iron Maiden—you know, Maggie Thatcher —is making it tough for the peasants, isn't she?"

"So they sent you over here? When?"

"Oh, earlier this year. In the wintry winds of January. There were notices in the parish about internships in the States. The 'p's' thought that this would be good for me. Get me away from my unsavory mates. It did sound rather fishy though: a farm on Cape Cod!"

"Where else have you been in the States?" Smith asked, leaning back in his chair.

"New York, of course. Started there, didn't I? Had a brief foray into New Jersey."

"Why?"

Cheeky looked confused. "Why what, sir? I mean sergeant."

"Why did you go to New Jersey?"

"Funny story, actually, sergeant. This bird that I met on the plane said that Garden City was just that. Like a garden. So I thought I'd have a look. It's confusing when they tell you it's Garden City in the garden state. I rather like gardens. I was looking to expand my horizons. But it's not much of a garden in January, is it? Have you been to New Jersey, sergeant? It smells rather, doesn't it? Particularly near New York. I guess there are a lot of refineries and things there."

"Yes, but why did you go there? I'm not buying the garden story."

Cheeky laughed. "A job, sergeant."

"You went to Garden City, New Jersey for a job. What kind of job?"

"A wedding, actually. The bird I met coming over was getting married in Garden City, New Jersey, and she saw my guitar, which I had wedged into the overhead bin, and she asked if I was a musician. I told her I was, and she asked if I would like to play at her wedding in Garden City. That mystique of British musicians since the Beatles and the Stones is still hanging on, isn't it? I asked her what kind of music she liked, and we ended up talking about many things. She had been carrying on a long-distance relationship with her boyfriend for years, and they finally decided to get married, which meant her giving up her life in England. I didn't think that was all that fair. I mean, why didn't he move to England? Well, she said that he had a career over here. Actually, I think she was trying to get away from England too."

Lisa could tell that the sergeant was getting impatient with Cheeky's ramblings. She was seeking for meaning among the flowers.

"Go anywhere else in Jersey? Atlantic City? Newark?"

"Why?" Cheeky asked.

"I'm asking."

"Oh, in that case. Yeah, I took a bus over to Atlantic City. Try my luck. Make my fortune. Trouble is that if you don't have a small fortune to begin with, it's tough to make it smaller!" Cheeky laughed. "I didn't get there jingling with change to drop into those machines. I would have. Trust me. They do a good job of promoting, don't they? It's hard to resist. ka-ching, ka-ching, dingle, dingle, dingle. The ocean looked nice, though, even in winter. I found a place on the boardwalk that sells these marvelous almond macaroons. They have what they call saltwater taffy as well, but those will pull your teeth out. Guess you have that here as well, don't you?"

Lisa wondered how far the sergeant would let Cheeky wander down this path. He seemed even more unlikely a murderer than Jon.

"So how was Atlantic City?"

"Splendid, sergeant!"

"You didn't happen to meet with Chris Kerchini while you were there, did you?"

Cheeky looked stunned. "What?"

"You met with Kerchini in Atlantic City, didn't you?"

"Who told you that?"

"That doesn't matter, Mr. Nando. Is it true?"

Cheeky looked at Lisa to find an answer to this riddle.

"Don't look at her, Cheeky. Look at me."

Lisa thought that Cheeky had slipped down a bit in his chair to make himself smaller.

"Well, yeah," Cheeky said quietly. "Did Mr. Megquire tell you that?" He looked at Lisa again, despite the sergeant's admonition.

"Why?" Smith asked.

"Why what... sir?"

"Why did you meet with Mr. Kerchini?"

"He happened to be in the bar at the casino," Cheeky said. "He was drinking at the bar. By himself. We just started talking. He is a handsome man... was a handsome man."

Smith waited for more, but Cheeky didn't elaborate. "That's it?"

"Sir?"

"That's all you're going to tell us? Don't you think that looks remarkably suspicious? That you just accidentally met Mr. Kerchini in a casino bar in Atlantic City and you somehow both ended up coming to this institute on Cape Cod—and now he's dead?"

Cheeky squirmed, but remained silent.

"I am wondering why you really went to New Jersey, Cheeky." Smith paused. "This is just a stinking pile of strange coincidences, isn't it? Of all the places that you could go in the United States, you just *happened* to go to New Jersey and then land on Cape Cod... with a dead man. Don't you think that sounds like way too many coincidences?"

"Not really, sergeant. For a wedding. Honestly. I want to tell you the truth here. I met the bride on the plane and she invited me to play music on my guitar. Sing songs, you know, like the 'Hawaiian Wedding Song' like Elvis—a British Elvis. And other lovely tunes."

"Would you say that you're a professional musician?"

Cheeky laughed. "I guess." He straightened his glasses.

Smith flopped back in his chair, which creaked in protest. Then he thrust himself forward and slammed his fist on the table. "BULL!" he shouted. "That's the biggest pile of shit I've heard in years!"

Cheeky recoiled—almost tipping his own chair over backwards.

"Did you kill Chris Kerchini, Mr. Nando? You were the one to find the body, weren't you? Did you have some sort of fight in Atlantic City and then follow him here to straighten him out? Did he insult you? Hurt your feelings? So you killed him?"

"I did not!" Cheeky screeched. "I'd never do such a thing. It was just a coincidence! Innocent coincidence."

Smith sat back in his chair and looked at Lisa as if to confirm that he wasn't losing his mind. "Am I just supposed to believe you?"

Cheeky shrugged. "It's the truth, sergeant."

Smith expelled an exasperated sigh. "So, what do you do here?"

Cheeky struggled to recover his composure.

"A bit of this and a bit of that. Organize, tidy, whatever needs to be done. It's shocking what people do in these rooms and cabins. They throw their clothes around, leave the water running in the bathrooms, and you wouldn't want to think about what they do in the beds. My god! People can be such animals."

"What about the people at this meeting? Are they better or worse than other groups?"

"Better than most, I think," Cheeky said. "But Miriam Leathe had her gun sitting on her dresser the other morning. Seems sloppy to me. I know Americans like to carry guns around like it's still the wild west. But you'd think she wouldn't leave something like that just lying around."

"Ms. Leathe carries a gun?"

"Well, it's not a very big gun. She probably keeps it in her handbag. But I was tidying her room, making her bed, changing the towels— that kind of thing, and she was probably at a session. I mean, that's what they're all here for, isn't it?"

"What kind of gun?"

"Ooh, I don't know anything about guns, sergeant."

Smith turned to Lisa. "Have they all gone home by now?"

"I believe most of the attendees have left."

"That's right," Cheeky said. "Checked out and shuffled off."

"What about Leathe? Is she still here?"

"She may have just left," Cheeky replied. "She looked a bit frazzled, if you know what I mean."

"No," Smith said.

"Well, after Mr. Megquire and that computer fellow got back, she seemed to kind of fall apart and then, like her head exploded, and she rushed off."

"What were they talking about?" Smith asked.

"Haven't got the faintest."

"We'll have to ask her about her gun. Do you know where she went?"

"She didn't say."

"Who *is* still here?" Smith asked.

"Well, the staff, of course, like me and Dr. Widner and the kitchen crew. We're providing meals to whoever is left. Mr. Megquire, the computer fellow, and Ms. Barker, I believe she has a flight out of Boston tomorrow morning. And Mr. Caruso, of course, because you told him not to leave and took away the keys to his truck."

Sergeant Smith looked at his watch. "Well, thank you, Cheeky. Do you have anything else to tell us?"

"Do you know who did it?"

"Besides you?" the sergeant said. "It's an ongoing investigation. Can't talk about it."

"Right," Cheeky said.

"Thank you, Mr. Nando."

"It wasn't me, sergeant. Honest. Since I know that, I don't have to worry about me murdering myself, but I do worry about someone else doing it. I wouldn't want to be murdered in my bed. Talk about things that go 'bump' in the night!"

"Have you heard something go bump, Mr. Nando?" Lisa asked.

"Always," Cheeky said. "Out here in the country, it's so very quiet. Occasional siren in the distance. Maybe a truck on the highway. You can hear a bird fart, it's so quiet."

"But you heard nothing on Monday night?" Lisa asked.

"Well, there were plenty of people here. Talking, drinking, you know how people are when they get together. But the cabins are pretty spread out."

"We were told that spray foam machine is pretty noisy."

"Oh," Cheeky said. "No, I didn't hear that. I was asleep, wasn't I?"

Lisa tilted her head at him. "Asleep? Bird fart? Were you asleep with someone, Cheeky?"

Cheeky got up.

"Who was it, Mr. Nando? Who were you in bed with that kept you from hearing the thump-thump of that foam machine in the middle of the night?"

"I prefer not to talk about it 'on the grounds that it might incriminate me'."

Smith stood up. At that moment, he reminded Lisa of a grizzly on its hind legs. She saw him pull his shoulders back and then angle his chin down so that he looked at Cheeky out of the top of his eyes.

"Where were you on Monday night?" Smith asked.

"In my room, of course," Cheeky said.

"In YOUR room?"

Cheeky blurted out, "I was with Dr. Widner. We were talking about the festival. That's all. We were just making sure that we were organized and prepared. He was worried about providing value, because these people came from a long way away and he wanted to be sure that everything was just right. That they would get their money's worth. That's all. We were just talking. He wanted nothing to go wrong, because he has an international reputation, you know. He has to maintain that. It's very important to him."

"Uh, huh," Smith said. He turned toward Lisa. "I guess that rules out the two of you as murderers!"

"Oh, certainly." Cheeky smiled. "Anything else, Trooper?"

Lisa shook her head and Cheeky slid out the door.

~

"So what do you think?" Smith asked Lisa as they drove home along Route 6, at the end of a long day.

Lisa was thinking about Jon and whether he was ever going to figure out what he wanted to do with his life. He needed more direction or more passion for a pursuit. Her crime fighting practical side told her that connecting her life to his was probably a bad idea. But she felt convinced she loved him and the unpredictable way his mind worked. That was a lot of thinking that had nothing to do with what the sergeant was asking.

Suddenly, she realized the sergeant had asked her a question. "Sure," she said.

Smith turned to look at her. "Sure? Sure we should arrest Caruso?"

"He seems like the most likely suspect."

Smith shook his head. "You can't arrest someone because they're a likely suspect. What proof do we have? What's his motive? Why did he do it?"

"Who else have we got?"

"What about your boyfriend?"

"What?"

"Forget about your connection to him. We still don't know what Megquire's doing here. He's not even a builder, and my understanding is that this is a builders' conference."

"Festival," Lisa corrected.

"Whatever. We connected all the other people here to building in various ways. Jon Megquire is the odd man out. So why is he here? I find that suspicious."

"He came up to see me," Lisa said.

"Well, if he came up to see you, why isn't he with you? Why is he here? What are we missing? I don't think you can be objective about this. Megquire is a sports promoter, right? I'm sorry, but I don't see how that connects to this in any way, shape, or form. See my problem here?"

It still challenged Lisa to move Jon from the personal files in her brain into the suspect files. For a moment, she tried to imagine him as a ruthless killer. But that would be like imagining her mother committing murder. The image of her mother in her apron and her sensible shoes wielding a foam spray gun while her victim writhed in pain on the ground was beyond imagining. Why would her mother do such a thing? Only to protect her family. But this was not a spontaneous act. You didn't suddenly bury someone in foam if you wanted to kill them. You would just shoot them. This was a crime of passion or abject cruelty.

It was equally hard for Lisa to imagine Jon doing this. "Jon couldn't have done it," she said.

"Why?" the sergeant asked.

How could she answer that question? Because she knew Jon was incapable of such a thing? She couldn't say that he wasn't there, because he had been. And Kerchini had been Jon's roommate. Another uncomfortable coincidence. Had Jon asked for that assignment?

"We need to find out how the rooms were assigned," she said. "Who handled that?"

"I think it was Nando," Smith said. "Didn't we ask him that?"

"I'll find out about the room assignments. But what motive would Jon have to kill Kerchini? There's no connection at all. Nothing."

"Well, maybe we missed something. Maybe Megquire is tangled up in drugs for financing his baseball project. Right? Maybe Kerchini—slick Chris Kerchini—was handling money laundering for the franchise and he stiffed the wrong guys and they sent Megquire up here to teach Kerchini's cartel a lesson. Burying someone in insulating foam would be like hanging a body from a tree as a warning. Not something you would forget, right?"

Lisa laughed. "That's crazy! You're hallucinating, Sergeant!" The thought of Jon as a drug lord was ludicrous.

"All right, but that would explain the viciousness of the crime, wouldn't it?"

They rode in silence.

"Who else?" Smith asked finally. "I mean, this can't be a pointless murder. What about Nando... Cheeky? What was that meeting in Atlantic City about?"

"Coincidences *do* happen," Lisa said. "It could have been just a coincidence."

"Not in my lifetime," Smith laughed. "There's always something more to a coincidence than just an inadvertent crossing of lives. Maybe it's subconscious, but if lives cross, something happens, and they come together again… in my book, that's not coincidence. That's intentional."

"So what happened in Atlantic City?"

"Damned if I know," Smith said. "But look at 'Cheeky'. Right? Slippery little sucker, smothered in a British accent, coming across all bouncy-bouncy. Pushing out his delicate feminine side. 'Oh, I'm too delicate to kill someone! Let's sing a song! All together now. One. Two. Three!'" The sergeant had taken on the voice of a children's entertainer.

Lisa laughed. "Come on, Sarge. You can't do that."

Smith kept driving. "I'm just saying Cheeky has yet to reveal all. Lovers' quarrel? I don't understand the gay stuff. Nando's gay, right? I can say that, right? It's just between you and me."

"We're not allowed to ask about sexual preferences," Lisa said.

"No, I know. Gay murders can be vicious. We don't have all those strings untangled: What about Nando and Widner, Nando and Kerchini, Kerchini and Widner? See what I'm saying."

That was a relationship knot that they hadn't untied.

"Almost everyone has gone now, right?" Smith asked.

"Right."

"But Nando and Widner are still here. We can be reasonably sure that it wasn't one of the speakers or lecturers. I mean, Hawkins is too old, and he's famous. I mean, he is supposed to have worked on the Manhattan project.

"The builder, Don Douthwaite, he's a Quaker. A conscientious objector, so forget him. What about Barker?"

"She's still here," Lisa said.

"What's her connection? What would make her do this?"

"She and Kerchini apparently had some research work connection. She didn't like him much, but I can't see her doing this either."

"Apparently innocent people are the worst kind," Smith said. *"Bang, bang, Maxwell's silver hammer up from behind. On the head."* The sergeant mangled the Beatles' song.

"Don't see a motive there either," Lisa said, ignoring the sergeant's lack of musical talent.

"Gotta be something in the backstory," Smith said eventually.

"But there were over fifty people here—including staff. We didn't talk to all of them. We didn't get all of their family histories," Lisa replied. "You bring together a bunch of random people in one place. One of them kills another. How are you supposed to pick out the killer?"

Smith looked over at Lisa. "You're smart. You studied for this. Put the clues together. Start at the beginning and work it through. What have we got? Let's focus on why and how Kerchini would let himself get buried in that foam. And we don't even know yet if that's what killed him. We haven't seen the autopsy. He could have been shot or strangled before he was foamed. Or how did the killer get Kerchini to lie there and let it happen?"

"Maybe he was drugged or drunk or a combination."

"What do we know about the vic?"

"Not much," Lisa said. She pulled out her notebook and flipped the pages to find her notes on Kerchini. "He lived in Waltham. Grew up there, in fact. Married. Catholic. He was in the army. They apparently called him 'Toad' because of his height or something."

"How d'you find that out?"

"His wife. He was married. With two kids."

"Jesus!" Smith said.

"He had a contracting company up there. Sold aluminum siding. Wanted to add foam insulation to the business, which explains why he was here."

Smith slowed his driving. "Drives people crazy when you slow down the cruiser like this. They all have guilty consciences, so they all slow down with you. Like you're going to cut one out of the herd."

"I gotta ask, Sarge. Have you always been this cynical?"

"It grows on you. Comes with the job," Smith said. "So, what do you think? Kerchini screwed one of his customers, who hunted him down here and killed him? That seems like a stretch. Did you find any army connections?"

"Nope. I checked his army records; he was honorably discharged. Stationed in Germany, he did office stuff. Procurement. Started his business with a couple of his army buddies."

"They weren't here?"

"No. I didn't get the impression from the people I talked to that he was particularly well loved."

"Who else?" Smith asked.

"Look," the sergeant said, "it had to have been someone at this event. And it had to have been someone who knew how to run that machine. So that limits the possibilities down to these people. Agreed?"

"That's what I said."

"So if we eliminate the dignitaries and hippy couples from California or Arizona who came here to learn about getting back to the earth, eating fish from big fiberglass tanks, and that Hare Krishna state of mind, that narrows it further. I think we can even rule out the guys from Connecticut, Vermont, and Maine who are following the sun and getting back to the earth. I might be wrong, but I don't think violence is part of that culture."

"You're jumping past a lot of possibilities."

"I am," he replied, "but there are no connections to any of those people. So, if it wasn't an enemy he made in the army, and it wasn't one the back-to-the-earthers, and it wasn't one of the festival dignitaries, and it wasn't your boyfriend, who's the most likely suspect?"

"What about Miriam Leathe? Nando found that gun in her room."

"She seems like an amiable lady. I mean, she's trying to learn things here to be a better real estate agent. Solid business reason. She thinks it will help her sell more houses."

"Yeah, but why is she carrying a gun?" Lisa asked. "Self-protection? From whom? She lives in Falmouth. As you say, this is not a high crime area."

"Did you find any connections to Kerchini? Anything?"

Lisa referred to her notebook again. "She lived in Hingham."

"So?"

"She said her son died when their house burned."

"Yeah. How did that happen? Let's talk with the Hingham police. See if they know anything."

"Will do, sergeant."

They pulled into the Yarmouth barracks parking lot.

Before opening his door, Smith said, "For me, all things point to Caruso. He's proved that he's violent. He certainly knows how to use a foam machine. And maybe he looked at Kerchini as a rival, or maybe they had some sort of beef in the past. Didn't Caruso used to live in Massachusetts?"

"That's right," Lisa said, referring to her notebook. "He hasn't left the institute yet, has he?"

"Nope. We took his keys and told him to stick around."

"All right. First thing in the morning, let's get him back in the room and make him squirm."

~

ITI WAS GETTING SPOOKY. Most attendees had left. The facility, designed for a crowd, was taking on a hollow vibe that Jon found unsettling. He was standing there with the remnants swirling around in the Cape Cod breeze on the plaza. All those people had come together, made noise, and now were gone. He should be gone too— but he wasn't. He wasn't sure he was welcome anymore.

Jon's head was full of unanswered questions. He hadn't had time to pin Lisa down before she left the Institute to find out if they were going to arrest someone.

Of course, Jon's principal question was, where he would go when he left? The answer to that depended on the status of his relationship with Lisa.

He found Gail Barker sitting by herself in one of the Adirondack chairs, nursing a beer. "The plane to Denver's out of Logan in the morning," she answered when Jon asked why she was still around. Jon thanked her for some great information. It impressed him how much Barker had accomplished in a mere twenty-nine years. She was an inspiration that excited the fire in Jon's belly to pursue an energy efficient construction career. It must have been hard for such an attractive woman to compete in such a male-dominated profession and be treated with respect.

Jon was about to sit down to talk with her further when Widner walked up to them, gave them a watery smile, and said, "It's over." He looked as though he were about to cry. "It's all over now."

"Yes," Jon said.

"It was a disaster," Widner said. "A murder in the middle of everything! And then the septic system..."

"Well, people won't forget it," Jon replied soothingly.

"Oh, that's for certain. And they haven't found the murderer yet! Few options now that people have gone home. How are the police going to solve it? I don't think much of their methods. It seems like they did nothing except talk to people and make them anxious."

"Have the police said anything about what happens next?" Jon asked.

"Oh, my," Widner exclaimed.

"Maybe you should sit down. I'll get you a drink."

Jon pulled a couple of beers out of the cooler and coaxed Widner into an Adirondack chair facing the evening sun. The air was redolent with the grass, the scrub pines and oaks that populated the lower Cape, along with the indescribable scent of cool ocean air. There was that insect chirp that seemed to surround everything at the end of the day. Jon thought that someday he would figure out what made that sound, the source that zeroed out the silence. A contrail painted a line across the darkening blue of the sky, the plane moving people from here to there—a million stories in progress.

"When I was in Saskatchewan," Widner began, "we had arguments. But no one ever killed anyone. I can't figure out why someone would do something like this. It just makes no sense."

"Well, that's the point. Figuring out the 'why' will solve the mystery. I'm not a detective, but in everything I've read, it's either love or money. Or love of money. Greed."

"Don't know where money fits into this," Widner said.

"Do you think the Wampanoag had anything to do with it? What about that curse story?"

"I don't think they like the institute being here. They believe that all this land belongs to them. That was what happened in Saskatchewan with the Métis. But I thought we were friends now."

"Why would the Wampanoag kill someone at this conference?"

"Maybe to discredit ITI. They might have thought that something like a murder would make the institute so distasteful to the locals that the town officials—or the ITI directors would withdraw the funding and shut us down."

"Seems pretty extreme to me," Jon said, taking a drink of beer.

"People can get very upset about things they don't understand. The townspeople don't understand the beneficial meaning of the institute's name. They think that because we're referring to a kind of magic, it's voodoo. Maybe they imagine we were sacrificing living creatures here. The popular press revels in such stories."

Jon thought Widner had more or less lost his mind and wished that he hadn't volunteered to sit and talk.

"So how is the fish raising going?" he asked, to change the subject.

"Oh, it's a wonderful process. It's amazing how nature closes all these loops. I'm sure you know that the first law says that heat is a form of energy, and thermodynamic processes are therefore subject to the principle of the conservation of energy. This means that heat energy cannot be created or destroyed."

Jon nodded.

"So we have those tanks in the Mycelium. The light from the sun passes through the roof glazing and the temperature of the room increases. Those big tanks hold seven hundred gallons of water. That water can hold a lot of heat and then slowly release it back into the space as the room cools. It's like a gigantic flywheel, you know. That's the second law of thermodynamics. So the tilapia are perfectly happy. Their waste is filtered out of the water and used on the gardens, and produce from the gardens returns to the tanks to feed the fish. Consider the fact that such an aquaculture/agriculture symbiosis is a system that enables a one-calorie energy input to yield five calories in perfectly edible fish!"

"Really?"

"Yes. It's extraordinary. The second law is miraculous. Things move from areas of higher concentration to areas of lower concentration like heat or moisture or pressure. We're all feeling the pressure here. How is nature going to relieve that and comply with the second law?"

Jon wondered how burying someone in expanding foam would relieve anyone's pressure.

"What's next?" Jon asked. "Any more festivals coming up?"

Widner looked around like he was taking a panoramic camera shot of the buildings, the grounds, the sunset, the trees—looking for an answer.

"Research," he said finally. "We'll keep doing the research until they shut us down. The work we're doing, Mr. Megquire, is important. Warm, low-energy houses are delightful, but it's the connection to the future that's most important. I'm not a crazy visionary who thinks that people are going to have huge tilapia tanks in their living rooms. And, although there is a lot of hype about it these days, I'm not even all that concerned that the world will run out of oil." He put his beer on the arm of his chair and guided the flow of sweat down the sides of the bottle and began picking at the label with his fingernail.

"The problem is that we won't run out of oil."

"What?" Jon asked.

"No, we'll just keep burning it, putting tons of CO_2 into the atmosphere, and dooming life on earth to enormous shifts in climate. Huge hurricanes, floods, earthquakes, tornados. Like the catastrophic end of times forecast in the Bible. The earth is not happy with us draining the blood from it, burning it, and destroying the ozone layer. The Indigenous people inherently understood the family relationship between nature and man. If we run out of oil, the burning would stop. It would have to."

Armageddon, Jon thought. What a jolly way to end the day. "You're not saying that we should stop making homes more energy efficient? That it's a bad idea to save energy?"

Widner stared at his beer bottle before he answered.

Jon had been expecting a rapid denial of that concept.

And then Widner laughed. It was a weird, hollow sound that gave Jon the creeps.

Widner said, "I have little hope."

That was even worse than the laugh. It triggered the smallest of thoughts: maybe Widner was despairing enough, crazy enough, to kill.

On the other hand, Jon knew that given what Ashton had discovered on his computer this afternoon about the fire in Hingham, as weird and unthinkable as it was, the solution to this murder was likely much more obvious than some crazy scientist with an end-of-times scenario.

AFTER LEAVING ITI, Miriam Leathe had a bitter taste in her mouth, the sense that her son Ian and her husband Ron were not satisfied, that something still needed to be put right.

She fussed about in her kitchen, tidying, then she mixed herself a gin and tonic and thought about how Ron would have made it for her —using lots of ice, the Tanqueray gin from the lovely green bottle, and a thin slice of lime. She pulled down her favorite copper pot and polished it until it glistened. Then she rehung it over the old black gas stove and, carrying her drink, walked out onto the deck. Summer was fully in control. The gardens were thriving. Bees were pollinating the squash plants.

She didn't have a view of the ocean, but most houses on Cape Cod didn't. The shoreline was too precious and reserved for the very wealthy. She hadn't come to Cape Cod for the ocean. She wondered once again about why she had come. Why hadn't she gone to Maine or North Carolina or Taos, New Mexico? If the point was to get away from Hingham, why not go further? She had in-laws in New Hampshire, but they rarely talked to her. They couldn't face what had happened to Ron and Ian. She got the distinct feeling that they blamed her somehow for what had happened, or that she should have been in the house when it burned, too.

Her brother in California wanted her to move out there. But she was convinced that California was going to fall into the Pacific Ocean, plus Californians seemed frenetic, as though they never sat still, never stopped to smell the roses or the warmth of the earth or the change of the seasons.

So she came to Cape Cod because... why not? She had to be somewhere. The real estate market was good on Cape Cod. Maybe not for selling hundreds of houses, but the commission on one of the million-dollar homes was enough. She liked the pace. It was like gardening. She carefully nourished her clients. She'd gained a reputation as a thorough and caring agent, bringing both sides together for mutual satisfaction.

Learning about houses and construction interested her and helped her to understand the craftsmanship as a work of art. She wanted to learn all she could about new technologies and their impact on old buildings, all of which had led her to the ITI festival—and Kerchini.

Suddenly, she dropped her glass on the flagstone patio. Her hand had just opened of its own accord and the glass plummeted, flinging glass shards and ice cubes everywhere. She felt dizzy, stumbled, and sank into one of the iron patio chairs. Kerchini's face loomed in front of her. The sun and the flowers and the smells of the earth around her disappeared as though the movie had reached a fade-to-black moment. She didn't feel regret. She didn't regret drugging him, persuading him to follow her, and then killing him. She was utterly convinced that he was the one who caused the fire that killed her husband and her son. He was so slick, so smug, so careless. She was actually pleased that she could do it. In fact, she would do it again if she had to. This was an unconscious, uncontrollable thought, and she didn't need to distance herself. She would proudly claim that she, Miriam Estelle Leathe, had slayed that personification of evil. If they had asked her.

But what were those men at ITI talking about this afternoon? What had they discovered about a fire in a house in Hingham? When the fire happened, she hadn't wanted to read the newspaper stories. She'd avoided them. She hadn't wanted to share in the moment's sensationalism. But maybe those men at ITI had seen something she should have seen—should have known. She should have stopped and asked them. She didn't doubt that what they found would confirm Kerchini as the cause of the fire. But what if he wasn't? What if she'd gotten it wrong? If she was so sure, why hadn't she stopped and asked?

Memories of the events of three years before had come flooding back. Their house in Hingham was just fine, and they should have left it alone. But Ron insisted they needed to do more to save energy. He'd been reading about the oil embargo and the predictions by MIT scientists that the country would be out of oil by the turn of the century.

Ron was a geek. He worked for Digital Computers. Digital was building machines that could crunch all the numbers in the world and tell you what you would wear in twenty-seven years… or maybe twenty-eight if they got it wrong the first time. They had plotted all the sources of oil in the world and what it would take to extract it and refine it and transport it, and Ron was convinced that the MIT guys were right.

They had to do their part, he told her. Right there—at home. Yes, the house was cheery, but it had an inefficient, oil-fired boiler that used way too much energy. Ron had added storm windows. Miriam hated those triple-track aluminum things that seemed to get stuck moving up and down. When they got dirty, you had to take the damn things apart to clean them.

Ron got Ian to write a report for his third-grade class on making houses energy efficient. The two of them spent several Saturdays measuring all the windows and doors. He taught Ian how to calculate the areas. Ron took all the numbers to his office to plug the information into his computer and gave Ian a pile of calculations for his report.

"You should write a book about all this," she suggested to her husband. "Do something useful with it."

"It's fun," he replied with a smile.

"Fun? Really? You are putting the fear of the end of the world into your son."

Ron looked at her. "You can't just stick your head in the sand and ignore the situation. Face it, Miriam. The facts are obvious."

She clearly remembered this conversation, the two of them standing in the kitchen of their lovely house with the morning sun pouring in the windows, windows that he informed her faced east, which was why they got so much morning sun! God damn him! He had to make a science experiment out of everything. He had indoctrinated her so she could never look at houses the same way. And it pissed her off.

Then he said they needed to increase the insulation in their house. He'd plugged the numbers into that damn computer model and that was what was missing. He'd been reading about how much better foam insulation was than fiberglass. "It was state-of-the-art," he said. "It would make their house cozy," he said. "Just like Squirrel Nutkin in his cozy nest," he said, and smiled.

Nutkin never had a nest, she'd replied, although she knew that wasn't the point.

Ron had arranged it all while she was off visiting her brother and his family in California. So it was really his own fault. He had arranged it and the contractor had come. She had never met him. He had come into their house with the equipment that he didn't know how to use. Sprayed foam insulation into their attic, packed up the equipment, and driven away. Three hours later, while Ron was probably making dinner and Ian was doing his homework, a fire started in the attic. And now she knew about the exothermic reaction of the curing foam. He'd probably put it on too thickly in the eaves, and he probably didn't mix it correctly, because that took knowledge and understanding of the process that the man didn't have.

Their pleasant house with the east-facing kitchen windows burned to the ground with her husband and son inside. And she had never known who did it. Until now.

After it happened, she shut down. She couldn't deal with it. Her mind moved into a different world, an alternate reality. Although she talked with a psychiatrist who prescribed medications, she buried her anger and her loss and reestablished herself in Falmouth, selling real estate. There was a connection there that she hadn't recognized. She hadn't connected herself to homes and Ron's interest until now. That was why she'd gone to this conference. Ron's or Ian's spirit had brought her to this festival to come together with their killer! It all made sense now.

But something still wasn't right. Pieces didn't fit right.

She pulled the twists out of her hair, ran her hands through the strands, and twisted them up again into an untidy knot. It must have been the thought that maybe Kerchini wasn't the ignorant contractor that caused her to lose the control of her hand and drop her glass. Otherwise, this would have been an unexplained, physical manifestation, and she didn't like unexplained physical events. It made her wonder if she was suffering from the early stages of dementia or Alzheimer's or cancer. She liked to believe that her personal discipline put her in full control of all the elements of her body. She had even coiled up the foam dispensing hose and put it back in the truck.

Ron had been disciplined and organized as well. He had kept a personal diary since he was twenty-two, noting important events and the names of people he met. She watched him write in it every night. Even on their honeymoon. God, that had pissed her off. "Dear diary, I got married today. It was a hell of a day. I can't begin to write the names of all the people who were at the wedding. When I finish writing this, we're going to have sex!"

That's what she imagined he'd written, but she hadn't read it. She had read none of the entries. She'd promised him she wouldn't, so he could write whatever crossed his mind. She still hadn't even read the old ones he kept in storage. What had he thought anyone was going to do with them? It wasn't as though he was a great diarist like Samuel

Pepys, chronicling the plague and Great Fire in London. But then again, she didn't know, so maybe it was brilliant prose.

They kept a fireproof box under his side of the bed with their passports, birth certificates, her grandmother's diamond bracelet, and Ron's latest diary. Why he thought the diary was as important as his passport or his grandfather's gold watch, she had no idea, but such were the mysteries in a long-term relationship.

She went back into the house and got a broom to sweep up the glass on the patio, while reprimanding herself for breaking one of the good glasses. It had been a Steuben glass, one of the "good" glasses they saved along with the "good" china for the special evenings that would never, ever come now.

She put the broom and the dustpan away, grabbed her keyring, and climbed the stairs to the bedroom. She sat down on the bed to gather her thoughts. The windows were open and the lightweight, yellow curtains billowed in the late afternoon breeze full of the scents of the garden with a touch of the distant ocean.

She hadn't looked in the black fireproof box since she had moved into this house, but she kept it in the same place under Ron's side of the bed.

Although she had tried to clean it off, the box still had soot on it. And the smell would never leave. That smell swelled her heart as she thought about Ron and her spectacular and utterly brilliant son, Ian. He would be eleven—approaching the teenage years. What would he have been doing, thinking, playing now? What songs would he have been singing? She choked, then reached down and pulled the box out.

She unlocked the box and lifted the heavy cover. Ron's diary lay on top. It was a common notebook of lined pages from an office supply store. Nothing fancy. Miriam wasn't sure she wanted to pick it up. She wasn't sure she wanted to slide into Ron's thoughts in the last days or hours of his life. Were his entries strictly factual? Or did he wax poetic each evening before they turned out the light and went to sleep, side by side, touching or holding hands? She'd never gone there before. She didn't know what she expected to find. Would Ron really have listed the name of an insulation company in his diary? Is that why he kept these things? God, that would make for dull reading by someone a hundred years from now. She was sure that Samuel Pepys never put crap like that in his diaries.

She picked up the diary and lifted it to her nose. Beyond the reek of the soot, she could smell just a hint of her husband's familiar fragrance. She flipped the notebook open to the first entry: *March 22, 1981.* Ron wrote in a quite legible style that was a combination of script and printing.

As she stumbled through his words and thoughts, she disengaged from her own reality and entered his three years in the past, not knowing that his days were truly numbered. He wrote about what was going on in the world, like the launch of the space shuttle, Columbia, in April and the appointment of Sandra Day O'Connor to the Supreme Court at the beginning of July, the same day that he noted they contracted to have the house insulated with expanding foam.

Miriam didn't remember talking to him about that. At the time, she was wrapped up in her real estate business, planning the trip to California and wondering if Ian should attend summer camp in Colorado. Insulating the house had not engaged her thoughts. Ron could handle it. And he obviously had. He had contracted with Joseph Caruso to do the job. *Joseph Caruso.*

The name jumped off the page and pierced her brain like a knife. She dropped the notebook. The heavy cover of the fireproof box slammed back down.

CHAPTER 11

ITI–THURSDAY AUGUST 9, 1984

"Yeah, the Discovery is launching at the end of the month," Jon said. "First launch of this one."

"What does your sister have to do with it?" Ashton asked.

"Don't know exactly. I only know she's going to be there in that big room they show on TV of the Kennedy Space Center, wearing a headset, staring at computer screens, and cheering like mad after a successful launch!"

Jon and Ashton were sitting on the plaza having breakfast. This morning it was eggs from the institute's chickens, homemade bread, and homemade strawberry jam. "I wouldn't be surprised if they grew the coffee beans for this coffee, too," Jon said. "It's great."

"No, but if you tell me it tastes like mud, I can use the old joke that it was ground this morning!" Ashton laughed.

It felt like a vacation morning—warm, calm, birds singing, the leaves susurrating in the gentle breeze. In contrast to the lives tourists left back home, a morning like this was pure paradise.

"So when you go back to Florida, are you going to watch the launch? Can you do that? Is there a viewing platform or something like that for a parade?"

"Not sure when or if I'm going back to Florida. It's nice here."

"It is that," Ashton said, looking around. "But you have a life there, don't you?"

"Well," Jon said, taking a bite of his toast. "I have sort of felt out of place there. Never really settled in. It's a bit like being back in college."

"A lot of partying? Hanging out with the sports stars and their glamorous women and fast cars?"

"In a way, but there's always pressure that wasn't there in college. Pressure to sell the deals. A lot of money pressure. People take money seriously."

Ashton nodded. "Better you than me."

"That's what I mean," Jon replied. "I don't want to do that shit. I don't think I would have that pressure here."

Ashton put down his coffee. "Are you kidding?" he asked. "Money pressure is everywhere. People are always wheeling and dealing—trying to be better than someone else. That's what makes the world go around." He pulled his legs out from under the picnic table, turned around, and leaned his back against the tabletop. "As much as it might look like it this morning, Jon, this place is not paradise. As witness the murder that just took place. And I know it wasn't here on the Cape, but look what happened to Miriam Leathe's family."

"It is amazing what you can find on a computer."

"It connects you to the entire world," Ashton said. "I can research phototropic mushrooms in Amsterdam or read a newspaper in San Francisco without ever leaving this table!"

Jon cocked his head..

"Well, I guess that's not quite true. I'd have to bring the computer out here and plug it in to power and a phone line. But it could be done. And the computer world is changing so fast. I bet your sister knows all about that. Love to pick her brain sometime."

"Good luck with that. She's always working." Jon got up from the table, then paused as a thought struck him.

"Could you find the name of the contractor who installed the foam insulation in the house that burned down?"

"If a permit had to be pulled, sure. If the town digitized the records to make them accessible online. Not all towns have gotten there yet. There are probably passwords to protect them, but they are public records, so the security probably isn't that tight. Why?"

"Well, maybe Kerchini caused the fire, and that's why somebody killed him."

Ashton mulled that one over for a minute. "Wow," he said. "You mean we could solve a murder using the computer? Wow."

Jon smiled. "That would be pretty amazing, wouldn't it?"

"Might take a while," Ashton said. "Phone line connections are not exactly lightning fast. But we could check it out."

"Let's do it."

ELLIOTT WIDNER HAD NEVER LIKED his small apartment. It was *too* small. He felt he deserved something grander. But ITI was not a religious organization that raked in millions from its parishioners every month. There was an underlying holy fervor in the back-to-the-earthers, but they eschewed money and that was a problem. Even supplicants need to make a living. This apartment felt like the cell of the senior monk—limited in ornamentation.

The space was also more modern than Widner would have liked, tucked as it was into the northwest corner of the Mycelium. It might have been designed as the chief gardener's quarters, because there was a small private balcony inside the greenhouse itself from which he could descend into the gardens. The apartment had a soaring ceiling that joined the peak of the Mycelium's glazing on the south side. It had a tiny kitchen. The bed was in a loft, which he had to climb by alternating step stairs. Coming down was challenging, especially if you were carrying anything. You always had to start with the correct foot. They told him it was to save space, but those missing steps made him nervous.

There was lovely light in the space and gorgeous sunsets from the western windows, and the woodstove warmed the place on wintry nights. But he couldn't escape the musty smell from the greenhouse gardens, and mold grew on his leather suitcase and just about every-thing else. After all, the primary purpose of the building was to grow things—not to live in.

The business side of the Mycelium was a natural growth factory. It was ninety feet long and forty feet wide, and the south-facing roof had trough-like glazing that soared to eighteen feet at the peak, providing access to operable vents. A steep set of steps in the north-east corner led up to a platform near the peak from which they could operate the vents. The north wall was built into the ground.

Dozens of vegetable beds positioned between wooden walking platforms covered most of the floor. A tomato and vine vegetable area with dozens of suspension strings attached to the glazing extended upwards like spider webs.

There were eighteen gigantic tilapia tanks holding seven hundred gallons of water each. The tanks were arranged in two rows, set far enough apart to allow walking space between them. The water in the tanks was an emerald green. More plants grew in trays along the tops of the tanks. The air in the building carried an overpowering odor of soil and plant life. On this August morning, the temperature inside was high, although both the top and bottom vents were open.

Widner knew he wasn't well suited to the growing part of the operation. He was more of a building scientist and manager, and his PhD, which helped in fund-raising, provided a properly academic tone to the operation. He did not, in fact, love the reality of growing things. The concept appealed to him, but getting his hands into the mud did not. The closed-loop nature of the plants and fish and waste treatment that mimicked the natural cycle of life had a harmony that sang to his theoretical soul. He was also good at balance sheets and the other mundane business activities that were an unfortunate necessity of any operation.

He was sitting at his desk pushing numbers around in his ledgers when Joe Caruso knocked on the glass of the sliding entrance door.

Widner walked over and pushed the door back to allow him in. "Mr. Caruso," he said. "Good morning. I think it's still morning, isn't it?"

"Yup," Caruso replied.

"Come in. Welcome to my abode. Can I get you some coffee? I only have instant."

"That's all I've got too. Thanks, but I don't want coffee," Caruso replied. "I just want my check and I want to get out of here."

"Ah, your check." For Widner, money changing hands was one of the most distasteful elements of the operation. He hated negotiating salaries or contracts. There was a level of antagonism in the process that offended him. Numbers in the ledgers were one thing. They were just marks on a page. But paychecks and contracts involved people. There was always friction in putting a dollar amount on the worth of the participants, which made Elliot queasy. Although Caruso's presence was of promotional value to his company, Foamrite, Caruso had also served as an instructor at the festival, and after a nasty bit of bickering, Widner had agreed to pay him for that service.

"Yeah, my check. I've been in this nuthouse long enough, and now I want to go home."

"Certainly," Widner replied. "Just curious. Have the police said that it's okay?"

"Haven't asked them and don't intend to," Caruso said. "They let everyone else go."

"But your truck. Isn't that a part of the crime scene?"

"Nothing happened in my truck. And that's another thing. Who's going to pay for all the foam? We had a deal about the training and that included some foam, but not all that stuff all over the parking lot. Who's going to pay for that?"

Elliott didn't have an answer. It didn't seem fair that ITI should have to pay for excess foam. "How much would that be anyway?" he asked. "Foamrite should be able to absorb that in their marketing cost."

"That stuff ain't cheap."

"Would you like to have a seat while I find the checkbook?"

Caruso dropped into an armchair that faced the main ITI buildings while Widner pulled out the checkbook. "Sure I can't get you some coffee?"

"Why not? I can handle a few more minutes."

Widner walked over to the kitchenette and put water on to boil. While he was waiting, he opened his file cabinet, ruffled through files, and pulled out the one for the festival.

Caruso's presence upset his equilibrium. He wanted the man gone. He felt something creepy about him. Working with the Métis, Widner had learned to sense or see a person's aura - a colorful haze, particularly around the head. Scientifically, it made little sense, but there were many things about people that science couldn't explain. Caruso's aura looked murky and brownish. Maybe a burnt umber color, which he didn't think was a positive sign. He watched Caruso out of the corner of his eye while he thumbed through the file, seeking the contract with Foamrite. Caruso was staring out the window.

"Ah," he muttered when he found it. He carried the file over to his desk and opened the checkbook. When the water boiled, he pulled two mugs out of the cabinet over the sink and spooned instant coffee into them. As he poured in the boiling water, it made a chuckling sound as it curled into the mugs, wrapping around the instant coffee crystals. He stirred the water. "Milk? Sugar?"

Caruso turned away from the window. "Both," he said. "You know. Regular."

Widner brought the mug over to Caruso, then sat down at his desk again. Was the man worth what he'd agreed to pay? He had his doubts. After all, if he hadn't been here with that infernal machine, this unfortunate murder would not have happened. Dead attendees were not in the best interests of the organization.

He wrote the check, tore it out of the register and was about to hand it to Caruso when the man jumped up and yelled, "Shit! Is there another way out of here?"

Widner spun around. "What?" he shouted.

"Is there another way out of here?"

"Through the Mycelium," Widner said. "You can go through that door into the greenhouse."

Caruso slammed down his mug, slopping some of it, grabbed the check from Widner's hands, and bolted through the Mycelium access door.

~

WHEN LISA and Sergeant Smith arrived at ITI and walked into the lobby, Cheeky was behind the counter, shuffling through a stack of papers. "Where's Joe Caruso, Cheeky?" the sergeant asked.

"Good morning, officers," Cheeky replied with a smile. "I believe he headed off to find Dr. Widner and get his check. Would you... gentleman, lady, care for some breakfast or coffee? I think there's a fresh pot brewing."

Lisa pushed her glasses up her nose and smiled at Cheeky. She declined breakfast but accepted coffee. She noticed Jon in the meeting room, huddled beside that Ashton character. They were staring at a computer screen.

Jon spotted her, smiled, and turned back to the monitor.

"Is there anything else I can get you?" Cheeky asked, handing them steaming mugs of coffee.

"Ah. The genuine stuff," the sergeant said.

"Do you think you'll have this wrapped up soon? It's hell on Dr. Widner's ulcers. He has a sensitive constitution, you know. And just about everyone is gone now. Scattered to the four winds." Cheeky made a dispersive gesture.

"No one wants to get this wrapped up more than we do," Lisa replied. She was indeed ready to have this whole sordid affair resolved. The evidence against Caruso was not rock solid, but it was still damning.

They carried their coffees out to the vacant plaza. Lisa felt awkward sliding back into one of the Adirondack chairs. It didn't feel very professional, so she perched uncomfortably on the edge, resting her forearms on her knees.

"We should talk to the local police before we talk to Caruso," Smith said. "Find out if Caruso has a history up there. Where did he say he was from before he moved to New Jersey? Quincy? Braintree?"

"Hingham," Lisa replied after checking her notes. "Said he grew up in Jamaica Plain."

"Uh, huh. Hingham." He scanned the property. "This is a pleasant spot," the sergeant said, sipping his coffee and looking up at the clear blue sky. "It's a shame to live in a place like this and never get to the beach. You get to the beach much, Prence?"

Lisa looked at him as though he had suggested swimming with snakes. She didn't have time to lie around on a beach. She barely had time for anything not related to her job. HR was always encouraging mental health breaks. There was a lot of stress being a cop. She was sure that the people who wrote the HR policies lived in a different universe painted by imaginative, best practices policies.

"Nope," she replied. "Not much time for that."

"Right. Why don't I go call Hingham police and you go find Caruso and get his ass up here? Hey, Cheeky," he shouted. "Where's Widner's office?"

Cheeky pointed to the Mycelium. Lisa put down her coffee and started off in that direction.

The building looked massive and totally out of place. It was all sharp angles, built of concrete and plastic and flanked by the gigantic water tanks filled with what looked like pond scum. Lisa had ruled out farming as a career long ago when her class had visited one in elementary school. The smell of the manure had stayed with her long after, and that distinctive tang was in the air here. She watched as one intern pushed the cover of a tank aside, reached in with a fisherman's net and scooped out a foot-long fish that twisted in its death throes.

Nope, Lisa thought, supermarket cooler for me.

"Lunch!" the intern called, waving the wriggling fish while he pushed the cover back onto the tank. Lisa waved back and kept walking.

She came around to the Mycelium entrance and the large, intricately carved double wooden doors. She'd been in greenhouses before, but never anything like this. Pulling the door open, she was greeted by a rush of hot, fetid air that reeked of biological activity. As soon as she stepped inside and pulled the door closed, she started sweating. She wondered how people could work in such conditions. What made the air so oppressive? Carbon dioxide? Or something else entirely? Plants grew everywhere she looked. Board walkways lay between the planted areas. Strings were connected to the sloped, glazed roof with plants clinging to them, turning the place into a jungle. There were more of those enormous water tanks, filled with scummy emerald-green water, undoubtedly populated by more fish.

Why would Dr. Widner live in this place? Wouldn't the humidity make his skin shrivel like a prune? It was all vegetation. There wasn't any place that a human being could live in this space—a bed among the tomatoes!

She was turning to go back to the entrance when she heard the muted thump of a door in the distance. "Hello!" she shouted. "Dr. Widner? Caruso? We need to talk to you!"

CHAPTER 12

MYCELIUM—AUGUST 9, 1984

At the same moment Lisa Prence was heading for the Mycelium to bring Joe Caruso in for further questioning, Miriam Leathe was back at ITI and storming toward Widner's apartment. She, too, was looking for Caruso, but with a very different purpose in mind. The night before, Ron's diary had injected venom into her veins. It was an understatement to say that she was angry. She was mad at herself for leaping to the conclusion that Kerchini was the murderer of her husband and son. Over the years, she had lectured herself repeatedly about the foolishness of grabbing at solutions. Since their murder, she had applauded herself about the controlled way she had behaved. She didn't cry every night anymore, and, until this festival, she had it all under control.

Fate had driven her to attend the event. Just a simple notice in the *Cape Cod Times*. It must have been a devil or a genie or some other evil spirit that urged her to go. Drawn to the insulating foam event, she was like a shark to blood in the water.

When she saw Joe Caruso's name in her husband's diary, she had dropped the book and stared out at the garden, her thoughts lost somewhere in the stratosphere. She envisioned using a butcher knife to stab the diary over and over. But those were Ron's words. Not

Caruso's. Yes, she was angry with her husband for initiating the whole insulating process. He had some misplaced notion of saving energy and saving the world, and it had killed him. And Ian! And that was the worst part. That conjured such intense pain in her heart that it was beyond description.

She wanted to jump in her car immediately, drive back to Tilley, find Caruso, shove the insulating foam gun down his throat, and fill him with foam. No, he would never sit still for that. She would have to shoot him first, just enough to immobilize him. Then fill him with foam and let that heat build up in his guts until he exploded. She pictured his stupid face with those dumb tortoise-shell glasses, eyes wide in horror as he as he felt his guts expanding and exploding.

She managed to get herself back to the kitchen without shredding her husband's diary and opened the last bottle of the Opus One wine she had bought on a trip to Napa with Ron, the bottle they'd been saving for some special night that would never happen now.

She poured herself a huge glassful, much more than was proper, sat at the kitchen table, and stared into the burgundy liquid. The kitchen clock ticked. The refrigerator cycled on, then off. All night she sat, getting up only to go to the bathroom. It was peculiar that even though time had stopped, bodily functions did not. Miriam's anger grew hotter. Eventually, the pressure in her mind reached a static state. She stopped thinking altogether and just sat in the dark, cradling her glass.

When the light of Thursday, August ninth, dawned, Miriam got up from the table, rinsed her glass, and loaded it into the dishwasher. Then she added coffee and water to her coffeemaker, turned it on, and cracked eggs into a pan, crushing the shells and dropping them into the trash. She added ham and goat cheese on top of the bubbling eggs, then green peppers and onions that she'd chopped fiercely on the cutting board. She poured herself a cup of coffee and set it on the kitchen table where she'd arranged her setting with a placemat, knife, fork, and folded napkin.

She settled herself in the chair after putting her omelet on a plate, ate the eggs, and drank the coffee.

After she was finished, she rinsed all the dishes and added them to the dishwasher. Then she went upstairs, showered, and put on fresh clothes, cinching her belt tightly. She checked her gun to make sure that it was loaded, then dropped it, with an extra magazine, into her purse.

She got in her car and drove to Tilley, ITI, and Caruso.

~

AFTER CARUSO RUSHED out the door into the Mycelium, Elliott had stood still with his mouth gaping like a tilapia out of water. He was glad to be rid of the odious man, but did not understand his abrupt and rude departure. Then he looked out the windows toward the main buildings and saw Miriam Leathe storming across the grass toward him—gun in hand.

"Oh," he said to the vacant apartment. "What is she doing back here, and why is she carrying a gun?"

Several courses of action came to mind. He had no desire to confront the woman. He knew that confronting a woman carrying a gun was not productive. Unplanned confrontations were anathema to him. He wasn't afraid of her. No, it was the gun. He was in control of this institute and had no reason to be afraid. But it was only sensible to be afraid of the gun. People who carried guns were dangerous, probably insane. It simply wasn't a normal activity. Criminals carried guns. Therefore, this woman had to be a criminal… or a killer.

He had an irresistible urge to hide. He looked frantically around the room and movie visions of lovers hiding in the closet or under the bed came to mind. But those, of course, weren't real. There was the loft bedroom, and he rushed over to the steep steps. If he got down behind the bed, she wouldn't see him. If he stayed quiet, maybe she would even have the decency to knock on the glass door, hear no response, and walk away.

He was halfway up the steps when he saw her out of the corner of his eye, standing at the slider. She didn't hesitate but pushed the sliding door back, the 'whoosh' making Widner's scrotum tighten, and he froze. If he didn't move, maybe she wouldn't see him.

She yelled, "Caruso!" and Widner almost lost his grip on the stair rail, barely avoiding falling off the steps. She saw him and calmly pointed her gun at him.

"No," he stammered. "No. He's not here."

"Come down," she said.

Widner eased his way backward down the damn alternating treads of the stairs—reaching for each step with his foot as he clung to the rail.

"He's not here," he repeated when he reached the floor. He tried to regain some composure, pulling himself upright and squaring his shoulders. After all, he was bigger than she was, and this was his home. "What do you want? You can't just come barging in here like this! This is my home!"

"I have permission," she said with a miserable smile, waving her gun.

It occurred to Widner that maybe he should know what kind of gun she was holding. But if there's dog shit in the middle of the living room floor, you don't analyze what kind of dog shit it is. You just remove it! Chances were good that whatever it was would emit bullets out of the barrel if she pulled the trigger. He knew enough to know that she was not holding a toy.

"Where's Caruso?"

"He's not here."

"I can see that. Where is he?"

"He was here."

"I didn't ask you where he was. I asked you where he is."

"I don't know."

"Cheeky Nando said he was here."

"Well, not anymore. He left."

Miriam turned her gun toward the sliding door and pulled the trigger. The noise was sudden and painful and Widner reached to cover his ears in a delayed reaction. The glass door fragmented, and the air filled with the smell of sweet charcoal smoke with a spritz of sulfur.

"Jesus!" Widner shouted. "You can't do that."

"I just did," Miriam said and calmly turned the gun back toward Widner, and pointed it at his head.

"He went into the Mycelium," he said, cowering. "I swear he's not here. Please don't shoot me. I don't want to die for vegetables!"

"What the hell are you babbling about?"

Widner clung unsteadily onto the railing for the stairs. "Do you mind if I sit down?"

"You don't need to sit down!" Leathe shouted. "Where's Caruso?"

"I just told you," Elliot said, as he felt his knees buckling. He did not feel at all well. It was not fair. It was not his fault. He knew nothing about this woman, and he knew nothing about Caruso. And he certainly knew nothing about a conflict between them.

Miriam moved closer. Despite the warmth of the room, Widner could feel heat radiating from the intense anger in her body. She lowered her gun until it pointed at his crotch. "Show me," she demanded.

"Oh," he gasped. "Oh, certainly. There." He pointed at the door to the Mycelium. "He went through there."

"Show me," she repeated. "Now." She emphasized this last word by bringing the gun up under his chin.

"I'll show you, but you really don't need to point that gun at me? That's dangerous."

"Shut the hell up and show me where Caruso went."

He moved sideways toward the Mycelium door, never taking his eyes off the gun. He nodded his head toward the door. "There."

"Open it." She stood back as though it might be a trap.

Widner twisted the knob and pulled the door open. A rush of hot, earthy-smelling air greeted them.

Miriam peered in.

"God, it's hot," she said. "Go."

"What?"

"You first. I don't know where he is in there. Or even if he's in there. You're going first!"

He didn't have any desire to walk in front of Miriam's gun. It felt like stepping into the middle of a high noon showdown on the main street in an old Western. If this woman had a gun, it made sense that Caruso had a gun as well and that they would point them at each other with him in the middle. They should take this outside.

Miriam shoved her gun into Widner's ribs. "Walk."

BACK IN THE main ITI building, Jon and Ashton focused on the computer screen. It was taking forever—poking through the connections, not knowing where to turn, what to open, what to leave alone. He leaned over Ashton's shoulder to watch the mysteries unfold on the computer screen. They had plugged the modem into the phone line, and the thing made a variety of chirps and gurgles as it connected to the invisible digital world. Ashton called it "shaking hands with the host.".

"Ah," Jon said.

"So, what are we looking for, exactly?" Ashton asked.

"We want to know if Kerchini was the foam insulation contractor for the Leathe house in Hingham when it burned down around 1981," Jon said.

"And season? Spring? Summer? Winter?"

"No idea," Jon said.

"So we're looking for a fire that might have taken place in Hingham sometime in 1981 to find the name of the contractor who might have caused it!"

Jon realized that this was pointless. Of the billions of pieces of information out there, they were trying to pull just the right, single page from all the information in the world about everything. "We need to set up a Johari Window."

"A what?" Ashton asked.

"A Johari window. My sister told me they use that at NASA to help people understand their relationships with themselves and others. It builds relationship blocks between the knowns and the unknowns. It's a psychological tool, but we could modify it so that we can categorize what we know and what we don't know. We know there was a fire. We know it happened in Hingham. We know it was caused by poorly installed foam insulation, right?"

"Right."

"What we don't know is exactly when it happened. We don't know if it was reported in the paper—although it seems logical that it would have been. We don't know if that newspaper report has been converted to an electronic document that we can find through your computer. The story may not exist and if it does exist, it may not be available to us."

"Right," Ashton said as he continued to type.

"We also don't know which newspaper it might be in if it was in a newspaper. And..."

"There's more?"

"And there are all the things that we don't even know that we don't know."

"So where does this Johari window come into this?"

Jon laughed. "I don't know. It was just one of those techno-babble terms I remember my sister talking about."

"What is the local paper in Hingham? The local papers aren't as easy to find on-line. It's the big ones that are digitizing everything."

"*The Boston Globe* then?"

After more clicking and whirring and waiting, they had made little progress. "As you said, the problem is that we might find nothing because there might be nothing to find," Ashton said. "Maybe it's one of the unknown unknowns or something like that. We have to come up with very specific search terms. We can't be vague about this. I don't think fuzzy logic is going to work for us here."

And they couldn't take all day to do it. Kerchini's killer was still at large. Jon had heard Lisa at the front desk asking Cheeky where Caruso was and set off to find him in the Mycelium. So the clock was running. Watching the hourglass flip around and around on Ashton's screen was a literal reminder that time was passing.

It stopped spinning, and a display blossomed on the screen. "Look at that," Ashton said. "*The Boston Globe* isn't electronic, but *The Middlesex News* is! I'll plug in 'house fires'." The hourglass started spinning again.

"This is taking forever," Jon said. "I mean where's Middlesex? I'm not good at Boston geography. Maybe Hingham isn't even in their coverage area."

"It says it's based in Framingham. That's west of Boston." The hourglass continued to spin.

"Isn't Hingham south and east of Boston?" Jon asked. His certainty that this was pointless was growing. Even if they found a press story, what would it prove? Lisa was out hunting a killer and he was sitting here watching a cartoon hourglass spin around and around on a computer screen, looking for something that might not even be there.

Abruptly, the hourglass stopped spinning, and a list of articles about house fires appeared on the screen. Porch fires that consumed the entire house. Electric space-heater fires. Kitchen fires. Stories about police chiefs and the fire departments and references to historical events all over the southern and western Boston suburbs. It was like walking into the New York Public Library and asking about one particular article in one particular newspaper somewhere in the world that happened at some moment in time. Way back when libraries were established, intelligent people realized that there had to be a way to organize all the information. There was simply too much electronic information, and looking for what they needed was painfully slow. It would be a miracle if they found anything useful.

Jon pushed back his chair. "I've got to go help Lisa," he said. "Thanks for this, Lash, but I don't know how this is going to help us."

But as he stood up, Lash tapped the solid glass screen of the monitor and said, "Look!"

Jon leaned back over. There was some gobbledygook that must have made sense to the computer, a line that mentioned the *Middlesex*

News as the source, and then a headline "Home Fire Linked to Foam Insulation."

"Bingo!" Ashton said.

Jon sat back down. "Open it! That's incredible. I never thought you'd find anything!"

Ashton clicked on the story, and the hourglass began spinning again. "I just hope someone doesn't interrupt this phone line before we get there," Ashton said.

The hourglass kept spinning. When it finally stopped, the article blossomed on the screen. They leaned closer and skimmed through the story. And there was Ron Leathe.

"Miriam's husband, right?" Jon asked.

And way down at the end, there was the name of the contractor: Joe Caruso.

"Oh, my god," Jon said. "Caruso caused the fire that killed Miriam Leathe's husband. Kerchini wasn't even involved. Not in any way! What does this mean? Is Miriam Leathe Kerchini's killer? Maybe she thought Kerchini did it. How could she make that mistake?"

"We could search for Kerchini," Ashton suggested.

"You can do that later. I've got to go tell Lisa." He stood up and rushed out the door.

JON DIDN'T KNOW if Caruso had killed Kerchini, and he didn't know why he would have done it. Caruso had not intentionally murdered the Leathe family. It had been an accident. Besides, burying someone in foam was crueler and more creative than Jon could give Caruso credit for. Killing someone that way would require imagining the pain, and Caruso couldn't imagine a well-crafted beer.

Lisa didn't know any of this. But she was in there with him, unaware of his motivations, believing that she just needed to ask him a few questions.

Jon almost tumbled down the hill to the Mycelium, reached the big wooden doors, and pulled the right one open to be greeted by the almost tangible barrier of moist, earthy heat. He stepped inside and began to sweat. When he called out Lisa's name, the dirt and plants muffled his voice.

"Lisa!" Jon yelled again. He thought he saw some movement and stepped cautiously along the wooden walkway between the tilapia tanks. "Lisa!"

He stopped and looked up. Way up ahead, he saw Widner emerge on a platform above all the plants. His hands were in the air, and as Jon watched, he saw Miriam Leathe appear behind him, waving a gun.

It suddenly became clear to Jon that Leathe had figured it out as well: she had made a mistake killing Kerchini, realized Caruso had killed her family, and she would right that wrong by hunting down Caruso. And now Lisa was somewhere in here as well, unknowingly in the middle of a critical situation.

For a moment, his heart leapt at the thought that maybe Lisa wasn't in the Mycelium. Maybe Cheeky had misunderstood, and she was still outside. Then he caught sight of the top of her head moving between the rows of water tanks. He yelled her name again.

And where was Caruso?

Caruso wasn't much taller than Lisa and could easily hide behind the tanks. If he knew Leathe was hunting for him, he wouldn't hang around this hothouse. He would try to get out of the building, probably heading toward the entrance behind Jon. It was just so damn hot. Jon wiped the sweat from his eyes. He realized it must be even harder for Lisa because her glasses would be fogging.

He kept shouting her name. The peculiar acoustics of the space distorted his voice. "Lisa!"

Widner just stood on the platform, holding onto the railing with Leathe beside him.

Then she lowered her arm and fired her gun with an explosive pop. One tank behind Jon began spouting green water.

"Hey!" Jon shouted as he ducked. He saw the dark shadow of a fish appear and disappear in the green water as it circled close to the skin of the tank beside him.

Jon assumed Leathe must have seen or thought she saw Caruso.

What the hell was she doing? Was she just going to shoot at anything that moved? Now she was pushing Widner ahead of her down the steps.

Jon moved as quickly as he could along the wooden path. He had no clear line of sight. The leaves of the climbing vegetables that stretched up to the roof glazing made the path narrow, and the support strings were like cobwebs. The space was arranged for plants —not people. "Keep your hands inside the car at all times." Water dripped off the roof glazing. The plants and the dirt around Jon's feet were wet and sweat dripped into his eyes.

The Mycelium was big, but it was a confined space and there were only two ways out—three if you counted the roof vents. Maybe Caruso would make a run for the steps up to the venting platform. The north side of the roof sloped down to the ground. Jon was blocking the main path to the east doors. But Caruso wouldn't care— he would just get out of the building and away from Leathe any way he could. He'd told Jon that he had a gun. So did Lisa.

This could end up being a wild-west shootout. But those shootouts took place in the open, not behind seven-hundred-gallon fish tanks and getting tangled in tomato vines. In hundred-degree, super-saturated air.

Suddenly Caruso appeared ahead of him between the tanks, waving his gun. "Out of my way!" he yelled.

In the distance, Jon saw Leathe coming behind Caruso. She fired another shot and another tilapia tank started pissing water.

Caruso stopped, turned, raised his gun and fired back. The space muffled the explosion, but still Jon covered his ears. The sulfurous smell of the gunpowder mixed with the perfume of the wet earth, but the bullet must have passed through multiple tanks because water was spraying in several directions. Jon saw Widner turn and flee back to the steps. Leathe merely ducked, but she was getting soaked.

And then Lisa stepped out onto the wooden platform about halfway between Leathe and Caruso. "Police!" she yelled. She too had her weapon drawn, but standing between the two combatants made it difficult for her to know whether to point left or right.

Jon could tell Leathe had no intention of stopping. She bobbed out from behind a tank and kept coming down the boardwalk. Lisa had no way of knowing the intensity of Leathe's motive to kill Caruso.

Caruso was bent over, running straight at him when Leathe fired again. The 'bang' was followed by the 'zing' of the bullet as it found a home in another tank and yet more water sprayed out. It was looking like an anemic Bethesda Fountain in New York's Central Park. Then Caruso stopped, turned, and fired back. His bullet shattered the structural integrity of a fiberglass tank's walls and seven hundred gallons poured out at once, carrying with it vegetables and flapping tilapia.

It wasn't martial arts training or even logical thinking that made Jon step forward as Caruso turned and rose from his crouch. Adrenaline and blind instinct drove Jon to wrap his arms around the smaller man, pinning his arms to his sides to immobilize him, and then to drag him, squirming like a tilapia toward the doors. They pushed through together, out into fresh air, and the contrast was startling.

But Caruso still had a death grip on his gun, and when Jon released him and stepped back, Caruso waved it at him. Both of them were soaked from sweat and tilapia tank juice. Their lungs were full of carbon dioxide and bio effluents. Caruso sank to his knees, trying to keep his head up, still pointing his gun at Jon.

Jon leaned over and spat some of the sour taste out onto the grass.

Caruso straightened up. "Get out of my way!" he demanded. "That woman is crazy!"

"Just drop the gun. I'm going back." Ignoring Caruso's gun might not have been the smartest thing to do, but Jon couldn't leave Lisa in the Mycelium with water spouting everywhere, fish flapping around her feet, and a crazy woman shooting at anything that moved. Particularly since Lisa wasn't aware of Leathe's fury.

Caruso started staggering up the hill, still waving his gun in the air.

"Drop the weapon!" Jon heard the barked command behind him. He turned and saw Sergeant Smith coming from the main buildings with his gun drawn. "Drop the weapon. Hands behind your heads. Down on your knees."

Jon didn't have a gun and at first he didn't accept that any of the commands were meant for him. "I've got to go back for Lisa," He called.

"On your knees, Megquire! Now!"

The command was explicit. Jon dropped to his knees and began explaining. "Lisa's still in there with Miriam Leathe. And she has a gun. It's crazy in there. There's water spraying everywhere!"

"Shut up, Megquire. Plant your face on the ground and put your hands behind your back."

"Sergeant, look. She's in serious danger. Leathe is crazy. She's randomly shooting at everything." Jon looked at Caruso. "Caruso was the contractor who foamed her house before it caught fire and killed Leathe's husband and son. She wants Caruso dead and doesn't care about anyone who gets in her way. Including Lisa!"

The sergeant leaned over and clamped his handcuffs on Caruso's wrists as he lay face down on the grass, whimpering.

Jon was infuriated that Smith didn't seem to be listening. He jumped up and ran back to the Mycelium's doors.

"Stop!" Smith yelled.

Jon ignored him and stepped back into the heat and humidity. With the pressures in the tanks relieved, the fountain-like flow of water had subsided to more of a dribble. Jon wiped the sweat from his eyes and yelled, "Lisa!" He stood by the doors, trying to determine which way to move. He couldn't help if Leathe shot him dead.

He began walking carefully back along the walkway. Green water lay everywhere. Tomato vines were twisted and tangled. Schools of fish huddled in the limited remaining water in several of the tanks. "Lisa! Where are you?"

Leathe stepped out from between two intact tanks, pushing Lisa ahead of her. Jon couldn't see it, but it was clear that Leathe had her at gunpoint. Lisa was holding her hands behind her head. Her glasses were missing. Both women were soaked to the skin, their hair hanging limply down over their faces, as though they had just climbed out of a lake after jumping in with their clothes on. The heat and the motionless air were overwhelming.

"She has a gun, Jon," Lisa said.

"I can see that."

"When the tank burst, it knocked me down."

Jon noticed the dying tilapia flopping around on the boardwalk.

"Let's get out of here, Miriam," Jon said, stepping backward toward the doors. "Maybe we can straighten this out outside."

"Bullshit!" Leathe exploded. When Jon had first seen Miriam Leathe, he thought she was a nice, middle-aged woman, the gentle sort who went to church on Sundays, garden club on Thursdays, and book club once a month. He had not expected a foul-mouthed, gun-toting, shoot-'em-up bitch. Well, maybe she wasn't a bitch, but she was most likely a murderer. "I want Caruso!" she yelled.

"Turns out that Caruso was the contractor responsible for the death of Ms. Leathe's family," Jon told Lisa as he continued to back up. "Mr. Caruso is outside," he informed Leathe.

"Yeah? Well, that's just great. Why don't you go out there and send him back in? I'll trade your trooper for him. Fair exchange. You get what you want, and I get the bastard who killed my husband and my beautiful son."

Jon stopped moving.

"Go!" said Lisa.

That did not seem like a good idea. Jon knew Sergeant Smith was not likely to send Caruso back into this jungle to die any more than Caruso would come willingly or that Leathe would just let Lisa walk out. At the same time, Jon was not about to let anything happen to Lisa.

"Miriam?" Jon asked. "You're not a killer, Miriam. You're a good person."

"Hah!" Miriam laughed. "That's funny!" It was a laugh without mirth—a hollow laugh. It was a deadly laugh. "After the first one," Leathe said, "the rest are easy. I buried Kerchini. Whoops! Sorry about that! My bad! That's more of a challenge than just pulling this trigger. I buried him in foam and that was a mistake. And maybe he didn't deserve it."

"You killed Kerchini?" Jon asked. "Why did you do that?"

"I didn't know, did I?" Miriam asked. "I wanted him to be standing up when he died, but he wouldn't cooperate. He needed to look like a foam-covered statue so you'd all come out for breakfast and there he'd be: a useless blob of foam." She pushed her wet hair back from her face again.

"Is this what your husband Ron would have wanted?"

"Shut up and go get Caruso."

"What do you think your son Ian would think about his mother as a killer?" There was so much water running down Miriam's face that Jon couldn't tell if she was crying. She ran her hand through her hair and twisted it as if she wanted to rip it off. She waved her gun at Jon. "Get him!" Leathe ordered. "Get Caruso! He's the killer."

"I think we have to do what she says," Lisa said as she smiled at Jon, and her bravery struck him in his heart and his throat.

"How old would Ian be now?" Jon asked. "The accident happened what, three years ago? That's right, isn't it, Miriam? It happened in August 1981? Do I have that right? This would be like the three-year anniversary, wouldn't it? So Ian would be ten now."

"Eleven," she said. "He'd be eleven. His birthday is in May."

Jon wiped his own sweat from his eyes. It was so hard to breathe and so damn bright.

"No," Jon said. "I don't think... If Ian was standing here right now looking at you... I don't think he'd want to think of his mother as an evil killer, despite what happened to him. I don't think he would want to think that."

"Shut up!" Miriam yelled and fired again, puncturing another tilapia tank, creating another geyser, and causing Jon to duck involuntarily. And in one spectacularly smooth movement, Lisa spun around, grabbed Miriam's arm and twisted her into the mud and the tomatoes.

OUTSIDE THE MYCELIUM, Jon could breathe again. The contrast in air density and temperature made it seem almost balmy. His shirt was sticking to his skin, but he knew it was worse for Lisa. He imagined she must have almost drowned when that tank collapsed. She had lost her glasses. Everything about her was soaked. She had come close to wearing one of Miriam's bullets. And she amazed Jon.

"You okay?" he asked. It was such a lame question. Like when someone is in a car crash lying on the pavement with a bone sticking out through their pants and someone comes up and asks, "Are you okay?" *Of course they're not okay*, Jon thought. *Of course, Lisa was not okay*. This was a day where people had come close to dying, and a lot of fish died!

But Lisa nodded. She handed over a weeping Miriam Leathe to Sergeant Smith, who had already dealt with Joe Caruso.

"I'll find them. I'll find your glasses," Jon said and began moving back toward the entrance to the Mycelium.

At that moment, Widner came running from the other end of the building. "What the hell happened? What the hell happened? Who's going to pay for all this? Years of research have been destroyed. Do you understand that? Years of research? How are we ever going to recover?"

Jon, Smith, Lisa, and Miriam stood together and stared mutely at this lunatic. Widner's universe did not intersect with reality, and for one strange moment, the four of them were united, wondering if Widner had the wrong script for this scene. Then they turned away.

Going back into the Mycelium was like returning to an underwater cave. It felt as though the whole place was going to collapse on him. He wondered if he could ever visit one of those garden center greenhouses again. And although he knew that the ground was solid underneath the board walkways, he moved cautiously, feeling as though he were balanced over a yawning abyss. He tried to picture where he'd seen Lisa come out with Leathe behind her. There was only one completely collapsed tank. That must have been where Lisa had been knocked off her feet and lost her glasses, allowing Leathe to take control. Dying fish flopped around on the boards and in the lettuce and zucchini. For a moment, the simple task of finding Lisa's glasses struck him as impossible. It was one of those stupid feelings when so many parts of life pile on at once and even breathing feels too hard and you just want to give up.

He had to regain control, so he stood still, closed his eyes, and listened to the sounds of the Mycelium. Except for the occasional flap of a fish and drip of water, it was remarkably peaceful. No sounds from the outside world intruded within these translucent walls. It was like being in a snow globe.

When he opened his eyes and turned his head, he saw Lisa's glasses lying in the mud, peeking from under some lettuce leaves.

~

JON HAD little to pack up in cabin 42. He showered and changed and packed up his things. Kerchini's car and belongings were gone. Jon never got to know the man whose body had been at the center of the turmoil, and who met such a gruesome end. He shuddered as he stuffed his laundry into his suitcase.

He stood for a moment on the front porch in the warm air. It was almost serene, a dramatic contrast to the insanity of the afternoon. He hoped that would be the last of gun shots and exploding fish tanks in his life. He had never realized how many people had guns and seemed ready to use them.

But then there was the promise of creating buildings that were connected to the harmony of nature, creating buildings that were connections—not interruptions of the earth, the wind, and the sun's bounty, creating buildings the way the Anasazi or the Wampanoag people had but adding modern materials and tools to make them even more comfortable. Computers, expandable foam, low iron glass, and inorganic fiberglass cloth could help. Orville Hawkins, Don Douthwaite, and Gail Barker had all talked about how to do that, and those challenges had infused Jon's mind with a desire to learn more, to do more. He recognized clearly that his future was not in Fort Lauderdale, Florida.

He leaned on the porch railing and looked up the hill to the main buildings of the Institute. Elliott Widner was an interesting man, but

Jon wasn't sure that he was the right person to lead a transitional construction charge into the future. It would take empathetic persuasion to convince old-time builders like Ace Wentzell to change. Change meant risk. It was difficult to take risks when it challenged your livelihood. What was the point of making a change when what you were doing worked? If it ain't broke, don't fix it.

Apparently, Maybelline wasn't eager to leave either. She didn't want to start. With his hands on the top of the steering wheel, he stared through the windshield into the trees. She was a fun car—when she ran. But Jon had reached the limit of her unreliability. He didn't have the time or the skill to work on her. He just wanted to get where he wanted to go.

And while he was sitting there, contemplating how to get to Lisa's, Cheeky appeared.

"Problems?" Cheeky asked.

"She won't start."

"Let's have a look," said Cheeky, and he popped open the hood.

Jon climbed out to peer into the engine compartment, standing beside Cheeky. He had a vague idea of how the components were supposed to work together, just like he had a vague understanding of how a human heart, lungs, and intestines worked together. Cheeky, however, had an intuitive sense of the system in its entirety—not as individual components, but how all the parts harmonized as a system.

"Let's change the oil," Cheeky said. "Her oil is tired. She's not getting enough compression. When was the last time you changed the oil?"

Jon could not conceive of the connection between the viscosity of the car's oil and its ability to start.

But they changed the oil. Cheeky had a supply of motor oil in his maintenance stores, and he went through the process without hesitation, while humming "Stayin' Alive" over and over. While the oil was draining, he pulled out the spark plugs and cleaned the tips.

Jon felt like an intruder while he watched Cheeky perform his magic

"Cheeky," Jon said when the man had pulled himself out from

under Maybelline's belly and was lying on the ground facing up to the sky, "I think it is time for Maybelline and I to part company."

"Really? Are you going to sell her?"

"Trade her in or sell her."

Cheeky stood up and wiped his hands on the rag he was holding.

"What do you want for her?"

They talked money for a moment and then Jon said, "You two seem like you were made for each other."

Cheeky dropped her down off the jack stands and closed the hood or "the bonnet" as he called it.

Jon got in the driver's seat, turned the key and she started up with an enthusiastic purr. He looked up at Cheeky and smiled.

"You've got a deal," Jon said. "Can't think of a better home for her to go to. I'll be back tomorrow."

~

THERE IT WAS. All of it. The finest of Cape Cod evenings. Barely four hours after all the shooting and sweating in the Mycelium. Jon was driving Maybelline with the top down, wind in his hair, a grin stretching his mouth from ear to ear, and Guess Who's "American Woman" pouring out of the speakers. Things were coming together. An explosive multitude of thoughts swelled his mind. His chest inflated with unprovoked joy. Even if this was to be one of his last rides in Maybelline. He forced himself to turn away from impediments to his happiness. Why would he feel happy about being shot at? It wasn't that. Maybe it was seeing Lisa standing strong, her hair hanging down on both sides of her head, holding a gun on the woman, who was both a killer and a victim of unfathomable pain.

But still, he grinned and slapped his hands on the top of the steering wheel. Why did it feel like he was going home? Lisa's apartment wasn't home—physically, anyway. But what made a place a home? Was it the wood, the glass, and the copper pipes? Was it the piece of land it sat on? Wasn't it the people that made it a home?

His thoughts were a jumble of flying fish, water fountains, dancing tomatoes, screaming bullets, and sports cars. And then there was Lisa. The miles hummed by under the little car's wheels. He was rushing home to see Lisa with her deep brown eyes, chestnut hair, silky shoulders, and dancer's neck, and absolutely brilliant smile. Oh, my God, he thought, and pushed the accelerator further toward the floor. What have I been doing? Why have I wasted so much time?

Suddenly, he was overwhelmed by the thought that there was so much he didn't know about her, so much he wanted to know. It was difficult to sit still and keep Maybelline on the road. He wanted all of her inside of him and all of him inside of her. And how, in the name of Jiminy Cricket, was he going to express all of that to her without sounding like a babbling idiot? And what the hell made him think about a cricket?

And then he was there. When he stopped driving, he noticed how amazingly warm the air was. He realized he should have stopped and bought flowers or wine—or two bottles of wine or four dozen roses— and he really had to stop gibbering to himself. And stop drooling. He wiped his chin.

Abruptly, he was afraid. He ran his hand through his hair and straightened his pants and smiled and waved to the family who sat in the parking lot watching him.

"Nice car!" one of them shouted as he walked up the steps to her door and rang the bell. He waited. He turned and looked around the lot. Maybe she wasn't home. Maybe she had a date. They hadn't officially settled anything. Sergeant Smith had just driven her away after Jon had handed her the glasses. Jon had noticed that they still had dirt on them, so he'd sort of grabbed them back and wiped them on his shirt. She'd pushed her wet hair back from her face, put on her glasses, and looked at his chin. And didn't say a word.

Shit, he thought. He simply assumed she would want to see him tonight. But maybe she didn't. Maybe he should find a phone booth and call her. That would give him a chance to get flowers, wine, dinner, whatever she wanted. And if he couldn't stay here tonight... he'd have to find a motel or something.

He knew the people in the parking lot were watching him,

expecting something to happen. He was the evening's entertainment. Better than television. Watching real life unfold in front of their eyes.

Maybe she couldn't hear the bell, so he knocked. And waited.

He was about to ring again when the door opened, and she was standing there.

"Hi," he said with a grin.

"Oh, hi," she replied.

She was wearing her glasses, a grey Red Sox sweatshirt, and cut-off blue jean shorts without shoes or sandals, a towel wrapped around her head. She held the door open with her left hand, and as he watched, she lifted her right hand to the towel, as though to be certain that it was secure. But she wasn't smiling.

"I'm sorry," he said. "I should have called." He grinned again. "I should have brought you flowers. Or wine. Or wine and flowers. I should have called. Are you okay?"

"Come in," she said.

And somehow that was enough to lift the terror of rejection off his shoulders, and he followed her into the living room, pushing the door closed behind him.

She assured him she was okay in response to his persistent questions, and then settled into a chair, leaving the sofa for him. She told him that the sergeant had been very empathetic, which she hadn't expected.

"Can I get you anything?" he asked.

She suggested he pull a couple of beers out of the refrigerator. He opened the utensil drawer, rattled around, found her church key and popped the tops off the beer bottles. He handed her one.

There were moments of uncomfortable silence as he tried to think of clever or comforting and reassuring things to say that didn't sound condescending or too clever or too comforting—until they got into the rhythm of their words and unraveled their mutual experiences of the day.

She told him how they had decided that they needed to interview Caruso further, and that was why she'd set off to find him.

He told her how Lash Ashton had used his computer to find the newspaper article that revealed Caruso's name.

They talked about the pain that Miriam Leathe must have been suffering.

They talked about the bizarre environment in the Mycelium and laughed about the flopping fish. And he reminded her about that crazy shooting in the restaurant in Fort Lauderdale with the lobsters scrambling for the doors. It made him think of the scene with Woody Allen and Diane Keaton in *Annie Hall* with the lobsters escaping and Allen suggesting that they attract one with a little dish of butter to get it out from behind the refrigerator! He wondered if you had to use lemons to attract escaped fish. And they laughed.

She unwound her hair from the towel, put on sandals, and they drove to the Lobster Shack down the road and ordered fish and chips. Jon touched her arm and said that the fries weren't as greasy as the ones at Clegg's in Tilley, and they laughed some more.

They stopped at a package store to buy a six-pack of Narragansett beer and a pint of Ben & Jerry's Dastardly Mash ice cream.

Back in Lisa's apartment, Jon told her about Maybelline not wanting to start and getting Cheeky's help. "I think I'm going to sell her to him," he said.

"But you love that car," she replied, resting her hand on his knee and tilting her head.

"I do," he said. "She's been good to me. I've put over a hundred thousand miles on her, but I need something more reliable."

They finished the ice cream, dipping their spoons into the container simultaneously and licking their lips. He wiped a dribble of chocolate off her chin with his finger.

"That's the first time I've been shot at," she said, leaning back on the sofa.

He didn't know how to respond.

"That's the first time I've been shot at," she repeated. "And it probably won't be the last."

He put the ice cream container down on the glass coffee table.

"I hope it is," he said. "I guess that's something you can't practice, is it?"

"No. Part of the job." She shook her hair back away from her face and tilted her chin up toward the ceiling. The trace of a tear appeared on her cheek.

Jon realized that this was real—her fear was real. He could feel it and smell it in the air the way an animal might. She was struggling to hide it. But it wasn't working. And so he had to take it away from her. He had to take her fear into himself and away from her.

So he wrapped her in his arms and drew her to him. He... And then she... And then he... And her skin touched his skin, and his skin touched her skin. Her face slid into his shoulder. The clean smell of her hair soared up his nose. Her glasses fell to the floor.

And they laughed. His hands touched the beautiful curve of her back. There was an urgency in their passion, as though the clock was ticking and time and bullets and lobsters and fish and tomatoes were flying until the water gushed out of the tanks and they lay back naked and spent between the sofa and the coffee table laughing.

CHAPTER 13

TILLEY–AUGUST 10, 1984

*T*he morning after, Jon and Lisa lay in her bed staring at the ceiling. Jon listened to the sounds of the house. He reveled in the light in her bedroom, the reflections on her ceiling, the smell of her perfume, the swish of the gentle breeze pushing back the gossamer light curtains over the open windows.

"Thanks for stopping by," she said.

He propped his head on his hand to look at her. "I'm not leaving." He wanted to know every line on her face that would tell him if she was serious or if she was kidding. He wanted to know every expression she would make in every situation, even if it showed her disapproval of him. He wanted to know what she really meant when she said, "Fine! I'm fine!" or "Nothing!" when he asked her what he had done. And he wanted to know her good faces, her soft faces when she was concerned about him or understood his fears or celebrated their successes.

And so he told her he loved her, which started the lovemaking all over again.

When they finally got up, Lisa said she was ravenous, and they walked down the street to the Canal Side Inn where they had first seen Joe Caruso's truck in what seemed like months ago. Jon found it hard to believe that not even a week had passed. The place was mostly empty except for one old guy at the counter reading the paper.

"Coffee?" the waitress asked when she came over to the table. "No work today?" she asked Lisa.

"Day off, Ethel," Lisa replied.

Jon could feel Ethel sizing him up, looking at him out of the corner of her eye, checking him out as a suitable match for this lovely woman.

"Do you eat here every morning?" Jon asked when she walked away.

"Nah," Lisa said. "Rarely during the week. Most mornings, I grab a piece of toast and maybe some cereal."

"If you're going to run around catching bad guys, you need to keep your strength up," he said with a smile.

As they ate breakfast, they talked about what had happened in the days before, Tilley, and the ITI festival. Jon asked her if she would find out what happened to Miriam Leathe or Caruso, if she would be privy to the rest of their stories. He said he would never find out the cause of the shooting at the Lobster Palace in Fort Lauderdale.

"Probably not," she said around a piece of toast, slathered with marmalade. "At least not all of it. I'll obviously be in court because of my involvement. What Leathe did was horrible. Murdering someone with expandable foam is going to go into the record books for sure."

A pair of elderly men came in, checked out Jon and Lisa as though they were infringing on their morning club. Jon wondered if they were old friends who sat together at the same table every morning talking about old times, sports, and the shocking things that the government had done. Ethel bustled about behind the counter, shifting pots on the coffee machine, adjusting the pastry display in the glass case, lifting the doors on the freezer case behind her to check the contents.

"Why isn't this place crazy busy?" Jon asked in a low voice. "It's high tourist season. Food tasted okay to me."

"Location," she replied. "The Mid-Cape Highway takes everybody down Cape—Hyannis, Dennis, Provincetown. The traffic just bypasses this place. Except on weekends. They serve a special break-fast brunch. Most of the locals avoid it. The tourists are just so crazy."

"I didn't tell you. My father remarried," Jon said.

"No, you didn't tell me. That's great!" He felt her studying his face. "Isn't it?"

"No. I mean, yeah. She's nice, I guess. And they have a baby. He's something like three years old already. I think that's right."

"Oh, my God! So, you're a big brother?"

"I am," he smiled.

"Brother Jon!" Moments passed while they ate in silence. "Do you want kids?"

Jon looked around the room and then down at his plate. He recognized that sort of question required a quick answer. To not answer or delay the answer could mean trouble, so the best solution was to respond with a question. "Well. I hadn't really thought about it. Do you?"

"My parents would really like it," she replied.

There, he thought. Her response was as evasive as his. But then he realized that he really wanted to know how she felt about children. In fact, he wanted to know how *he* felt about children, about being a father, about settling down with a family, about all the other stuff that came with shouldering all that responsibility that went way, way, way beyond happy times and great sex. He suddenly felt queasy, and it wasn't the grease from his fried eggs.

Ethel interrupted to ask if there would be anything else. "If you don't mind my saying so, sir, you're looking pale. Are you okay?"

The "sir" hit him like a ton of bricks. Right there was responsibility and aging. Was he really a "sir" now? It wasn't the first time he'd been addressed as "sir". It was the timing. Being called "sir" sucked in all the other thoughts about kids and mortgages and family vans and fatherhood.

∾

BACK AT LISA'S APARTMENT, Jon called Ace and asked if he was feeling well enough for visitors. Ace and Babs happily agreed. Maybelline cooperated, and they drove down Cape with the top down, the sun shining, questions of children and responsibility blown away by the music and the warm summer air. Lisa said, "You can't sell this car. You love this car!"

Jon laughed and said, "When she runs."

Even though five years had passed, arriving at the Wentzells' house on Bartlett Street in Tilley was another kind of homecoming. Ace's old pickup was parked in the driveway, and Jon slid Maybelline up beside it. It was like two old dogs, smelling each other, getting reacquainted.

Jon and Lisa walked up to the front screen door and knocked. Babs came bustling up from the back of the house, wiping her hands on her apron, calling out, "Come in. Come in."

She hugged Lisa, and then she hugged Jon.

"Ace is out the back. I've made him sit. He didn't want to. He wanted to go to a job site, but I wouldn't let him. They let him out of the hospital, but they said he has to take it easy. And I have to watch his diet, and that doesn't make him happy either." She grinned and shot a conspiratorial look at Lisa.

They followed Babs through the house and out to the back deck, where Ace was ensconced in a deck chair with his feet up. "This is bullshit," he said, holding out his hand. "Rest and recuperation! My heart's as solid as a train conductor's watch! Never better."

Babs asked what she could get them to drink—coffee, lemonade, ice water, soda? She and Lisa went back into the kitchen.

Ace asked Jon how things had gone at the festival at ITI.

"It was great," Jon said. "Crazy yesterday… but the festival itself was good. I learned a bunch."

"Anything about foam insulation? That guy from Florida that you sent my way… Marty Robbins. Thought he was the singer at first! He's from Toledo. He wants all the latest and greatest in his vacation home. State-of-the-art shit. I don't know if I'm ready to do that. There aren't a lot of foam insulation contractors around. I had to get in touch with some guy in Waltham. Chris Kerchini. I don't know enough to know if he knows what the hell he's doing."

Jon dropped into one of the folding green and white nylon webbed garden chairs and asked, "Kerchini?"

"That's his name. Can't remember his company's name at this point. Wonder if you lose parts of your memory when you have a heart attack."

"That was the name of the guy that was killed at the festival! He was the one that got buried in the foam that I told you about at the hospital."

"No shit!" Ace said. "Guess we're not going with that guy, at least. Maybe there really is a curse out there! I'm not sure if I really want to do this house, anyway. I'm not good with new stuff. Houses last a long time, and we don't know if any of these foams or any of that stuff is going to last ten years... far less, a hundred. I don't want to be experimenting on someone's million-dollar home."

Lisa and Babs came out of the house. Lisa handed Jon a glass of lemonade.

"Hey, you want a beer?" Ace asked. "You're old enough now." Jon laughed.

"Too early. But thanks."

"So tell us about all that stuff that happened yesterday at your institute."

Jon and Lisa went back and forth describing the events in the Mycelium. Jon talked about working with Lash Ashton and his computer skills. Lisa said that she and the sergeant had realized that there was more to Caruso's story than he had revealed in their interview, and how she had set off to find him. And how Miriam Leathe showed up waving a gun from one end and Caruso waving a gun from the other, and Jon appearing in the doorway and Leathe shooting and puncturing the big tilapia tanks and water spraying out. She said Jon was so good at talking Leathe down, relating her to her dead son. Jon described how amazingly brave Lisa was and how smoothly she'd disarmed Leathe. And Lisa said that she could empathize with Leathe's terrible pain.

"Her anger must have been stewing all those years. I can't imagine what it would be like to lose a child that way," she said.

"Yes," Babs replied. "There's nothing worse than losing a child." After a moment's pause, she asked, "So what are you two going to do now? When do you go back to Fort Lauderdale, Jon?"

"Not sure," he said.

"Do you enjoy what you're doing down there? That's the point, isn't it? You have to enjoy what you're doing, or it's not worth doing it. Life is too short."

"Life is too short," Ace agreed.

"Not really... no," Jon said, answering Babs. "No, I mean I guess you're right about life, but I mean the job. I don't enjoy the job. It's frustrating. I'm not making progress, and I don't see the point. I'm not crazy about Florida, but maybe I've just never seen the good side. It feels like a temporary place to be. Know what I mean? A place for vacations or retirement. This feels more like home." He looked around.

There was a moment when the world seemed to stop, and then Ace asked, "How d'you like to work here with me?"

Babs put her hand up to cover her mouth.

Lisa placed her lemonade on the glass table and said, "Oh!" and smiled.

"I could use a hand with this building science stuff."

Jon looked at him. He looked at Lisa. And then he said, "That'd be good, sir. I think I'd like that."

REFERENCES

Music in Second Law

- REO Speedwagon - "Back on the Road Again"
- Cindy Lauper - "Time After Time"
- Billy Ocean - "Stay the Night"
- The Seekers - "Kumbaya"
- Peter, Paul, and Mary - "If I had a Hammer"
- Chumbawumba - "Coal not Dole"
- Aretha Franklin - "RESPECT"
- Chuck Berry - "Maybelline"
- Stevie Wonder - "I Just Called to say I Love You"
- Tina Turner - "What's Love Got to do with It?"
- Sade - "Smooth Operator"
- Jimmy Buffet - "Cheeseburger in Paradise"
- Ethel Merman - "There's No Business Like Show Business"
- Linda Ronstadt - "Desperado"
- Kenny Loggins - "Footloose"
- Van Halen - "Jump"
- Bee Gees - "Stayin' Alive"

Literary References

- Sun/Earth Buffering and Superinsulation - Don Booth with Jonathan Booth and Peg Boyles
- Double Sheet Solar House - Don Booth
- Air-to-Air Heat Exchangers for Houses - William A. Shurcliff
- New Inventions in Low-Cost Solar Heating - William A. Shurcliff
- Super Insulated Houses and Double Envelope Houses - William A. Shurcliff
- *Spray Foam Insider* - Jay Davidson
- History of Spray Foam Insulation
- The National Digital Newspaper Program

TRIBUTES

Building Science

When you work in a discipline every day, it seems so obvious—all the acronyms, terminology, and systems. It seems like everyone should know what you are talking about. And one forgets that simply isn't true.

Building science has been around as long as we have built buildings. It just was. And it was nameless. Until it needed a brand. You can be a geologist or an astronomer or biologist. But there still isn't a Nobel Prize for Building Science! Like any of the sciences, building science did not spring from nothingness to whole cloth. Many wonderful people and organizations labored to generate the masses of information that built the fundamentals.

I can't celebrate all of them, but I am honoring three of them here who have left us and should be included when a history of building science is written so they won't be forgotten.

Don Booth: In the 1970s, Don Booth ran a company called Community Builders in New Hampshire. He was a creative perfectionist and not always easy to work with, but he attracted a crew of smart and curious workers who wanted to learn how to build better.

By the 1970s, Don's awareness of the need

for more energy-efficient homes became the single-minded focus of his business. Each new home incorporated lessons learned from the last, as well as adding new ideas to better harness the heating capacity of the sun and the earth itself. Don offered seminars for owner/builders and, at conferences, he freely shared his experiences and enthusiasm for the solar options he pioneered.

That was a particular challenge because of his vocal cord dysfunction which often left unaccustomed listeners struggling to understand his words.

He was a lifelong activist for peace and justice and stood on the Mall in Washington in 1963 to hear Dr. King proclaim his dream. His books Double Shell Solar House and Sun/Earth Buffering and Superinsulation are landmark works.

Rob deKieffer: Rob was a farmer, eagle scout, Cub Scout leader, singer, performer, and treasurer for *Up With People!* He was also one of the twelve people tasked by then Vice President Joe Biden with crafting a new national energy policy. Rob worked at the Solar Energy Research Institute (SERI) which became the National Renewable Energy Laboratory (NREL) in 1991, when it became

the only sole-purpose national laboratory. He was the managing partner of Boulder Design Alliance and was involved in applied research, development and application of innovative energy conservation programs from 1978 forward. Rob wrote papers with titles like "Combustion Safety Checks: How Not to Kill Your Clients" for *Home Energy Magazine.* He actively took part in Affordable Comfort conferences, talking about "Energy Consumption as a Diagnostic Tool" with Michael Blasnik and "The Road to High Performance Construction". I'm proud to have known him as a friend.

William Shurcliff: The Northeast Solar Energy Association (NESEA) had a chapter in Massachusetts that had monthly meetings at MIT that Dr. Shurcliff attended. I had the distinct honor of meeting him there, as I was just starting to think about solar heating. He had worked on the Manhattan Project (the atomic bomb). He worked for Polaroid, and he played an outspoken role in defeating plans for supersonic passenger planes in order to prevent Super Sonic Transports (SSTs) from flying over populated areas. In the 1970s, he became an advocate for passive solar building design and superinsulation. He wrote numerous books on the subject, including a seminal book on air-to-air heat exchangers.

In that book, he has a chapter on controls which includes the unique concept of controlling the rate of exchanger air flow by the exterior wind speed. He points out that infiltration increases with increases in windspeed. "What is important in keeping the levels of pollution low is the total rate of fresh air input: the greater the natural input, the smaller the input needs from the exchanger." What a concept!

ACKNOWLEDGMENTS

The title of this book came to me almost before the story. Pressure. People under pressure. Lives pushing on lives, until a release of pressure resolves the differences. Having settled on *Scrivener* as my writing software, I started putting it together in April 2020. By early July, Second Law was in my head. By mid-July, the story was keeping me awake.

There was much to learn:

• how to use an Apple iPad to allow me to sit on the front porch in the early morning light to develop characters;

• about the early years of spray foam;

• early years of superinsulation;

• about the Métis and the "October Crisis"; and

• police procedures in 1984.

And there were all the crazy real world distractions like the 2020 elections and COVID-19. By September, the story and the characters were still forming in my thoughts, but by the end of September, I started writing the rough draft. By the end of March, 2021, I printed out the rough draft to have a read through. Then I began editing.

By mid-June it seemed ready to send out to my wonderfully tolerant beta readers: Bill Boyer, Jason Wolfson, Jim Weber, David Goehring, Rana Belshe, and my wonderful wife, Kate Raymer. I sent excerpts of the book to Jay Davidson of *Spray Foam Insider* to verify what Joe Caruso was teaching and Marianne Gonsalves to clue me into state police procedure.

With that brain trust of input, I set about editing some more and then seeking the skills of a professional editor. They are busy people.

By the end of July, I connected with Nancy Doherty and convinced her to look at the book.

By the end of August, she had gotten back to me with some excellent story line revisions, which I implemented, and got back to her by mid-November. (And Kate got to read it again!)

At that point, Nancy dug into the mechanics of the words and the grammar and returned it to me by early January, 2022. With all the insertions and deletions and adjustments, I ran the book through *ProWritingAid* software, chapter by chapter.

Finally it went out again to the eagle eyes of Jason Wolfson (again), Rana Belshe (again), Jim Gunshinan, Cindy Young-Turner, and Bill Sims for that one last look before it is off to the press and the June 18, 2022 official launch. Special thanks goes out to Chef John Marcellino and his wife Marion for hosting us at the Station Grill in Falmouth.

With the help of all these wonderful people and brilliant minds, I have learned a lot in this process. When I typed out my first novel in 1972, I had no idea how much there was to learn or even a hint of how the world of publishing would change over the next fifty years. Maybe there are people who can write a story while secluded in a remote cabin, experiencing no human contact. But that's not me. The story is the confluence of the thoughts and lives of the characters both within and without the covers of the book. I am eternally grateful for all of you—both real and imaginary!

Falmouth, MA–April, 2022

ABOUT PAUL H. RAYMER

Paul H. Raymer was born in New York City. He has worked as a teacher in a one-room school, an assembly-line worker in a television factory, a quality control manager for an under-water acoustics company, inventor of twenty-five different product lines, founder of ten companies, a building scientist for forty years, and the father of three excellent children.

He is the author of Recalculating Truth a tale that describes what happens when developing a product that uses computer integrated human tells to discern the truth—a far more benign and effective process than water-boarding. Even candidates for the Supreme Court can tell lies.

Death at the Edge of the Diamond introduces Jon Megquire to the world, bringing him to Cape Cod in 1979 to play baseball in the premier summer league. Unfortunately, it turns out to be less than a peaceful Cape Cod summer visit when a client uses the family mansion as a murder weapon.

Seeing a need for better understanding of the air quality in houses (indoor air quality or IAQ), he wrote <u>Residential Ventilation Handbook</u> which was published by McGraw-Hill in 2010, quickly becoming the go-to source for many building science training programs. He updated and self-published a second edition in 2017.

While he was trying to figure out what to do with his life, he moved temporarily into an old, seventeen room inn on Cape Cod in 1975... and never left. His wife, Kate, joined him seven years later, and she never left either. Their three children grew up there but they figured out ways to move on.

SALTY AIR PUBLISHING
NEWSLETTER & WEBSITE

Salty Air Publishing, bi-weekly newsletter
Subscribe here

Salty Air Publishing Website
https://www.paulhraymer.com/

Made in the USA
Middletown, DE
20 May 2022

66003963R00139